THE CROWN OF SHADOWS

*The Queen's Defiance Against
the God of Light*

PART I

ECHO EVERGREEN

Table of Contents

CHAPTER

ONE

"To place a crown upon a woman," someone once remarked, "is as absurd as setting a saddle upon a wild bull."

Yet, into the grand hall stepped Laurent, her presence as delicate as a whisper upon the wind. The walls, swathed in brocade rich with history, seemed to lean in, bearing witness to the momentous occasion.

With a reverent bow, she inclined her head, allowing the Divine Messenger to rest a golden crown, studded with the light of a thousand stars, upon her brow. A scepter graced one hand, a pearl the other, as she turned to meet the gaze of nobles and ministers gathered in solemn assembly.

At a mere sixteen summers, Laurent possessed hair as dark as raven's wing, skin as fair as porcelain, and eyes wide with innocence, fringed with lashes that caught the light like morning dew. Her lips, red as the roses of legend, completed her ethereal visage. Petite and delicate, she seemed more like a child in a tapestry of dreams than a monarch upon the throne.

None among them envied her; instead, they cast upon her a gaze of pity.

A woman upon the throne? It was an anomaly, as unnatural as a fish taking to the land. Surely, it was but a matter of time before some ambitious man would seize that crown from her slender grasp.

The tapestry of Laurent's life was woven with threads of misfortune. Only a year had passed since her father, King John II, succumbed to a mysterious ailment. Physicians, armed with magnifying glasses and the wisdom of ages, had examined him relentlessly, yet their search yielded nothing—a mystery as elusive as the morning mist.

In the realm of the Holy Light Empire, where every heart beat in devotion to the sanctity of light, the rites for King John II culminated in the cleansing flames of cremation.

On that fateful day, the king's body seemed to defy death itself—sweat glistened upon his skin, his lips quivered, and his limbs twisted, as if life stubbornly clung to him. Some swore they heard chilling screams, echoes akin to the laments of tormented souls adrift in the abyss.

Yet, this eerie tableau stirred not a ripple within the palace walls. In time, it was relegated to the realm of ghostly tales, a mystery left to linger unresolved in the shadows of history.

Only days hence, tragedy struck once more, claiming Prince Branvilliers, the first heir to the throne.

On the day of his demise, he stood before his courtiers, reciting a eulogy with fervor, when madness overtook him. With eyes alight in a crimson fervor, he lunged towards his father's coffin. On hands and knees, he descended into a primal state, gnashing his teeth against the wood before collapsing into death's embrace. His fate mirrored the legendary kings of Babylon in their moments of madness.

Laurent's visage turned ghostly pale, tears cascading like a relentless waterfall. In her grief, she nearly joined her brother in his wooden sepulcher. Yet, with the crown prince gone, the late king left behind only a tiny prince, not yet three years of age. Thus, with sorrow etched upon her heart, she undertook the solemn duty of overseeing the funerals of her father and brother, tears mingling with the resolve in her eyes.

It seemed as if misfortune had singled out poor Laurent, weaving a tapestry of woe around her life. A mere week after the cruel hand of fate had claimed her father and brother, her little sibling vanished as if spirited away by unseen forces.

Upon hearing the dreadful news, Laurent's heart nearly faltered. She gathered her heavy skirts and, with a determination born of desperation, searched the labyrinthine corridors of the palace through the long night. Whispers reached her ears—a maid spoke of the Little Prince, perhaps taken by a wet nurse driven to madness. But why such caregivers lose their wits is a mystery to all.

Two days hence, word reached the palace of a stout woman seen at the docks, clutching a golden swaddle as she boarded a ship bound for the east.

In a frenzy, Laurent dispatched her people with haste to pursue them. Yet, despite all efforts, they could not overtake the ferry that vanished, swallowed by the mist and lost to the world.

With this sudden turn, Laurent found herself the final bearer of the royal bloodline.

By the laws of the land, two paths lay before her: to wed and yield the kingdom to her husband, or to don the mantle of queen herself.

History, inked in the blood of dynasties, imparts a singular lesson: the throne's heir must be appointed without delay, lest chaos descend like a storm.

Yet Laurent, steadfast in her resolve, refused the crown and all its burdens.

Laurent held a belief, shaped by the ancient doctrines of her faith, that women bore an inherent guilt. It was whispered through the ages that had it not been for Eve's temptation by the serpent, the tasting of forbidden fruit, and the subsequent fall of mankind, humanity might still dwell in the blissful embrace of Eden. In atonement for this primordial sin, a woman was destined to serve a man and nurture his progeny. How, then, could she aspire to wield the power reserved for men?

The ministers nodded in solemn agreement. Yet, beneath Laurent's unexpected leadership, the empire, once on the brink of ruin, flickered back to vibrant life.

First, the scourge of leprosy that had plagued the kingdom was miraculously contained. None could say what Laurent whispered to the medical official, but he proclaimed that it was by her influence the disease was halted.

Then, as she perused state documents by candlelight, a flame toppled onto her. Instead of igniting, her gown unveiled a majestic golden double-headed eagle—the emblem of the fabled Byzantine queen.

Lastly, during her inaugural recitation of the "Ode to Light Sutra" over one gravely ill, she invoked divine power to restore them to health.

These wonders seemed to affirm that Laurent was indeed God's chosen queen.

However, shadows of rumor began to creep, threatening to mar her image.

Some whispered that beneath her innocent facade lay a ruthless demoness who had poisoned her father and brother. How could the kingdom entrust its fate to such a venomous heart?

Others claimed that women were inherently fragile, and Laurent, the frailest among them, was no exception. To have such a delicate hand steer the kingdom's course was more terrifying than the prospect of falling into the clutches of non-believers.

As the slander spread like wildfire, the queen's image in the public eye warped and twisted, becoming a grotesque reflection of the woman she truly was.

Two months passed, and the rumors swirled ever stronger, like a tempest gathering within the palace walls. Some swore that their kin, who toiled within those very walls, had spied the queen weaving a crown of serpents, dipping gloves in black venom, and staining her lips with the blood of mandrakes and salamanders. It was whispered that every man who ventured too close to her met a grim fate, reduced to a heap of bones in her garden.

Hearing these wild tales, Laurent was bewildered and distraught. She hastily summoned the venerable professor from the seminary, pouring out her heart to him in a torrent of tears.

It is said that upon seeing the professor, her eyes brimmed with tears, soaking through her delicate white lace gloves. Anyone who witnessed such a scene could never believe the malicious gossip. The queen appeared so fragile and endearing; how could she possibly have poisoned her own father and brother?

Her father and brother were men of great strength and vigor, her father especially, once hailed as the empire's bravest warrior. He had drunk from the skulls of enemy generals in times of victory. How could a frail young girl like Laurent topple such mighty lions?

The professor, clutching his heart, vowed to the queen that he would extinguish these vile rumors in the name of the God of Light.

With this promise, Laurent reluctantly departed. She cast lingering glances over her shoulder, her large eyes swimming with fear and tears, as she made her way toward her chamber.

Each step she took seemed to resonate with her profound helplessness, a silent echo of her solitary struggle.

"Women are indeed not suited for power," the professor mused. If only she had realized this sooner, found a husband, had a son, and ruled the Empire of Light with her husband, perhaps she wouldn't be facing such humiliation and slander.

The crown on her head was not a symbol of glory but the sword of Damocles, ready to fall at any moment.

What a poor woman—no, she's not even a woman, she's just a little girl.

The professor shook his head, sighed, and left the palace.

Laurent entered her bedroom.

The tears in her eyes had long vanished, replaced by a cold, sharp expression.

She opened her arms, allowing the maid to remove her cloak, gloves, heavy skirt, and crinoline, and put on a lightweight nightgown.

Beneath her coat, she wore a thin suit of armor. This soft armor, made of thousands of tiny rings of Demon Forbidden Stones, felt like a hard undergarment, offering protection without being noticeable.

Laurent had a peculiar habit. No matter where she went, even if she fell asleep beside her mother, she always wore her soft carapace.

This armor had indeed saved her life once.

On a cold winter day, Laurent and her brother, Prince Branvillier, went to the theater to watch a play.

Despite her own superb acting skills, she couldn't appreciate the opera performers. She couldn't fathom why these talented individuals didn't strive for higher status but instead played comical roles to make the audience laugh.

Laurent didn't understand.

From the moment she became conscious, she knew exactly what she wanted: the throne, the glory of all the kings in history, and immortality recorded in the annals of time.

While her brother wandered aimlessly in the realm of dreams, blind to the world of ambition, Laurent's gaze was unwaveringly fixed upon the throne.

She believed with unshakable conviction that one day, it would be hers to claim. Where her brother stood bewildered by the shadowy specter of poison, Laurent possessed the uncanny ability to discern a tainted apple amidst a basket of ripe fruit.

Her naive brother never suspected that the maid who attended him was a clandestine agent from a rival kingdom, intent on sowing ruin through the dark arts of voodoo, aiming to curse the fertile land. But Laurent, upon unveiling the plot, swiftly dragged the maid to the grim confines of the torture chamber. There, she employed harsh methods — forcing a funnel into the maid's mouth, pouring cold water to drown her senses, reviving her only to repeat the torment.

Under such relentless interrogation, the maid quickly broke. She revealed her name as Margo, a witch of the Roman Empire, who had lurked within the Empire of Light for five long years. Laurent, astute and calculating, spared Margo, binding the witch's service to her own designs. She took the enchanted ring and wore it upon her thumb, a trophy of her cunning.

Laurent was naturally self-assured and ambitious, aware that her intellect and resourcefulness surpassed those of ordinary nobles. Yet, she also understood the peril of revealing her full capabilities, choosing instead to cloak herself in the guise of a meek and powerless girl, watching the intrigues of the palace with a detached eye.

At the tender age of fifteen, Laurent realized she had blossomed from a charming child into a beauty of extraordinary allure. Curious about altering her appearance, she inquired of Margo whether magic could achieve such transformation.

In the Holy Light Empire, a realm devoted to the worship of the God of Light, magic was strictly forbidden, save for the clergy and royal blood who might occasionally wield divine power. The penalty for dabbling in magic was death.

Margo, having witnessed many a devout soul prefer death over the use of magic, found Laurent refreshingly different.

The young queen appeared utterly indifferent to the supreme deity who granted light and held dominion over all creation. Her morning prayers, when offered, were little more than a formality—an act devoid of true devotion.

Once, Laurent stood beneath the grand dome, its celestial frescoes depicting the god's incarnation as a radiant sphere surrounded by angelic hosts. Her gaze defiant, she declared, "God is merely a tool wielded by the king to govern his people."

Margo, taken aback by such audacity, felt a chill run down her spine, nearly causing her to faint.

Yet Laurent merely smiled, her attention returning to the pages before her.

Margo was awestruck by Laurent's meticulousness. The young queen had lined the walls with soft sponge, crafting a chamber so ingeniously soundproofed that unless she screamed, not a whisper could escape to the outside world.

From that moment on, Margo understood that survival in the Holy Light Empire meant aligning with Laurent, for she was the sharpest, most decisive, and ruthlessly pragmatic woman Margo had ever encountered.

That fateful day at the White Tower Theater, as Laurent enjoyed a play with her brother, a band of pagans stormed in, intent on capturing her. They had heard of Princess Laurent's presence and perceived it as the perfect opportunity for abduction.

Mistakenly assuming her to be a fragile girl, reliant on maids for every step, they dismissed her as a threat, turning their focus to ransom negotiations.

But Margo knew better. Her mistress was more formidable than many men, akin to a serpent cloaked in vibrant scales.

Laurent harbored a fascination with poisons, delving into ancient manuscripts, modern alchemical writings, and sacrificial rites in pursuit of knowledge.

The nobles of the bygone dynasty had imbibed mild toxins to build resistance—a practice abandoned by her father from fears of infertility.

Laurent entertained no such fears. Her resolve was unmatched. During a blistering summer, she ingested poison for the first time, resulting in vivid, blood-red sores across her skin. Adorned in a wide-brimmed hat and thick garments, she walked beneath the scorching sun, never once crying out in pain or confiding in another soul. Had Margo not glimpsed her undergarments, soaked with pus and blood, she would have remained oblivious to the depths of Laurent's silent suffering.

Margo often pondered whether this seemingly delicate girl might indeed ascend as the first queen of the Empire of Light.

Naturally, the band of infidels was ill-prepared for Laurent's cunning.

With a calm demeanor, she deftly slipped strychnine into their meals, observing with a detached curiosity as they succumbed, one by one.

What piqued her interest was the pagan leader, a man versed in the art of poisons like herself, who exhibited some resistance. He collapsed, convulsing, yet with a final burst of strength, he hurled a dagger at Laurent.

The blade found its mark, piercing her chest.

Yet her stride remained unbroken.

The leader's eyes widened with disbelief and terror.

Laurent approached him with unyielding poise, lifted the hem of her gown, and mercilessly crushed his fingers beneath her heel.

The leader's scream rent the air.

Silent, she half-knelt beside him, pried open his mouth with a swift, practiced motion, and activated the mechanism on her thumb ring, releasing two drops of venom into his throat.

Her movements were precise and assured, reminiscent of an alchemist who had conducted countless experiments.

Choking and gasping, the leader stammered, "You... aren't you just a weak little girl? They say you're a rose that shatters at a touch⋯"

Her smile was sweet, her voice as melodic as a silver bell, "Who said the thorns of roses cannot kill?"

With that, she stepped aside, divested herself of the cumbersome overskirt and crinoline, unfastened the garter buckle, withdrew the dagger embedded in her armor, placed it in the leader's hand, and drove it into her own thigh.

"Puchi—"

Crimson splattered forth.

Her decisive, fierce courage stood in stark contrast to her innocent visage, leaving the pagan leader utterly confounded. Until his dying breath, he no longer dared to mock the seemingly fragile girl before him.

Prince Branvillier, in contrast, was indecisive and timid. Though tall and strong, he was consumed by a passion for beauty and art, ever enveloped in the scent of fine perfumes.

When Laurent was abducted, he saw the direction the captors fled but dared not pursue. Instead, he vented his frustration upon the knights, berating them for failing to protect the princess.

When the knights sought his command to pursue, he hesitated, more concerned with his own safety.

After Laurent was retrieved by the tardy rescuers, she recounted how the pagan leader had tormented her until she lost consciousness, only to awaken amidst corpses. The knights, noting her pallor and wounded thigh, accepted her tale without question, just as Margo had informed her they would.

Yet Laurent was indifferent. She knew her brother for what he was: mediocre and ineffectual. In his leisure, he chased butterflies with nets and servants. Had he led the charge to rescue her, she might have feared him and conspired against him.

Family affection meant little to her; power and the bejeweled crown were her true desires.

She aspired to rule the land, not merely serve as a pawn for marriage or an unknown consort.

Her ambition burned brightly, not just for a crown, but to conquer bountiful lands and expand her domain as no man had done—or rather, to surpass any man's achievements.

Her ambitions flared like a flame, unwavering and eternal.

To realize her dreams, she donned the guise of an innocent, guileless girl, disarming those around her. She did not hesitate to eradicate any obstacles in her path.

At last, she claimed the crown.

But who could have foreseen that she would lose her hard-won throne to a deity that existed only in the minds of men?

CHAPTER

TWO

"The divine has decreed that the Empire of Light forbids women from assuming the role of regent," the pronouncement echoed through the halls of power. "Should you yield to her governance, the Almighty shall unleash calamity upon you. In that dire time, cities shall lie in ruin, barren of vegetation, livestock shall wither to mere skeletons, and all unborn infants shall perish within their mothers' wombs. Is this the fate you desire?"

"The Almighty shall not permit a woman to serve as His vassal! Should you disregard His sacred teachings, His wrath shall be kindled, and He shall extend His hand to obscure the sun, casting a pall of sin upon your very being!"

"None can absolve the transgressions condemned by the divine! Reflect upon your kin and progeny; if you overthrow the queen's dominion, there remains a glimmer of hope for restoration."

On December 3, 1782, Queen Laurent was unceremoniously stripped of her right to inherit the throne. The charges laid against her were as heavy as they were numerous: murder, contempt of law, violating divine will, and, most grievously, angering the gods.

Simultaneously, the Temple of Light issued a decree that henceforth, no woman would inherit the throne or serve as regent. A double blow that reverberated through the land.

The very next day, the temple judge signed the queen's sentencing order: death by fire.

Execution day dawned, and throngs of nobles and commoners alike converged upon the Fire Court. This building, the most foreboding in the royal capital, was hewn from dark stone, with an eerie dark blue light dancing along its eaves. Inside, only a front hall and a main hall existed, devoid of any side corridors. Dozens of large gray windows allowed in a dim, cold natural light.

The crowd stood on tiptoe, craning their necks and jostling against one another, all eager to witness the queen's final moments.

They knew nothing of her true character, but the temple judges had branded her "vicious, cruel, rough, hypocritical, and blasphemous." Thus, they perceived this as a righteous retribution for evil deeds, anxiously awaiting her fiery demise.

Yet, when the executioner solemnly unveiled the prison cart, to the crowd's astonishment, it was empty.

The queen had vanished, leaving behind only whispers and speculation.

Meanwhile, the fugitive queen sat serenely at the marquis's estate, indulging in afternoon tea as if the world beyond was not in pursuit. Her demeanor was one of calm, as she meticulously spread butter upon a slice of bread.

Laurent's tastes were extravagant and indulgent: the bread was dusted with sugar as fine as snow and layered with angelica leaves, almonds, grapes, and candied strawberries. After adding a generous spread of cream and honey, she parted her crimson lips to devour this decadent creation in a single, graceful bite.

A young man burst into the room, his voice a mix of urgency and disbelief. "Your Majesty, didn't you say someone would take the blame for you? The entire capital knows you've escaped! Furious believers are hunting for you like bloodhounds⋯ What's your plan?"

"Don't worry, they won't find me," Laurent replied nonchalantly, licking a stray dollop of cream from the corner of her mouth. "Do you have chocolate sauce?"

"⋯ Yes, I'll have the chef prepare it," the young man stammered, visibly unnerved. The thought of opposing the temple filled him with dread. If they discovered he was harboring the queen⋯ the mere thought was terrifying.

Yet, he found himself unable to betray her. Laurent was entrancingly beautiful. When she had appeared in the garden last night, her soft fingers pressed to his lips, he was utterly captivated.

She had stood in the cold dawn, her black hair cascading like a waterfall, adorned in a red velvet robe trimmed with lace, her feet adorned with black silk slippers, her dainty, fair toes peeking out, rendering even the most vibrant flowers dull in comparison.

He would gladly face the temple's wrath if only to kiss those exquisite toes, such was the depth of his infatuation.

As he stood there, entranced, he remembered she was supposed to be under house arrest, not in his garden. Before he could inquire, she had flung herself into his arms, weeping.

Like many nobles, he dabbled in perfumery to mask the scent of sweat. But Laurent's fragrance was unlike any other—an enchanting blend of nutmeg, patchouli, and roses. He had encountered it on many women, but none wore it as enchantingly as Laurent.

She was akin to a rare, ethereal creature born from the petals of a green leaf rose.

No wonder the poets, before her ascent to the throne, had penned verses likening her to a rose nourished by the blood of poetry.

In that moment, though he knew the peril of harboring her, he concealed her in his chambers, driven by an inexplicable courage.

Had the penalty order not been signed, he might have shielded her longer. But once it was issued, doubt crept in. The judge's words rang in his ears—calling her a cold-blooded, ruthless serpent poisoning the realm. Could it be true? Had she truly committed such atrocities? Poisoned her own kin and blasphemed the God of Light? She seemed so delicate, how could she harbor such audacity?

The next morning, his father invited him to witness the queen's execution, but he declined, feigning illness. Naturally reserved, he disliked social gatherings and even avoided eye contact with the servants. His father left without suspicion.

Living on the same estate as his father meant that sheltering the queen would soon be discovered. What fate awaited him? A trial in the Fire Court? A death sentence? No, he couldn't risk it—despite his shyness, ambition coursed through his veins. If he fell, his title and estate would pass to his younger brother, and he would be the subject of ridicule. The elite would sip their wine, jesting over his downfall for a condemned woman. Too tragic.

Yet all such worries evaporated in her presence.

Her porcelain skin dazzled his senses, and the aroma of nutmeg and roses enveloped him, intoxicating as ivy. Her raven hair, alabaster skin, noble eyes, and delicate, doll-like lips burned through his mind like an eternal flame.

Should he lose her, he knew he would never again encounter a woman so graced by a crown. She embodied the very essence of the Holy Empire of Light, and to possess her was to hold dominion over the empire itself. Who among men could resist such perilous allure?

Last night, Laurent's actions were a masterclass in manipulation, blending vulnerability with intention as she draped herself into the marquis's embrace. It was a silent invitation, a signal that she was his for the taking, should he muster the courage to claim her.

The young marquis, overwhelmed by a mix of excitement and disbelief, approached her with bated breath. Laurent, ever perceptive, caught the fervor in his eyes and returned his gaze with a thoughtful, enigmatic expression.

This moment of perceived acceptance sent a wave of intense joy crashing over him. The realization that this enigmatic, once-queen was amenable to his advances was intoxicating. His imagination raced ahead, envisioning a future where he could be her savior and partner, the one who would stand by her side as she navigated the perilous waters of her predicament.

The exhilaration was palpable, shaking his very core and leaving him on the precipice of giddiness. He was entranced, caught in the web of his own desires and ambitions, seeing in Laurent not just a woman to be desired, but a queen to be won, a prize that could elevate his status and fulfill his wildest dreams.

Yet, in his eagerness, he overlooked the depths of Laurent's cunning. For her, this was more than a simple exchange of affection; it was a calculated move in a larger game, a step toward her ultimate goal of reclaiming power and rewriting her own fate.

In that charged moment, the marquis stood on the brink of a decision that could alter the course of his life, unaware that to Laurent, he was just another piece on the chessboard, ready to be moved or sacrificed as her plans demanded.

At that pivotal moment, Laurent set aside her knife with deliberate grace, her cream-stained fingers slipping into her mouth as she thoughtfully savored the sweetness. Her calm, unhurried manner was disarming, and the young marquis was utterly captivated, as if reason had suddenly deserted him.

The room seemed to echo with a deafening crash, a stark contrast to the quiet intensity of their interaction. His gaze locked onto hers with a fervent eagerness, his voice emerging as a raspy whisper, "Your Majesty, I yearn to kiss you... may I? May I? Just for a fleeting moment, I beseech you, just a moment. I am prepared to offer any sacrifice, even the severing of my limbs, if only I might press my lips to yours."

Laurent's smile was teasing, her eyes dancing with intrigue as she posed her question, "Would you be willing to face the guillotine for me?"

His mind was a tempest of visions—Laurent, with the cream on her lips, her pearly teeth, her scarlet tongue, and the alluring scent of roses that enveloped her. He was reduced to a mere puppet, his strings pulled by his overwhelming desires, the aspiration to conquer this imperial rose burning fiercely within him.

"I am willing, I am willing," he exclaimed anxiously, his desperation palpable. "Please, please."

Laurent scrutinized him with an intense gaze, assessing the depths of his infatuation before extending her hand with deliberate grace. Her voice was soft, commanding yet gentle as she said, "Kneel before me, and I shall grant you the privilege of kissing me."

Overwhelmed by a mix of gratitude and crude desire, he knelt before her, pressing his lips to the back of her hand with reverence.

"How rude," Laurent remarked with a wry smile. "Do you mind if I'm rude too? I'm not a good girl; I have many bad habits, like a man."

Her words hung in the air, laced with a challenge and an invitation, hinting at the complexity and unpredictability that lay beneath her composed exterior. The marquis, caught in her web, was both entranced and ensnared, unaware of the intricate game being played and the formidable player before him. Laurent, ever the strategist, knew precisely how to wield her charms to keep him—and others—under her spell, all while advancing her own enigmatic plans.

His heart raced with an intoxicating mix of excitement and desire, caught up in the romantic allure Laurent exuded, an enchantment known to few. He was eager for what the future might hold—if he could claim her, he envisioned giving her a new identity, spiriting her away to a secluded village where they could revel in their secret joy. Once his father had passed, he would return to the capital to assume his rightful title, with Laurent by his side.

Yet, as he was lost in this vivid fantasy, he failed to notice the knife lying on the table—until it was too late. In one swift, chilling motion, it sliced across his throat. His eyes widened in shock and disbelief as he collapsed at Laurent's creamy white instep, the life draining from his body.

With a casual air, Laurent discarded the knife, picked up a napkin, and wiped the blood from her hands with an unsettling grace. She slowly finished the last piece of her sweet, greasy bread, unfazed by the chaos she had wrought.

"I said I would be very rude," she remarked, her voice calm and composed. She kicked his lifeless body aside with disdain and elegantly sucked her fingers clean as she walked into the bedroom closet, her mind already on her next move.

Margo never imagined that the queen's escape plan would involve masquerading as the marquis's eldest son.

Even more astonishing—it worked seamlessly.

The marquis's eldest son was naturally shy, always averting his gaze while speaking or traveling. His pale, delicate features, reminiscent of a girl's, were a perfect match for Laurent, allowing her to adopt his identity with ease.

Laurent had refused Margo's suggestion to use magic to alter her appearance. The capital was laden with Demon Forbidden Stones, which would illuminate like signal fires if they detected magic, betraying their location to those hunting them. Instead, Laurent opted for a more traditional disguise, using ink, charcoal, and a wig to transform her appearance.

She removed her earrings, necklace, and bracelet, donning a man's triangular hat, a crisp white shirt, a snug vest, and a dark blue jacket. Without the constraints of her usual attire, her steps were more agile and confident than ever.

Laurent's transformation was complete; she was no longer the fallen queen, but a cunning chameleon ready to outsmart those who sought her downfall. Her cleverness and adaptability ensured that she and Margo could navigate the treacherous landscape of the Empire, always staying one step ahead of their pursuers.

Laurent cast one last glance at the young man lying lifeless in a pool of blood. With an air of noble arrogance, she draped a white cloth over him, concealing the evidence of her decisive action. With unwavering confidence, she left the bedroom, her mind focused on the next steps of her escape.

By the time the marquis's eldest son was discovered, Laurent and Margo had long vanished from the capital, leaving behind only questions and chaos.

Maintaining the guise of the marquis's son would have been imprudent, drawing unwanted attention and making her an easy target. Instead, Laurent and Margo deftly switched identities, adopting new personas as easily as one might change clothes. They became peasant women, noblewomen, refugees, circus acrobats, gypsy girls, troubadours—always staying one step ahead of their pursuers. In their most daring disguise, they posed as expelled leprosy patients, donning white cloaks and ringing bells to warn others away. This guise proved more effective than any other, as people avoided them like the plague.

Ironically, it was Laurent herself who had decreed strict control over leprosy patients in the capital, a measure intended to maintain the health and safety of the populace. Had it not been for this decree, the drastic step of assassinating the marquis's eldest son might have been unnecessary.

By the time they reached the border village, two months had passed.

The journey was arduous, with magic strictly forbidden and the kingdom feeling as isolated as a prehistoric land. News from the capital trickled in only through the temple networks, which served as the empire's primary channels of communication.

During her brief three-month reign, Laurent had been consumed by a desire to uncover the secrets of the Supreme Temple, rumored to house the true statue of the God of Light. Yet, when she sought access, the divine messenger had rebuffed her with a firm decree that no woman had ever set foot within its sacred walls.

Sensing a dark omen in this rejection, Laurent turned her attention to her father's alchemy chamber, devoting countless hours to studying the arcane and mysterious knowledge contained within. It was a place filled with secrets, where her father — a man driven by ambition and the pursuit of immortality—had conducted his experiments and gathered knowledge from witches and legendary herbs.

In the solitude of the chamber, Laurent honed her understanding of the court's dangerous intricacies, devising new strategies to reclaim her power and challenge the temple's authority. Her journey was far from over, and she was determined to emerge victorious, regardless of the obstacles that lay ahead.

Laurent's father, John II, was a formidable and fearsome figure whose obsession with power knew no bounds. Determined to wear the crown eternally, he enlisted witches to concoct elixirs that promised to extend his life. Yet, his ambitions stretched further, as he sought to ensure his dominion by feeding his own son poison to stifle his intellectual growth and eliminate any threat of usurpation.

Laurent managed to escape the same grim fate as her brother, not out of any paternal fondness, but because John II regarded women as insignificant — foolish, ignorant, and cowardly. The Holy Light Empire had never known a woman in power, which rendered her a lesser threat in his patriarchal view.

Ironically, it was her father's eccentric pursuits that inadvertently paved Laurent's path to the throne. His relentless quest for immortality through alchemy led him to overindulgence in mysterious pills, culminating in a death-like state that prompted Laurent to cremate him swiftly. His obsession with witches and legendary herbs introduced her to Yin Chen, an herb with a sinister reputation for madness, one that had afflicted a Babylonian king and, ultimately, her brother.

Initially, Laurent harbored no intent to kill her brother; John II's machinations had already rendered him ineffectual. Her goal was simply to strip him of dignity before the court.

However, when she retrieved the Yin Chen from the depths of the basement, an accidental spill of poisons—crafted from toads, vipers, salamanders, and scorpions—sealed his fate.

Her brother's death, while accidental, was a product of their family's dark and melancholic dynamics, a tragedy born from a legacy of intrigue and manipulation.

Though Laurent had become morbidly indifferent, shaped by the upbringing under John II's oppressive shadow, it was this very indifference that shielded her from potential threats—a fate that could have easily resulted in her demise at the hands of unknown poisoners, sudden assassins, or a mysterious drowning.

In this perilous court, Laurent learned the art of survival, mastering the delicate balance of power, secrecy, and strategy. Her journey was marked by cunning and resilience, as she navigated the treacherous waters of a legacy she never chose but was determined to outmaneuver.

The real twist of fate came when Laurent, during her explorations of the Chamber of Secrets, stumbled upon a hidden passageway. This secret corridor led directly to the backyard of the Marquis of Carlisle, a discovery that would prove invaluable.

For three months, Laurent took advantage of this clandestine route, wandering through the marquis's garden under the cover of night. With her sharp and analytical mind, she meticulously memorized the intricate paths and escape routes, preparing herself for any unforeseen circumstances.

So, when the time came and the temple convicted her, Laurent faced the ordeal with unshakable composure. As the judge leveled the charges against her, expecting fear or contrition, Laurent instead met his gaze with a serene smile. "I am indeed a venomous snake," she declared, her voice steady and unyielding, "and a venomous snake that wants to wrap around the statue of Light."

Her words were both a declaration and a challenge, revealing her defiance and her unwillingness to submit to the temple's authority. It was a moment that encapsulated her resolve and her cunning, a testament to her willingness to embrace her dark reputation if it meant reclaiming her power and challenging the status quo.

Her confidence unnerved the court, for they realized that Laurent was not a woman to be easily subdued. Behind her calm exterior lay a mind that had already planned her escape, a mind that understood the power of perception and the art of manipulation.

With the secret passage as her trump card, Laurent was ready to defy the temple's judgment and secure her own destiny, proving once more that she was a force to be reckoned with—a true queen in exile, poised to reclaim her throne.

Laurent's audacious words were unlike anything the judge had ever heard, leaving him livid, his face flushed with anger as he rattled off a litany of charges against her.

Her response, however, was calm and unrepentant, accepting the accusations with an air of serene defiance.

The temple, in its hypocrisy, allowed her the comfort of her own bedroom as she awaited execution. This decision, born of arrogance, proved to be their undoing. It afforded Laurent the time to utilize the secret passage she had discovered. With Margo's help, a simple pillow was transformed into a decoy of the queen, and together, they made their escape, leaving behind a room that seemingly held the condemned queen.

The charges were grave: conspiracy to usurp power, desecration of the God of Light, use of forbidden magic, and public humiliation of the temple's authority. The rift between Laurent and the temple was now beyond repair, a chasm that neither side wished to bridge.

Laurent harbored no desire for reconciliation.

She held no reverence for the temple's deity, doubting the very existence of such a god. To her, the notion of a god who would deny women the right to rule was unworthy of worship, a construct she was determined to dismantle.

As she pondered this, a bold and daring plan began to take shape in her mind—a plan to reclaim the throne and topple the temple's oppressive influence.

The cornerstone of her strategy was blasphemy.

Complete and utter blasphemy.

She envisioned a campaign that would challenge the temple's dogma, expose its hypocrisies, and rally those who had grown weary of its tyrannical hold. She would use her cunning and charisma to gather allies, weaving a narrative that questioned the divine right of kings and the exclusion of women from power.

Her goal was not only to regain her throne but to incite a fundamental shift in the empire's beliefs, to create a world where power was not dictated by gender or divine decree but by merit and vision.

With Margo by her side, Laurent set out on this perilous journey, determined to forge a new path for herself and for the Empire of Light, a path illuminated not by the false light of a distant god, but by the brilliance of her own ambition and resolve.

CHAPTER

THREE

"**I** plan to sneak into the temple," Laurent declared suddenly, her voice firm and resolute.

Margo, caught off guard by the bold statement, blinked in surprise. "What are you saying?" she asked, unsure if she had heard her correctly.

"I don't want to repeat it a second time," Laurent replied, her tone leaving no room for doubt.

"But..." Margo began to protest, but Laurent silenced her with a gentle gesture, raising a finger to her lips.

Laurent walked over to the window, drawing back the blinds to gaze out at the bustling street below.

They were staying in a grimy little hotel, where every surface seemed perpetually coated in a layer of grease, and the peeling paint revealed patches of black lime beneath. The atmosphere was far from luxurious, but it served their purpose.

Nearby, the rhythmic pounding of a pestle at a laundry released a swirling vortex of hot, soapy water into the street, which the crowd navigated with practiced ease. People moved like an unperturbed river, stepping over the soapy mess without a second thought, for them, it was just another day in the neighborhood.

Across the way, a lively restaurant buzzed with activity. Inside, priests in pristine white robes and silver crowns enjoyed their meat soup, their laughter punctuating the air as they twitched their mustaches and slurped noisily. They were a stark contrast to the austere Puritan priests of the capital, who eschewed meat and other earthly pleasures.

"Can monks eat meat?" Laurent mused aloud, observing the scene with interest.

Margo, ever ready with an explanation, replied, "They're not ordinary monks, but priests. Priests hold a higher status and can spread God's word. Except for the devout monks who swear lifelong devotion to the God of Light, most believers can live normal lives. Some priests are so wealthy they're practically dripping with oil. After all, who wouldn't want God's favor?"

Laurent nodded thoughtfully, her lips curling into a playful smile as she blinked her eyelashes and revealed charming dimples. "I want to earn God's favor too," she remarked, a hint of mischief in her voice. "I hope they won't reject me."

Margo was taken aback by the queen's unexpected stance. "Your Majesty, are you really planning to sneak into the Temple? The Temple of Light's hierarchy is even stricter than the old church. You must be recommended by a diocesan priest to enter the diocese temple. Many monks have spent their entire lives in the church without ever seeing a diocesan priest."

Laurent shrugged, her demeanor casual yet determined. "Then let him recommend me," Laurent declared calmly.

She pulled off her headscarf, letting her thick, lustrous black hair cascade down her back.

The mere thought of infiltrating the temple filled her with a thrill she hadn't felt in a long time, painting her cheeks with a bright blush that gave her an almost shy allure.

This excitement was a rare sensation for Laurent. From a young age, she had known she was different. While other girls were drawn to embroidery, music, and painting, Laurent found herself captivated by the shooting range, mesmerized by the guards as they practiced their marksmanship. When a bullet was fired, she would lower her head, hiding the gleam in her eyes, not wanting anyone to witness her thrill.

While others praised each other's skills, Laurent discreetly tucked a small flintlock pistol into her pink skirt, bringing it back to her room to study in secret, all the while indulging in cream cakes. She was a born rebel, with little regard for tradition or deities, and a restless, almost violent energy coursing through her veins.

At the same age, her brother was lost in dreams of butterflies, beauties, and fine wine, while Laurent's fantasies revolved around a perfectly calibrated flintlock gun and the graceful fall of an antelope. She craved excitement and challenges, feeling an acute sense of unease and frustration when life grew too calm.

Before she ascended to the throne, her father, John II, had been her sole adversary. In his youth, he was a formidable warrior, a visionary sage, and a wise ruler. But in his later years, he succumbed to incompetence, weakened by his obsession with longevity elixirs, leaving him vulnerable to Laurent's ambitions.

After she seized the throne, Laurent anticipated a period of boredom. Yet, unexpectedly, a new adversary presented itself: the Temple and the so-called God of Light. The temple's power was vast, dwarfing that of the royal family. While people feared the monarchy, they revered the temple, entrusting it with all aspects of life—from birth to death, and everything in between.

The God of Light, or "Father God" as he was known, was believed to be the creator of all things, including abstract concepts like time, order, power, fate, laws, and wisdom. This reverence made the temple a formidable opponent, one that Laurent was eager to challenge.

For Laurent, the temple represented not only a new challenge but also an opportunity to redefine power dynamics within the empire. With her rebellious spirit and strategic mind, she was poised to confront this mighty institution, ready to disrupt the status quo and carve out a place for herself that defied both tradition and divine decree.

The image of the God of Light was omnipresent, looming from the domes of palaces, courts, and churches—a deity depicted with compassion, holding the light of order. During Laurent's coronation, she felt the weight of his cold gaze from the palace dome as she gripped the pearl of light, a symbol of her supposed eternal servitude. Yet, despite this vow, she was stripped of her right to the throne, accused of disrespecting the sanctity of this distant and oppressive deity.

From the very beginning, the God of Light had been a constant barrier, an unyielding force that seemed intent on keeping her shackled, preventing her from advancing further.

It wasn't just Laurent who felt this heavy hand; everyone lived under the shadow of this divine figure.

In times of hardship, people instinctively turned to him, seeking protection through prayer, whether or not their pleas were ever answered. In the face of disaster, their immediate response was to kneel and beg for mercy, hoping for him to retract his punishing left hand, rather than taking action themselves. For repentance, they flocked to the God's forgiveness centers, avoiding introspection and personal accountability.

The grand image of the "God of Light," cold and majestic, was like a cunning parasite, subtly eroding the minds of the populace, rendering them pliable and easy to manipulate. The first to devise such a mode of governance was indeed a genius.

Laurent couldn't help but admire this system of control, even as she sought to dismantle it. She bit her lower lip, a rare expression of vulnerability for someone usually so composed. In that moment, she was acutely aware of her rapid breathing, the fiery rush of her blood, and the pounding of her heart.

Her desire for the temple's power was as fierce as her childhood longing for a flintlock gun. She relished the challenge presented by the temple and the God of Light, finding excitement in having a formidable new rival.

The diocesan priest was an elderly man, his cheeks sunken, eyelids swollen, and skin tinged with a waxy yellow hue. Yet, his eyes were strikingly clear and sincere, perhaps a reflection of a lifetime of good deeds. Unlike the other priests adorned in pristine robes, he wore a slightly yellowed robe and tortoiseshell-rimmed glasses, his beard meticulously groomed.

With Margo waiting for orders at the hotel, Laurent, cloaked in white with her hood drawn, watched the bustling street below. After two or three days of patient observation, she finally spotted the priest's carriage.

Seizing the moment, she rushed forward, extending her palm for the horse to sniff a tranquilizer, ensuring it would halt without panic or harm. Her quick actions brought the carriage to a stop, and the priest, relieved to see no harm done, leaped out to assist her.

As she rose, Laurent took the opportunity to pull back her hood, revealing her face—a stunning blend of strength and beauty. Without the aid of magic, her features lacked the innocence of youth, instead embodying the allure of a wild rose in full bloom, vibrant and compelling.

Her dark hair and striking eyes only amplified this beauty, elevating her presence to something extraordinary, irresistible, and commanding. In that moment, she was no longer just a queen in exile but a force to be reckoned with, ready to confront the temple with all the power and cunning she possessed.

The priest stared at her, wide-eyed and nearly speechless. He had encountered noblewomen who used cashmere fat, milk, and egg whites to care for their hair, but none possessed hair as thick and lustrous as this girl's. Her raven-black hair, dense like crow feathers, cascaded over her pure white robe like a waterfall. But it was her eyes that truly captivated him—more mesmerizing than her hair. They glimmered like the legendary gold of Ophir, with a blue glow reminiscent of a tranquil pond reflecting a golden-orange sunset.

Laurent appeared particularly nervous, biting her rosy lips. For devout believers of the Light, this red was seen as evil and unhealthy, akin to the shocking blood of the devil, and it fiercely captured the priest's heart. He couldn't help but grasp her cold, delicate hand, asking with genuine concern, "Miss, have you encountered anything bad? Where is your family?... Oh, your hands are as cold as ice! Poor child, you must have had a very unfortunate situation to walk the streets so absentmindedly."

Laurent lowered her eyelashes, casting a calm glance at the priest's hand—she disliked the old man's touch, which felt warm and slippery, like wet worms in the mud after a rain.

Her heart filled with disgust, but she pouted and choked out, "I... I don't have any family anymore."

The words were genuine, though her tears were feigned.

"Poor child," the priest sighed, gesturing for the coachman to lower the small staircase and inviting her to sit inside. "Hurry up, child. God wouldn't bear to see you stand in the cold wind for so long. If you stand there a little longer, you might faint."

His enthusiasm was unexpected and unusually warm. Laurent didn't worry much; she was confident in her ability to handle any sudden changes. If this old man dared to harm her, she had plenty of ways to deal with him.

Once she was seated in the carriage, the priest joined her. The space was narrow, and she could clearly see the ugly warts on his eyelids. She could feel his gaze slowly examining her features, as if savoring her appearance while pondering her origins.

Then, he handed her a miniature statue wrapped in red silk. The priest spoke kindly, "Kiss the hem of the statue, and God will save you from the quagmire of misfortune."

Laurent took the statue gently, murmuring a soft thank you. She gazed at the miniature statue in her hands. Though only the size of a palm, it appeared lifelike, especially its cold, dignified eyes, reminiscent of those seen in the domes of palaces, churches, and courts.

With her eyes closed, she feigned a reverent kiss on the statue's hem.

She wasn't sure if it was her imagination, but as soon as her lips touched it, a vast, serene, and shimmering ocean materialized in her mind.

Before the golden ocean stood a tall, upright figure.

While she couldn't discern his clothes or face clearly, she sensed an overwhelmingly powerful force emanating from him, so intense that her hands trembled with fear.

She felt that this figure was not a god but perhaps an incarnation of one. A wisp of black mist swirled around him, his gaze cold and venomous.

When Laurent tried to observe further, a sharp pain pierced her mind.

It seemed God did not want her to continue watching. The shimmering golden ocean vanished.

Laurent opened her eyes, finding herself back in the carriage.

She looked at the statue in her hand, bewildered and incredulous.

Had she just seen a god? Could there truly be a god in the world? How was this possible?

She had once stayed with the ruler of the Supreme Temple, a man rumored to be the incarnation of a legendary god, possessing a hint of divine holiness. Yet, even he had not allowed her to witness miracles. How could a border priest enable her to see the God of Light?

"God didn't allow you to kiss his hem, did he?" the priest seemed to read her thoughts and gently reassured her. "Don't be sad or try to comprehend God's thoughts. His actions are beyond mortal understanding. God is in heaven, and you are on earth. He sees, knows, and controls far more than you can imagine. Don't overthink it. No matter what you've faced in the past, as long as you remain devout, loyal, and pray on time, the Spirit of God will save you."

Laurent paid no heed to his words. She fixated on the statue, bringing it closer, her nose twitching as she tried to detect any scent of illusion drugs.

The priest's expression suddenly shifted as he snatched the statue away, angrily reprimanding her, "What are you doing? This is a great disrespect, you know?! Only heretics would treat the statue like that! Considering your youth and ignorance, this is just a warning. The next time I see you doing this, I will take you directly to the court."

Nothing more was said during the journey.

Laurent sat silently, her mind racing with possibilities, her heart still pounding from the vision she had experienced. She needed to understand what she had seen and what it meant for her plans. The temple was no ordinary opponent, and this encounter had only deepened the mystery surrounding its power.

CHAPTER

FOUR

Two hours later, the carriage arrived at the priest's residence, a place surprisingly opulent for a man of the cloth in a municipality. The Palladian architecture was elegant, surrounded by lush flower beds in the back and emerald fields stretching out in front.

The priest humbly attributed this luxury to the love and affection of the people, and he offered a sincere apology for his earlier rudeness in the carriage.

Laurent quickly shook her head, her dark eyelashes trembling as she feigned fear and insisted it was all her fault. Her submissive demeanor seemed to please the priest, who gently inquired, "Child, do you believe in God?"

Though Laurent didn't truly believe, she quickly conjured the image of a devout lady she once met. This lady believed that joy was a gift from God, while negative emotions like sadness, anger, and disgust stemmed from a lack of piety. She prayed upon waking, thanked God before meals, and eagerly read the temple's compilations of God's words and deeds. Despite her devotion, the temple never permitted her to enter and worship inside, allowing her only to pray on the steps, an act for which she shed many grateful tears.

Laurent had never disdained the lady's piety; instead, she felt a disconnect. Normal emotions — happiness, sadness, anxiety, despair, satisfaction—often eluded her. Instead, she was driven by an insatiable greed and pulsating ambition. She excelled at imitation, observing, remembering, learning, and deploying emotions as tools to build a bridge to power.

In a soft voice, Laurent replied, "My mother told me faith shouldn't be something to show off... As long as you have God in your heart, God will remember you. No need to proclaim your devotion."

"You have a good mother," the priest nodded with approval.

As they passed through the garden and entered through the gate, Laurent felt a peculiar sensation. Behind the door were four large locks with iron bars, and a small wind chime on the doorframe made a crisp clanging sound. In the shoe cabinet, several pairs of women's shoes of varying sizes were placed alongside men's shoes, catching Laurent's attention.

The priest explained, "On weekends, several distinguished ladies come here to pray."

He led her to the innermost room on the first floor. As they passed the spiral staircase, Laurent noticed the second-floor corridor was empty, with all doors locked.

She blinked and asked innocently, "Is anyone sleeping upstairs?"

The priest responded smoothly, "Yes, my wife is sleeping there. Thank God for his mercy, priests can marry. My wife suffers from severe insomnia and only sleeps during the day. Don't disturb her; she has a bad temper, and even I am afraid of her. If you hear any noises at night, don't come out; it's probably her moving around."

Laurent nodded obediently, concealing her skepticism.

The priest ushered her into the room and then left.

Whether intentionally or not, he treated her as an orphan without a family, ignoring her origins and not even asking her name. While this oversight provided Laurent with considerable convenience, it seemed incongruous with the tenets and duties of a "priest."

In fact, it felt as though he would have taken her in regardless of whether she had stopped his carriage. Reflecting on this, Laurent didn't feel fear; instead, she smiled playfully, like a nocturnal predator catching the scent of prey.

She thrived on danger, excitement, and the thrill of conquering the unknown.

Her heightened excitement led her to bite her nails, which Margo had meticulously trimmed and polished. Now, they were bitten to shreds once more.

Laurent eagerly anticipated the moment when the priest's true nature would reveal itself. If he turned out to be a genuinely kind-hearted person, she would be disappointed. She was prepared for whatever lay ahead, ready to navigate the intricacies of this new environment with her characteristic cunning and resilience.

In the quiet hush of evening, when shadows began their gentle dance upon the walls, the maid arrived with the evening meal.

She was a grand and stately figure, an elderly woman of round form, her hair a cascade of silver strands, her face adorned with age's gentle markings. With patient hands, she kindled the kerosene lamp, casting a warm glow across the room, and set before Laurent a steaming bowl of meat soup, urging her to partake before the sun's descent.

Laurent, with a slight furrow of her brow, lifted the spoon, allowing the thick broth to swirl before her gaze. "And should the sun set before I finish?" she inquired with a touch of mischief.

"As you wish," the maid replied, her tone as cool as the evening breeze. "Once the sun has bid the day farewell, my duties call me home. You may tend to the dishes yourself, if it pleases you. Be warned, however, that the madam will soon descend for her nightly rituals. The master, with his generous heart, offers refuge to wayward girls such as yourself, providing shelter and sustenance. But the madam, she has little patience for those with voices that pierce the air. So, mind your supper and spare yourself her ire."

With that, the maid turned, the dining cart creaking softly as she made her exit.

Yet, as she reached the threshold, Laurent let forth a scream, sharp and sudden, a mere trick of whimsy to startle the maid. And startled she was, pausing in her step, eyes wide with alarm. Upon realizing no harm had befallen, she turned back, bewildered, to face Laurent. "What mischief is this?" she demanded.

In a voice as sweet as honey, Laurent replied, "I wished to know if my voice could indeed carry such a shrill note." She returned to her soup, savoring it with deliberate grace.

The maid, casting one last incredulous glance, departed swiftly, as if to flee from some strange apparition.

Left to her own devices, Laurent closed her eyes, tasting the soup with care before letting it slip back into the bowl. She dabbed her lips with a napkin, rose with a languid grace, and began to wander the confines of her chamber.

The room was ordinary in every sense—its furnishings unremarkable, its secrets well concealed. She examined the lampshade, finding no hidden scents, and shifted the room's adornments, uncovering no hidden doors or chambers as those of her palace home. This was but a simple room, yet the peculiar behavior of its inhabitants piqued her curiosity.

As the sun dipped lower, painting the room in hues of crimson and gold, evening drew near.

A thought stirred within Laurent, reminding her of the world outside her window.

She approached and gazed upon the garden below, where each flower and leaf was washed in the eerie glow of the dying day, like a tapestry of blood and shadow. Yet more unsettling was the nature of these plants—each a vessel of poison, a deadly secret cloaked in beauty.

Laurent's heart quickened, her breath shallow, as she leaned closer, her eyes transfixed by the dangerous allure of belladonna, aconite, and foxglove. Who would suspect that the revered priest of this outpost would nurture such a deadly garden? The thought amused her, and if not for the chance of being overheard, she might have laughed aloud.

This place, shrouded in mystery and peril, had nearly led her astray from her original mission—to secure the priest's endorsement for her entry into the temple. Yet now, she found herself drawn to the intrigue of the household itself.

Nightfall arrived, and with it came not the madam as anticipated, but the priest himself. He entered clad in simple attire, his demeanor amiable, casting a glance at the untouched soup before resting a hand upon Laurent's shoulder. "Does the supper not please you?" he inquired, his voice a curious blend of warmth and command.

His hands were strong, the hands of a laborer rather than a priest, and the truth of his garden was revealed in the hard, stained nails, reminiscent of an alchemist's toil amidst fumes and concoctions.

Laurent met his gaze with a serene smile. "I find myself with a taste for sweeter fare, such as cream cake," she replied, her words laced with innocent charm.

The priest chuckled, amused by her candidness, yet his laughter quickly faded, replaced by a stern countenance. "Do you take this place for a refuge of indulgence? I gathered you from the brink of peril, saved by my hand, and offered you the blessing of the sacred statue. Show gratitude, as you would to the divine, and consume what is given. Spare me your demands, do you understand?"

His temper flared, his eyes intense, as he leaned closer, delivering his commands with fervor. Laurent, her expression one of feigned submission, nodded and drank the soup to the last drop, concealing her thoughts beneath a mask of compliance.

Beneath her calm exterior lay a mind quick and calculating, ever pondering the soup's potential secret—a poison brewed by the hand of her unpredictable host. But she bore no fear, for she knew well the art of patience, waiting for the right moment to tip the scales of power in her favor.

Were it not for the old man's potential utility, Laurent might have hurled the soup bowl at his head. Yet, she harbored no anger—for anger, in her mind, was a luxury for those with power and privilege.

Without status or authority, one often faced indignities, a reality she had come to accept.

In situations where strength was unequal, she practiced restraint; for there would always be time for bold actions when the scales were balanced in her favor.

Her thoughts lingered on a singular concern—whether the meat soup had been poisoned. Though she detected no obvious signs, she knew well that some poisons were as elusive as shadows, like the infamous Tofana Fairy Liquid, which was as clear as spring water. When administered gradually, it left neither trace nor suspicion upon the deceased, confounding even the most astute coroner.

Yet such a poison was rare and costly, unlikely to be squandered on someone like her.

Observing her compliance as she finished the soup, the priest's temper cooled, and he offered an apology, reminding her to wash the dishes before he departed.

As he turned to leave, the sun completed its descent, and the last vestiges of crimson light faded from the sky. Night enveloped the world, and the stars began their eternal vigil.

Laurent rose, taking the empty soup bowl in hand. She cast a nonchalant glance at the darkened garden outside, where the poisonous plants lay cloaked in shadow, before stepping out of the room.

With each step, she carried with her a growing resolve, her mind keenly aware of the intricate dance of power and deceit that lay before her.

FIVE

The hallway stretched before Laurent, dark as a moonless night, as if laying a snare for her every step. Yet she moved with the ease of one undaunted, her memory guiding her through the shadows toward the kitchen.

A small, dim lamp flickered on the wall, casting eerie shadows over the copper stove, which still pulsed with a faint, red-hot glow from the coals. She turned the faucet, and hot water flowed—a luxury.

This priest was no ordinary cleric. The copper stove and on-demand hot water suggested wealth and influence beyond the reach of most priests, who would never dream of such comforts. Coal was costly, and even some of the affluent could not afford the luxury of hot water at their fingertips.

Though Laurent was clever and composed, she was somewhat naive—her life had never truly been touched by poverty. During her flight, she encountered many struggling souls but only received aid from those who could afford to part with a little money. She had never met an ordinary priest, one clad in threadbare robes, subsisting on meager offerings from marrying the poor and praying for the destitute.

Casually, she rinsed the soup bowl with hot water and placed it back in the cupboard. Instead of returning to her room, she removed a candle from the wall lamp and began to explore the kitchen. The lavish setup surpassed her imaginings. Beyond the glowing copper stove, two pots of hot water simmered gently. The cupboard was lined with exquisite Eastern porcelain. Washed thistles and asparagus hung in the sink, and a half-cut cured ham lay invitingly on the cutting board.

With candle in hand, Laurent searched for the spices, her curiosity piqued. She tiptoed and sniffed each jar: salt, sugar, pepper... and then, the ominous scent of bufotalin powder, a deadly poison.

Just as she made this discovery, footsteps echoed down the hallway. In a swift motion, she hid the poisonous powder in her skirt pocket and returned the candle to its place on the wall.

The priest appeared, his transformation startling. The whites of his eyes were veined with angry red streaks, his eyelids trembled uncontrollably, and his nostrils and wrinkles twitched like those of a deranged old monkey.

He seemed particularly agitated, his face taut and eyes burning with ire. Muttering to himself, "He's ignoring me, he's ignoring me..." the priest spotted Laurent in the kitchen, and his suppressed fury erupted. "Why are you still here? Get out of there!"

Laurent's hand tightened around the blister powder hidden in her pocket. She tilted her head, adopting an air of innocent confusion, like a curious kitten. "I just finished washing the dishes. Who upset you?"

Despite her stunning beauty, her feigned innocence and childlike demeanor exuded a disarming charm—a skill she had honed over time.

The priest regarded her with a sinister gaze. It had been long since he felt the allure of a young girl, not since he brought that tiny idol from the parish shrine into his home.

Laurent was the first this month. She was strikingly beautiful, like a translucent ruby, radiating a natural and gorgeous glow, yet hinting at a playful, impure, and discordant undertone. In her presence, the priest felt a surge of conflicting emotions, drawn to her beauty but wary of the unknown forces she seemed to embody.

When Laurent first stepped into the carriage, the priest had allowed her to touch the revered statue, hoping to divine the deity's disposition. The God remained silent, which the priest took as tacit approval to pursue his monthly indulgences with women.

Yet, when he later reached for the statue, there was no divine response. The deity ignored him! The silence of his God was deafening.

Though his livelihood did not rely on the priesthood, he reveled in the prestige and power it conferred. He thrived on the admiration, reverence, and fear of those who called him "priest." While wealth afforded him comfort, it was faith that bestowed the true power he craved.

In this small town, he was seen as the divine messenger, the embodiment of the God of Light. The townsfolk approached him with their deepest pains and secrets, hanging on his every word. A mere gesture from him brought them immense solace. Here, he reigned as a god among men.

After stealing the miniature statue, fear gripped him, dreading the day the parish priest would discover its absence. Yet, the diocesan temple remained silent, as if the statue had never existed.

Days later, a wealthy lady came to confess, and he had her touch the statue. As her fingers brushed the divine hand, she trembled with reverence and awe until she fainted. Upon awakening, she knelt before him, tearfully proclaiming him a true messenger of God. "Compared to you, the incarnation of the god in the Supreme Temple is nothing at all."

"Please, keep this to yourself," he urged with solemn gravity. "Do not flaunt your faith."

The devout noblewoman promised secrecy. Yet, it was the priest himself who let the secret slip.

As his reputation soared, so did the status of the local clergy. Once pale and thin, they became rosy and robust. Missionaries came from afar to study under him, recording his every word as though it were divine scripture. His influence seemed to double overnight.

He understood that his newfound prestige stemmed from the miniature deity statue. In response, he adopted a life of purity and restraint, severing ties with his former mistresses.

He was resolved to be a true priest, until Laurent came into his life.

To him, women were temptresses, and Laurent was no different. The moment she touched the statue, the god turned away, leaving him alone in his turmoil.

His anxiety was overwhelming; his body shook, his chest heaved, and his eyes burned with anger and confusion. But the mistake was done, and it could not be undone.

The irony was not lost on him. He had never been a good man; he and his wife were corrupt and greedy. They lured innocent girls into their home, where his wife would poison them after he indulged in their beauty. They mixed the girls' blood, oil, and white wax into wrinkle-removing rouge for old, faded ladies. They sold abortion pills and elixirs made from the fat of the young, promising to restore lost youth in a single dose.

For over a decade, they committed these heinous crimes. Why, then, would taking in Laurent cost him the favor of the god?

And the statue... it had appeared in his leather box of its own accord.

Why had the deity chosen him? Certainly not for his piety; even he did not believe that. It became clear that the deity had chosen him for his wickedness. No wonder the god turned a cold shoulder when he attempted to mend his ways!

Once he understood this, he relaxed and gently apologized to Laurent, asking her to return to her room.

Laurent noticed the subtle shift in his demeanor, reading the change as easily as one reads a book. She saw the conflict within him, the surrender to his darker nature, and she understood that the game had just begun.

Clearly, this man was no saint; the malevolence within him was almost palpable. This place was far from safe. Logic dictated that Laurent should leave at once, but she still clung to the hope of a recommendation letter from the priest. Deceiving another priest seemed tiresome, and who knew if the next one would be any better?

Each with their own thoughts, they approached one another.

"Mr. Priest, can you do me a favor?" Laurent asked, her voice laced with a hint of desperation.

"Of course, child," the priest replied with a practiced gentleness.

"My mother is a devout believer," Laurent said weakly, her eyes pleading. "Her greatest wish was for me to become a faithful goddess. But you know, the goddess enters the temple around the age of seven and dedicates her entire life to the God of Light. I'm already past that age and need your recommendation letter to enter the temple. Can you fulfill this small wish? It's my mother's wish and my only wish in life."

Tears glistened as they trickled down her face, tracing a path to her thin, red lips. The temple taught that a pure girl should have pale, plump lips, but hers were thin and sharp, with a natural, wicked crimson hue. Yet, it was precisely this color that had ensnared the priest, compelling him to bring her here.

Without her presence, he might never have uncovered the secret of the miniature statue. His only regret was that she was too thin, lacking the fat that would make her a prime ingredient for the nourishing pills he and his wife brewed.

The priest hesitated, then finally spoke, "I know your piety, but a goddess must be a pure girl. If you've done anything immoral, recommending you to the temple could implicate me."

"Of course, I am a pure girl!" Laurent insisted, her expression a mix of bewilderment and intimidation. "I am truly pure; how can I prove it?"

"Purity or impurity is not just talk," the priest said. "Tomorrow evening, I will come to your room. Don't worry, I will bring the letter of recommendation. As long as you are a pure child, you can take the letter that symbolizes light and glory."

"Okay, I'll listen to you," Laurent nodded, tears of joy streaming down her face. "Whatever you say, I agree."

"Good child," the priest said, observing her tearful face. Her lips glowed even redder after crying, her cheeks and nose a delicate pink.

Was it his imagination, or did he catch a glint of cold light in her eyes, like a bullet from a flintlock gun, smoke and flames rushing past his face? When he blinked again, her face was once more filled with childlike sobbing.

She wasn't as innocent as she seemed.

But whether she was innocent or not, it mattered little to him. He had the miniature statue of a god, and his wife was an alchemist. He doubted this delicate girl could do anything against him, let alone cut his throat.

Thinking of this, he couldn't help but laugh. Cut his throat? Had she ever even wielded a knife or killed a chicken? He doubted her legs would hold at the sight of blood.

If not for tonight's guests, he might have dealt with her then and there.

The priest escorted Laurent to the door, advising her to sleep on time. Just as he was about to leave, he heard her whisper, "Since my family passed away, I've been having nightmares every night... Could you give me a Demon Forbidden Stone? Without one, I'm afraid I won't sleep well."

How could he provide a Demon Forbidden Stone? He had chosen this remote location to avoid the influence of such stones in town.

The priest gave her a dismissive pat on the head, his arrogance unmasked: "Don't be afraid. You live in the most powerful priest's house on the border. No demons or monsters dare harm you here. If you seek a Demon Forbidden Stone, I am the living one."

After the priest left, Laurent's demeanor shifted as swiftly as lightning. She coldly lowered her lashes, biting her thumbnail in contemplation.

The priest's intentions were clear, yet he hadn't acted immediately, suggesting more pressing concerns occupied him. Returning to her room, she cast a glance at the second floor. One locked room emitted peach-colored smoke—likely the alchemy chamber.

The absence of a Demon Forbidden Stone was her only solace. Her inquiry was merely to confirm her suspicion. Perhaps she could reach Margo through witchcraft, though the town's interference might hinder communication.

Her only tool was cantharidin powder, insufficient for immediate poisoning.

She needed a weapon, but all the kitchen knives were put away.

Perhaps she shouldn't have entrusted her ring to Margo for safekeeping. Yet even with it, the effect would be minimal. Surely, the priest had measures against toxins like her.

Taking him down wouldn't be simple.

Just then, she kicked something, glancing down to find the precious god statue the priest treasured so dearly.

There was no way the priest had left it here voluntarily. Even if he wasn't devout, his disdain for women would prevent him from allowing the statue to share space with her.

The only explanation was that the statue had found her on its own.

What is HE?

HE doesn't know.

HE seems to have been a cold, hollow, and gloomy black mist since birth. He feeds on desires, and whenever HE sees desires, He wishes to hold them in his mouth.

The priest's desires, steeped in impurity and corruption, exuded a musty stench that wearied him. Yet, in the midst of his discontent, he saw her.

To the world, she seemed a beautiful girl cloaked in innocence, but he knew better. Beneath that facade lay a cold, calculating nature, devoid of emotion yet driven by primal instincts and insatiable greed.

In this, he found a peculiar fascination, a hunger that stirred within him.

So, obeying his instinctual urge, he drew closer to her, compelled to grasp her desires and hold them within his grasp, as if they could satiate the void within his own being.

This attraction was not born of affection, but of a shared understanding, a recognition of the dark currents that flowed through them both.

CHAPTER
SIX

Laurent picked up the statue, lying on her bed, and examined it with a skeptical eye. She even shook it vigorously near her ear, as if expecting it to divulge some hidden secret.

It seemed to be an ordinary statue, unremarkable in every way.

She pressed her lips against its base, recalling a moment from her carriage ride, but the illusion she once felt was now absent.

"Is this truly just an ordinary deity statue?" she mused aloud.

But ordinary idols didn't "grow feet" and wander into her room.

"What are you?" she whispered, narrowing her eyes and bringing the statue closer to her ear. "Are you a demon or a creature conjured by the Romans? Why did you come to my room? You understand me, don't you?"

She waited, but silence was her only answer.

Laurent frowned, tossing the statue aside with a sense of disappointment.

For a fleeting moment, she had believed the statue might be sentient, capable of conversation. How absurd. Why had she entertained such a fanciful notion? It was as whimsical as children believing flower petals could predict the future. She forgot for a moment that she herself was just sixteen.

She stretched out on the bed, contemplating how to deal with the priest.

The poisonous plants in the flowerbed were not a viable option—if she possessed such lovely yet lethal flora, she would surely lay traps to ensnare thieves. Even without traps, some toxic weeds emitted shrill cries when touched. If the priest heard them, the outcome would be as dire as falling into a trap.

Was she really going to resort to applying cantharidin powder to her lips and hands, using such a base and repulsive method to kill him?

As she pondered, she turned over, only to find the statue had quietly moved behind her.

Laurent remained unfazed, not screaming or even widening her eyes in surprise.

"Is sneaking around all you can do?" she asked, propping her cheek with one hand while gripping the statue's throat with the other. "If that's the case, why hide in a statue? Wouldn't a cursed doll suit you better?"

The statue remained silent.

Laurent's eyelashes fluttered twice. She suddenly sat up, pulled off her white underskirt, and wrapped the statue in it.

If there had been an audience, they might have thought she was scared, trying to hide the statue with a clumsy trick.

But once wrapped, she slammed it hard onto the floor.

Bang.

A muffled sound echoed in the room.

The statue shattered.

Laurent's expression remained unchanged, but her pupils dilated slightly with excitement at the impending destruction.

This wasn't an ordinary statue. Inside, it was hollow, and nestled near the hem of the garments at the base was a small, round crystal that glowed like black jade.

As she reached out to touch the crystal, she immediately felt a cold malice, akin to the presence of a venomous snake.

In an instant, the malice transformed into a visible black mist, which began to chase, entangle, and invade her fingers.

At the same time, behind her, a thicker and more sinister black mist slowly filled the entire room.

The black mist slithered like a dangerous serpent, covering all the glowing spots inside the house.

In an instant, the entire room was engulfed in darkness.

She was swallowed by the cold, surging darkness, immersed in an abyss beyond reach.

Throughout it all, Laurent remained calm and composed.

Yet, in the next moment, she furrowed her brow and asked, as if on the verge of tears, "What are you? Are you going to kill me?"

The black mist loomed over her without any hint of emotion.

It was clear she was feigning innocence.

Her first reaction when confronted with unknown entities—whether potentially good or evil—was neither surprise, fear, nor blind worship. Instead, she treated them as humans and used little tricks to tease them. Should we say she was smart, arrogant, or foolish?

The black mist swam up to her, gazing down at her face from a high vantage point, intrigued by her audacity and composure.

Laurent's face was a study in contradictions—her beauty starkly contrasting with the hypocrisy lurking within. Her black hair framed white skin, her forehead was plump yet not prominent, and her nose was a perfect, elegant bridge. Her golden eyes shone brilliantly, and her lips were thin, small, and red, like a vivid stroke of paint.

The black mist observed her pale, slender fingers, attempting to mimic their form. But to grasp her throat, it required a hand large and strong, with the joints and spikes of a wild beast.

With a grotesque extension of its form, the black mist conjured an ugly hand, gripping Laurent's throat with force. The spikes on its knuckles pierced her skin, and beads of red, agate-like blood seeped out.

Laurent finally frowned, releasing a painful "sizzle." Was her expression, her gaze, her voice real or fake? Her desire was so potent that even her blood carried the scent of greed.

The black mist observed her perfectly sculpted nose, mimicking its shape as it leaned in to sniff her bright red wound.

Laurent remained silent, her teeth biting deeply into her lower lip.

Her blood was as sweet as her desires.

A thirst rose within the mist. "How can I taste her blood?" it pondered.

It fixed its gaze on her mouth for a few moments before decisively, mercilessly parting her upper and lower jaws to reveal her pristine teeth, bright red tongue, and soft palate.

It seemed the mist had crafted such a creation before, for it instantly comprehended how to replicate it, forming an identical tongue and mouth.

With the imitation lip and tongue, reminiscent of a black venomous snake's, it snaked through her thick black hair to lick the bloodstains on her neck.

Laurent pressed her lips together, remaining silent.

At this moment, she had to concede that mysterious and unfathomable powers, akin to gods, truly existed in the world.

She had seen Margo perform magic before, but it seemed more like a trick—sleight of hand, like pulling a pigeon from a top hat.

When Margo recounted legends of witches, monsters, and various guardian gods of the Roman Empire, it all sounded like supernatural fairy tales.

Gods, magic, and sorcery seemed mere explanations for the inexplicable forces people believed in. Who would have imagined beings like this black mist truly roamed the world?

The mist before her observed, imitated, and mocked her.

Despite lacking a tongue, it fixed its gaze on her mouth, replicated an identical organ, and licked the blood from her neck.

As it tasted the blood, it appeared immensely satisfied, the black mist swirling like a beast contentedly belching.

The gap between her and the Black Mist was vast.

When its grotesque palm gripped her throat, even the thought of resistance vanished, much like an antelope trapped in a cheetah's jaws — an antelope would never dream of gripping the cheetah's throat.

She loathed this feeling.

Since she had developed a thirst for power, she rarely felt powerless. The last time was in the fire court, where the judge unjustly stripped her of her right to inherit the throne on the absurd charge of "blasphemy."

She had thought that would be the final time she felt powerless.

Unexpectedly, not long after, she found herself a hostage once more. This time, to a shapeless black monster.

Was she truly that weak?

How could she break free from this vulnerability, where anyone could hold her captive?

Black Mist was taken by surprise. He hadn't anticipated that after threatening Laurent, she would not only remain unafraid but also become even more driven by her greed.

Desire radiated from her, carried on her slightly somber breath, fresh, potent, and vibrant as it flowed, creating a sweet breeze that mingled with every particle of his misty form. Even in the face of life-and-death situations, she didn't lose her resolve; instead, she burned with a fierce spirit like a wild beast.

She wasn't a perfect puppet, but she would be the sweetest indulgence he had ever experienced.

Perhaps he shouldn't have been so harsh with her.

Her greed was richer and sweeter than any desire he had ever tasted. If she were to end her life out of anger or fear, it might take him ages to find another like her.

At that moment, Laurent suddenly asked, "Are you a puppy? Have you licked enough?"

Her anger made her voice icy.

He needed to calm her down.

So, he pondered for a moment and placed his coarse palm on her forehead, capturing her happiest memories.

She was a composed and controlled individual, rarely experiencing extreme joy or sorrow. Her happiest moments included savoring delicious cakes, feeding pupating poisonous insects, stealing the perfect flintlock gun, and wearing a jewel-adorned crown.

Though he was still weak and couldn't please her with a crown, he could offer her a delicate flintlock pistol.

Laurent waited for a response, but none came. She frowned and glanced over, only to see Black Mist mimicking human hands and presenting a small pistol.

After she took the gun, Black Mist nuzzled her cheek like a playful puppy or kitten.

Laurent focused all her attention on the flintlock pistol, completely oblivious to his affectionate gesture. She thought she was doomed, believing this black mist was inhuman and incapable of communication. Unexpectedly, as if he knew her deepest desire, he handed her a delicate flintlock pistol that fit perfectly in her palm, as if custom-made for her.

What exactly is this black mist?

Is he conscious?

Does he possess wisdom?

Can he communicate with her?

She lifted her gaze and looked directly at Black Mist. "Why did you give me this gun?"

Silence.

No voice answered her.

Was she overthinking? Or was it true that this creature lacked the wisdom to communicate with her using words?

Laurent lowered her eyelashes and attempted to load the gunpowder into the barrel of the flintlock pistol. Black Mist seemed unable to understand her words, yet he cooperatively handed her the necessary accessories for the pistol.

"Will people outside hear me if I fire this handgun indoors?" she asked.

Still, there was no response.

Just as she was about to abandon her attempts to communicate with him, a low, hoarse, strange, blade-like voice emerged: "They... won't... hear."

He seemed to have just learned the language, struggling with the pronunciation. It took him several seconds before he could smoothly say the next sentence: "I sent it... to please you."

"Please me?" Laurent squinted her thick black eyelashes, her tone neither surprised nor sarcastic. "Why do you want to please me?"

Black Mist took a moment to contemplate the reason, then began to swirl around her.

Without a specific shape, his entire form was a bundle of senses, absorbing her beauty. While slowly learning language due to his weakness, he also absorbed the priest's desires. The priest's desires were vastly different from Laurent's, filled with vile thoughts towards innocent girls, imagining mistreating them like livestock.

He absorbed the priest's foul thoughts and couldn't help but feel restless.

At this moment, he regarded Laurent with his all-encompassing senses, and the sensation changed completely.

She became as enticing as profound evil, making every one of his senses come alive and wriggle.

"Because... I crave you," he said bluntly, his gaze enveloping her, describing her, feeling her. "I long for your skin, your bones, your organs, your desires... You are the sweetest feast I have ever encountered."

Laurent's eyes widened slightly, not in fear, but in understanding. She realized that this creature, this presence, was unlike anything she had encountered before. The black mist was drawn to her not just for her physical form but for the essence of her being, her desires, and her unyielding spirit.

In that moment, she felt a strange kinship with the mist, an understanding that they were both creatures driven by desire, though in vastly different ways. And perhaps, in this shared understanding, there was an opportunity—a chance to turn this unexpected encounter to her advantage.

CHAPTER
SEVEN

The priest was in an exuberant mood, basking in the success of his latest transaction.

Last night, he had skillfully convinced a wealthy lady to purchase his so-called nourishing pills, a concoction with a dark and sinister origin.

The noblewoman, draped in a wide-brimmed hat and a black veil, had rushed in with urgency, tossing a bag of Golden Johns his way, her voice a hushed whisper as she demanded the finest product. In the past, he might have hesitated at such a request, for the delicate and tender fat of young girls was not easily obtained. But now, a peerless beauty with black hair and porcelain skin was under his roof. How could he not see the potential for an excellent product?

The next morning, after a luxurious breakfast in bed, he summoned the maid—not the elderly Black woman who worked in the shadows, but a charming and melancholy beauty—to oil his hair. With practiced precision, he used a badger hair brush to lather soap foam, applying it to his temples and jaw before shaving his emerging beard with a razor.

The priest was acutely aware of his advancing age, knowing that his days of reveling in wealth and indulgence were numbered. Yet, he chose to live extravagantly, sparing no expense on food, clothing, and the finer things in life. He even harbored a pathological habit of equating his expenditures to the cost of young girls' lives.

For instance, in his twisted economy, a young girl was worth one hundred Golden Johns. One Golden John equaled twenty silver coins, and one silver coin equaled twenty copper coins.

His annual rent was a hefty 1,400 silver coins and 70 Golden Johns. Each year he resided in his lavish villa, more than half of a girl's life was metaphorically sacrificed for it.
He considered himself a connoisseur with an exquisite palate: fresh and tender veal, pricey caviar, and delectable boletus mushrooms graced his table. His daily meals cost a mere hundred silver coins, a sum that could sustain an ordinary person for two months. Tragically, the sparkle in a poor girl's eyes dimmed to satiate his insatiable appetite.

Moreover, he employed a carriage driver with noble bearing, paying him two hundred silver coins a month——a staggering sum of one hundred and twenty Golden Johns annually.

Whenever he traveled in his four-wheeled carriage, preaching sanctimoniously in the name of God, the weight of his hypocrisy was crushing. With each journey, another young girl would metaphorically perish beneath its wheels. It seemed that even the cost of maintaining his private carriage demanded more than one life.

His world was one of decadence and darkness, where the value of a life was reduced to mere currency, and innocence was a commodity to be consumed. In his eyes, the world was a ledger of debts and payments, where each indulgence was balanced by the extinguishing of another's light.

Despite his wife's skills as an accomplished alchemist, she had yet to create a genuine elixir of immortality. Consequently, the priest resorted to abducting young girls, finding cruel satisfaction in extinguishing the light in their vibrant eyes and relishing their vitality.

Though he couldn't extend his life, the perverse pleasure of ending theirs was enough for him. Tonight promised yet another occasion for this grim indulgence.

Initially, he had no desire to spend time crafting recommendation letters. But when he noticed the cold glint in Laurent's eyes, he realized she wasn't as easily deceived as the hundreds of girls before her. Without a genuine letter, she wouldn't allow him to touch her soft, fair hands.

As the priest was writing, a knock on the door interrupted his focus. The maid had come to report something missing in the kitchen. Annoyed, he retorted, "Can't you see I'm busy?! What's missing from the kitchen? Does it concern me, or do I look like the new cook?"

The maid quickly closed the door, deciding not to bother him further.

Thus, until the priest finished writing the recommendation letter and tucked it into his robe, he remained unaware of what was missing from the kitchen.

That evening, he drank a large bowl of aphrodisiac soup, though reluctant to consume such an expensive concoction. Made from a blend of exotic ingredients, it was a popular item due to concerns over declining fertility. If not for the desire to enjoy Laurent's beauty, he wouldn't have spent so extravagantly.

He instructed his wife to collect the body in half an hour and briskly headed toward Laurent's room.

Laurent had prepared herself, wearing a light pink dress and combing her hair into thick braids. She was eating a cone cake lavishly topped with almond milk ice cream, sugar, raisins, and cherries—expensive end-of-life care.

The priest asked gently, "Is it delicious?"

"Do you want me to be honest?" Laurent replied, licking the cream from her fingers. "Not particularly; I prefer vanilla. But you've managed to find such a sweet cake in the countryside. Well done."

Her dining manners, combined with her sweet yet superior tone, made the priest laugh uncontrollably.

He approached her, placing a hand on her shoulder, half-threatening and half-suggestive: "You're such a beautiful, strange, tempting little girl! My God, I want to devour you in one bite... Who taught you that poise? You looked like a queen just now! Are you the queen who fled?"

Laurent responded, "I am indeed."

Delighted, the priest engaged in this role-playing game: "So, Your Majesty, should I kneel down to you?"

Laurent turned and, with a casual glance, simply said, "Kneel down."

The priest was ready to jest but was captivated by her fierce eyes.

Her golden eyes, framed by mysterious black lashes, radiated purity and beauty when she smiled. But when she stopped, they transformed into deep wells of darkness, radiating a cold light that sent shivers down his spine. Concepts like "terror," "hell," and "cruelty" replaced thoughts of beauty.

The priest felt a chill.

He must have been mistaken. How could she, at her age, possess such terrifying eyes?

To regain control and boost his confidence, the priest pulled out the recommendation letter, waving it before her: "This is your letter. Do you want it?"

As expected, the intense look was merely an illusion.

Laurent's attention shifted to the letter, her golden eyes following his hand with innocent curiosity. She seemed like no more than a young girl, devoid of deeper schemes.

After all, what fortress could a sixteen-year-old girl have? Noble girls, confined indoors for needlework, rarely encountered men. How could she have a gaze more ferocious than theirs?

The priest felt his earlier fear was absurd. Being afraid of a little girl—it was ridiculous.

He said, "Do you want this letter? If so, just follow my instructions and remove your skirt."

He opened the letter, showed its contents to Laurent, and placed it on the cabinet. Then he sat back, watching her, anticipating her response.

In these situations, girls often fell into despair, sobbing as they undressed. Some fainted from shame and fear, while others who had experienced the forbidden might feign calmness and ask for sponges or sheep intestines to avoid pregnancy.

This was one of his favorite scenarios, observing life's facets from the comfort of his home. Witnessing these girls, held hostage and forced to please him, filled him with superiority and satisfaction.

The priest, a man who preached the glorious deeds of God and His messengers, found his true power not in spreading faith but in the cruelty he inflicted on those unfortunate girls.

The effects of the aphrodisiac began to take hold, sending a feverish heat through his veins, turning his eyes red and his breath hot with urgency.

Yet, Laurent remained unmoved, calmly licking cream and sugar from her fingers, seemingly oblivious to his commands.

He repeated himself, his patience thinning, then snapped, "Stop licking! Come and serve me. If you please me, I'll buy you any cake you desire."

Laurent tilted her head and chuckled softly. "Really? Weren't you going to knock me out, peel off my skin, cut away the fat, and throw it into the alchemy furnace to make medicine?"

Her words reverberated in the priest's ears, shocking him into silence. He stared at her, bewildered, as if the prey had suddenly turned predator.

For a moment, he tried to regain control, forcing a calm tone. "Where did you hear such nonsense? I would never do that to you... If I did, not only would those around me disapprove, but God would punish me with His wrath."

Laurent smiled, finishing the last of the cream on her fingers, wiping them clean with a napkin. From under the table, she retrieved a flintlock pistol, and the priest's eyes widened once more in disbelief.

He had seen such weapons only with high-ranking guards, certainly not in the hands of a girl. He relaxed slightly, convinced she wouldn't know how to use it, even if she dared try.

"Do you really plan to use that on me, my little angel?" he taunted. "I doubt you even know how to load it. Stop struggling, and obey me. I'll give you what you desire..."

His voice trailed off as Laurent expertly loaded the pistol with bullets, her movements sharp and precise. The priest's face went rigid, a chill creeping up his spine as she raised the gun, aiming it directly at him.

Frozen in terror, he stood there, the effects of the medicine making him appear grotesque, his face flushed, sweat pouring down, limbs trembling.

Laurent tilted her head, slowly pulling the trigger with her slender fingers. Just as she was about to fire, she leaned forward, pouting her lips with a playful "Bang~," mimicking the sound of a gunshot.

The priest's heart eased, momentarily relieved. He chuckled dryly, wiping sweat from his brow. "My little angel, my little kitten... you're so naughty. I've never seen a girl as playful as you."

But his laughter died in his throat as Laurent pulled the trigger for real.

Bang.

Smoke filled the air, and the priest collapsed into a pool of blood.

Calmly, Laurent stepped onto the chair, retrieving the recommendation letter from atop the cabinet. Thanks to the meticulous priest, the envelope remained pristine, untouched by bloodstains.

With the letter in hand, she glanced back at the lifeless body, an image of concluded justice. Laurent had reclaimed her power, and the priest's reign of terror had come to an abrupt and well-deserved end.

CHAPTER

EIGHT

L aurent folded the envelope carefully, tucking it securely into her bra, and donned her white cloak. Without sparing a glance at the priest, now entirely engulfed by the black mist, she gracefully made her way to the second floor.

Her mission extended beyond retrieving the recommendation letters; she sought the priest's accumulated wealth and valuable alchemy materials. The second floor, seldom visited, was even more lavishly decorated than the first. Rose-colored velvet wall coverings lined the corridor, adorned with inlaid paintings and gilded frames. Under the candlelight, colorful pottery shards, enamel, and ink sparkled brilliantly. A treasure cabinet displayed valuable items from around the world—porcelain, jade, shells, ivory carvings, copperware, and more.

Laurent was acutely aware that the priest's wealth came at the expense of young girls' lives. While she lacked personal sympathy for these unfortunate souls, she despised the priest's methods of exploiting them. She recognized the hypocrisy in his actions, reminiscent of the nobles who opposed female autonomy yet depended on women's tender presence.

Her thoughts turned cold as she glanced at the treasure cabinet. If Margo had received her message, she should be on her way by now. Laurent planned to take what she needed and have Margo return the remaining items to the victims' families.

The first room she entered was a dressing room. Laurent went straight to the long wardrobe, pulling open the silk curtain to reveal about ten neatly ironed white robes and several woolen cloaks with large hoods. She needed a cloak to conceal her identity and quickly pocketed one.

The wardrobe drawers were filled with luxurious items: collars, neckties, shirts, and vests—useless to Laurent. She wouldn't bother exchanging them for money but intended for Margo to use them to aid the poor families oppressed by the priest. She rifled through the drawers, selecting only a few shiny gem cufflinks, precious gold ones, and a pair of fragrant goat leather gloves.

As she concluded her search, Margo arrived just in time. Upon learning of the queen's plight, Margo was shocked by the priest's wickedness, his cruelty towards young girls.

"Fortunately, His Majesty is even more ferocious than he is," Margo thought with some relief.

"What are you thinking?" Laurent asked thoughtfully.

Margo quickly replied, "I was thinking, fortunately, Your Majesty was clever enough to avoid the priest's clutches." She then asked, "Your Majesty, should we return those fine linen shirts and silk morning gowns in the drawer to the victim girls' parents?"

Laurent responded nonchalantly. She had no use for the priest's personal clothing; they were tainted. But those clothes, stained with the priest's disgusting fluids and soaked in the tears and blood of young girls, were better returned to their rightful owners than left for strangers to claim.

"But how can I find the parents of those girls?" Margo asked.

"The priest, nearing old age, lusts for young, vigorous girls. Do you think it's just lust?" Laurent said lightly. "He believes that by killing them and consuming their bodies, he can control his fate. In reality, he gains nothing but sin and the fat on his body."

Margo was silent, recognizing the sharp accuracy of Her Majesty's words.

"For him, those girls are not only a source of vitality but also the foundation of his power," Laurent calmly conveyed the priest's mindset as she slipped on the leather gloves, "He likely kept a record of the names and addresses of every girl he harmed, probably so he could reminisce and savor his misdeeds. Find that name book, copy it, and use it to distribute the priest's property accordingly. Keeping the original version will be useful to me."

Margo nodded earnestly and promptly set off to locate the name book Laurent referred to.

Laurent looked at the alchemy room filled with peach-red smoke, put on her cloak and hood, and opened the door.

The room was empty.

The priest's wife had fled.

Laurent tilted her head slightly, a lively expression crossing her face. A small smile played on her lips. She knew that she had taken the first step in dismantling the priest's cruel empire, and with Margo's help, justice would be served.

At the moment the priest fell into a pool of blood, his wife, Marina, sensed something was amiss. As one of the top alchemists in the Holy Light Empire, her instincts were finely tuned. The empire, with its strict laws against magic, witchcraft, and the raising of magical creatures, allowed alchemists like Marina to practice their craft within regulated boundaries. Her expertise was unmatched, giving her a heightened awareness of her surroundings.

The faint scent of gunpowder mixed with the metallic tang of blood reached her nostrils, alerting her to the dire situation. Marina knew immediately that something had gone terribly wrong. Despite her position and skills, she felt no urge to investigate or seek vengeance for her husband; their marriage had been one of convenience, a mutually beneficial arrangement rather than one of love or loyalty.

The priest's death was a signal for her to flee.

The girl, Laurent, was an enigma—odd and dangerous.

Marina had drizzled a knock-out drug over the cake, expecting the priest to signal if needed. No signal came, which meant Laurent had managed to kill the priest with a flintlock gun while consuming the drugged cake. The situation was far beyond her control.

Now was the time to flee. She packed swiftly, grabbing only essentials, and wrapped herself in a gray cloak and hood before darting toward the forest bordering the villa.

In her haste, she failed to notice the black mist trailing her like a predator in the night.

As Marina ran, fear and regret gnawed at her. She regretted her involvement in the priest's vile deeds and the decision to incorporate the bodies of young girls into their alchemical products. The priest had convinced her it would enhance the pills' value and profit, a notion she had accepted without question. But now, she realized the horror of their actions. Those girls' lives had been sacrificed for empty promises, and guilt weighed heavily on her conscience.

"It was all the old man's idea. I was forced..." she murmured, trying to absolve herself. "If you want revenge, don't come after the wrong person... I'm innocent."

Yet, her protests rang hollow. Marina conveniently forgot her own role in leading those young girls to their doom, in preparing their remains for the alchemical furnace, and in enjoying the wealth built on their suffering.

Despite her self-deception, deep down, Marina knew she had no right to claim innocence. Her hands were stained with the blood of the innocent, and she knew retribution would inevitably find her. But in the moment of her flight, she clung to the lie she told herself, seeking solace in the false belief that she was not to blame.

As Marina neared the edge of the forest, her breath came in ragged gasps, each step fueled by desperation and the instinct to survive. She could see the faint outline of the path leading away from the villa, a promise of freedom just within reach. However, the black mist trailed her, a silent and relentless pursuer, weaving through the trees with an eerie grace.

The mist was more than just a shadow; it was a manifestation of justice, set into motion by Laurent's decisive actions. It moved with purpose, ensuring that all those who participated in the priest's sinister activities would face the consequences of their actions.

Marina felt its presence, an unsettling chill that seemed to seep into her very bones. She quickened her pace, but the mist remained close, an inescapable reminder of her past transgressions. Her mind raced with thoughts of escape, but deep down, she knew there was nowhere she could hide from the truth.

With a resigned sigh, she turned to face the mist, understanding that the time had come to acknowledge her part in the darkness and to accept the justice that Laurent had set in motion.

Terrified, Marina asked, trembling, "What are you... why are you pursuing me? I have no grudges against you."

The black mist remained silent.

HE was contemplating the conversation with Laurent from the previous night.

When she learned of HIS longing for her, she smiled angelically—sweet and full of intrigue.

HE desired everything about her: her desires, her skin, her blood, her bones, her internal organs... yet she sought nothing from it.

Thus, she gained the upper hand and led the conversation.

With innocent-looking eyes filled with undisguised malice, she said, "You long for me, you want me to be your food, right?"

Yes.

But not entirely right.

HE yearned for her blood and desires as precious as delicacies but did not want to kill her.

HE wanted to enjoy her forever.

As he pondered how to convey this, Laurent stepped forward, right into the mist. Her assertiveness was overwhelming, her mind incredibly sharp, and her fierce, predatory nature was simply irresistible to him. If he were human, he might have found himself falling for her allure.

Once his initial surprise faded, he became acutely aware of everything about her.

Her long, black hair cascaded like a waterfall, her skin was strikingly fair, her internal organs gleamed with clarity, and her blood vessels resembled seaweed. He noticed the graceful curve of her back, the occasional tension in her shoulder blades, her elegant and slender neck, and her two pure yet dangerously alluring golden eyes.

In the enveloping dark mist, he could sense every detail about her.

"I can agree to your request," she said, a smile playing on her lips, "but you must serve me. As long as you are loyal to me, I am yours."

To a human, these words might have sounded like a dizzying declaration of love.

But he was not human.

To him, it was a straightforward transaction.

He agreed.

"I will be loyal to you," he replied in a low, hoarse voice, "as long as you provide me with the sustenance I crave."

Laurent smiled faintly and extended her hand.

He was momentarily stunned, unsure of his next move. Was he supposed to kiss her? How would he go about it, shifting his form as he had once done —into head, neck, and hands—to kiss the back of her hand?

In an instant, Laurent withdrew her hand and remarked, "Since that's the case, we'll save it for next time."

But when would that next time be?

In his memory, he had never encountered such a confrontation with a woman. Laurent had disturbed his mist entirely.

After she had eliminated the priest, he behaved like a devoted hunting dog, first devouring the priest's body entirely, and then setting off in pursuit of the escaping Marina.

If he could bring the woman back, it might please Laurent. His thoughts were simple. He commanded the mist to spread toward Marina—only Laurent could safely reside within it, for the mist was a deadly miasma for ordinary people.

Suddenly, Marina screamed, "Don't kill me, don't kill me... I had a deal with the Skeleton Society, you can't kill me!"

The black mist halted its spread and asked in a cold, hoarse voice, "What is the Skull Society?"

Marina, taken aback, replied earnestly, "You can speak? How is that possible?" She continued to explain, "The Skull Society is a group that worships darkness. They believe that light is extinct and that only by embracing darkness can they achieve eternal life. They consider miasma to be a miracle of the God of Darkness, and wherever there is miasma, they are present... You are the only miasma I have ever encountered that has the ability to speak."

The black mist seemed to consider this.

Marina swallowed hard and pleaded, "I can take you to meet the leader of the Skeleton Society. They'll make you a god and worship you! I've shown you the path to godhood... Please, don't kill me."

Becoming a god?

The black mist pondered briefly, but then mercilessly strangled Marina, transforming into a black python to drag her body back.

His first thought wasn't about becoming a god, but to use her as a bargaining chip to please Laurent.

When she was happy, she provided many delightful offerings.

Such as desire.

Such as blood.

NINE

Margo quickly found the name book in the priest's bedside table, just as Laurent had instructed.

The priest, who had committed numerous evil deeds, seemed almost eager for others to uncover his crimes, hiding evidence of his wrongdoings in the very place he slept, with his head turned towards it each night. Wasn't he afraid of retribution? Didn't he fear that the souls of the girls he had wronged would come back to haunt him?

Margo frowned, struggling to contain her anger as she opened the name book and was horrified by the extent of the priest's wrongdoing. In less than a decade, he had poisoned nearly seven hundred girls. These victims were treated like dismembered elk, with everything from their hair to their nails sold as commodities.

Remarkably, the priest felt no guilt. He even went so far as to annotate their facial features with short Latin letters next to their names, ensuring that their identities would be vividly remembered in the future.

Margo's fingers trembled as she read.

Being executed by Her Majesty was too lenient for this old man. Villains like him deserved to be cast into a terrifying purgatory, boiled in magma, tortured by demons, and corroded by poisonous swamps for eternity.

Determined to report the matter to the queen, Margo closed the name book and turned to leave, only to find a giant python standing in front of Laurent.

The python's devilish scales emitted a nightmarish black mist, yet it possessed a pair of beautiful eyes—unlike any Margo had seen.

Typically amber, these eyes were a stunning blend of purple and blue, like a mysterious purple morning mist, rainbows after a storm, or purple-blue gemstones splashing on the sea.

The python's eyes were strikingly beautiful and soft, like a captivating dream. Yet, when it suddenly hurled the priest's wife's body, Margo was taken aback.

Despite its beauty, the python exuded an overwhelming sense of danger. It was a powerful evil creature, its sharp vertical pupils revealing its true animalistic nature. Without needing to attack, its emotionless gaze alone was enough to create an oppressive atmosphere, like a tsunami crashing down.

Margo's instinct was to protect the queen. Despite Laurent's harsh interrogation, which had left Margo on the brink of death, she knew Laurent aimed at the spy of the

Roman Empire, not her personally. Over the years, she had also benefited from Laurent's rule.

Although Laurent was inherently cold and indifferent, she had a clear sense of love and hate. Those who were loyal to her could expect their loyalty to be rewarded a hundredfold, even a thousandfold.

Margo always remembered one crucial fact: if not for Laurent, she would have long since perished at the hands of assassins who meticulously targeted the Roman Empire's spies, or from the endless palace poisons. She never knew how such an abundance of poison found its way into the Empire of Light. Even during something as simple as a handshake, she had to be wary of gloves that might have been soaked in poison.

Perhaps even worse, she could have become a scapegoat in the ongoing power struggles between nobles, falsely accused and sent to the guillotine.

She was resolved to save Laurent, no matter what.

But as she rushed forward, the massive python unexpectedly lowered its head, allowing Laurent to stroke its flattened head.

Margo was stunned - Laurent, you truly are remarkable.

Laurent gently caressed the snake's head, looking at the corpse on the ground with interest. "Are you trying to please me with this?" she asked.

Only then did Margo realize the queen was speaking to the python.

How could she explain to the queen that no demon, even the highest level kept by the Roman monarch, could communicate with humans or possess emotions, unless enlightened by Roman gods?

However, in Roman culture, power was revered, and anyone sufficiently powerful could be deified. True deities had long been forgotten in history's tide.

Margo wanted to warn the queen about the dangerous python. But to her surprise, the python spoke in a low, hoarse voice, "I... want to... please you."

Margo was left speechless. The day's events felt utterly surreal.

Laurent smiled faintly, neither confirming nor denying the python's intention.

Without turning around, she extended her hand toward Margo, requesting the name book.

Margo quickly handed it over. Laurent opened the book, her cascading black hair falling naturally, revealing her elegant neck.

The moonlight filtered through the leaves, highlighting her thick, rich hair, which, even when loose, accentuated her petite, adorable face.

Her way of tracing the notebook's pages with her fingers, coupled with her smile, exuded warmth and affection. If Margo hadn't known the queen's true nature and the contents of the book, she might have been deceived by the apparent sweetness.

But she knew better. The queen's smile was not sweet but sinister.

"So, it turns out he intended to strip my skin, extract the oil, and even sell my hair and nails as commodities," Laurent said, closing the book with a frown. "He's truly despicable. Simply killing him would be too easy a punishment."

"The opportunity to please me has arrived, little snake," she said, "I want you to help me seek revenge."

Her eyes twinkled with cunning, actual nonchalant. She didn't care about the priest's wickedness; she just wanted to test the python's power.

He—absorbing the priest and his wife's evil thoughts—felt slightly less weak, enough to grant some of her wishes.

If she could deduce his origins, he would be grateful.

The essential point was that he remembered how sweet and alluring her blood and desires were. As long as she provided him with abundant sustenance, he would remain loyal.

"How do you want me to help you?" the python asked.

Laurent's eyes curved into a smile, dimples appearing on her cheeks. Her red lips whispered coldly, "An eye for an eye, blood for blood. By law, the priest should be burned. But that's too lenient. I want him to be deprived of reincarnation and suffer eternally in purgatory. Can you do it?"

—The simplest request.

His initial thought: what was he before, to consider life, death, and depriving reincarnation as simple matters?

His status seemed incredibly high, beyond life, death, or reincarnation. But paradoxically, he was also perpetually unsatisfied.

He is indifferent to order and fate. If he were complete, the entire world would be under his control.

However, despite this potential power, his status seems quite low, as he has never truly satisfied his appetite.

He is like a nocturnal predator, roaming through forests, mountains, and lakes in search of the most delectable desires.

Had Laurent not shattered the statue, he would never have imagined becoming a tangible being, much less conversing with humans. It seems he has long been accustomed to being omnipresent, like light and mist.

"Sure," he said, locking his vertical pupils onto Laurent, curious about her thoughts regarding his identity.

"That's amazing," Laurent praised, then posed an unexpected question. "Why did you transform into such a beautiful snake? Is it because you know I like snakes?"

He had no idea. His only desire was to quell the restless mist. Initially, he controlled every strand of black mist, but after consuming the priest's desires, they began to writhe chaotically.

The mist absorbed the priest's desires, gaining intelligence akin to low-level demons. Like hot blood surging through veins, the mist burned and boiled, urging him to explore the intricacies of human relationships.

Transformed into a python, he had calmed down, but Laurent's casual words stirred the foolish mist once more. The mist writhed silently, desperate to escape his sturdy scales and move toward Laurent, to invade her senses and relish every part of her.

To silence these shameful impulses, he swiftly extracted the priests' souls, ravaged them, and cast them into fiery purgatory before Laurent.

Depleted of energy, the restless mist naturally subsided.

Laurent clapped her hands in delight. "Wow! Amazing," she exclaimed. Without hesitation, she cut her palm with a dagger and offered it to the python. "Drink! Your reward."

The scent of her blood made the black mist on the scales even more restless, twisting and leaping like a wild flame, eager to break free and reach the sweet crimson pool in her palm.

The python gazed at the blood for a few moments before transforming into a slender black snake. It wound its way up her skirt, across her waist, and along her arms until it reached her palm.

As it neared, its animalistic instincts became more pronounced. Finally, like a venomous snake ready to strike, it opened its jaws and bit into her wound, drinking deeply and savoring the taste.

Margo, watching nearby, was extremely concerned. To her, the scene resembled a cult ritual.

Laurent tilted her head, watching the savoring snake with interest in her eyes.

Margo dared not remind the queen to be cautious, fearing that such a warning would only excite her more.

Once the little snake finished, the wound healed instantly.

"Do you have a name, little snake?" Laurent asked, gently tapping the snake's head with her index finger, her tone sweet as if she had discovered a beloved caterpillar. "Would you like me to give you a name, or do you prefer to be called 'little snake' forever?"

"I don't have a name," he replied, feeling momentarily exhausted after consuming Laurent's exquisite blood. "You can call me 'Loire,' and I will always be loyal to you. When I wake up, there's something else I want to tell you."

He had one more thing to offer her.

After saying this, he transformed into an elegant black bracelet around her wrist and drifted into a deep slumber.

Laurent, intrigued, called out to him several times but received no response. Her initial excitement at capturing an intriguing creature was suddenly dampened.

Absentmindedly playing with the snake bracelet, she turned to Margo and instructed, "Copy the name book. Return the property the priest has plundered over the years in the order I've marked. In half a month, we'll visit the parish temple."

"Your Majesty, half a month might not be enough time to manage the aftermath and distribute the assets," Margo cautioned.

Laurent smiled. "Who said I need to handle the aftermath?"

Margo, shocked, asked, "You don't? The priest has many disciples, and news of his disappearance can only be hidden for a month or two at most. Once it spreads, everyone will know he's missing. How will you present yourself at the parish temple? They'll all remember you were recommended by the priest and might suspect you of murder."

Laurent nodded, smiling sweetly. "I know. That's exactly what I want."

Margo couldn't help but shiver. Every time the queen showed such a sweet smile, it heralded trouble. The last time she smiled like this, the priest was consigned to hell, never to reincarnate.

CHAPTER
TEN

Margo, once a notable spy of the Roman Empire, had a revelation as she pieced together Laurent's intentions.

Laurent aimed to exploit the priest's death to tarnish the temple's reputation.

Imagine a time when society held the temple in the highest regard. Suddenly, a scandal erupts, revealing that the most respected priest at the border is actually a murderer. For over a decade, he had poisoned nearly 700 girls and planted deadly plants in his courtyard. He meticulously documented each girl's name and details, hiding these records in his bedside table and admiring them daily. Such a revelation would profoundly shock the public.

If Laurent were to reveal this scandal herself, the temple would likely suppress it through its considerable influence. But if the temple initiated an investigation upon her joining, the dynamics would change.

When the diocese's priest suspects her of murder, his outrage is inevitable. The very words "goddess," "priest," and "murder" combined would wreak havoc on the temple's reputation.

The temple's immediate reaction would likely be to silence her through assassination. Hence, Laurent needed to ensure she was memorable and beloved before the priest's disappearance was uncovered.

Under public scrutiny, while she couldn't evade punishment, she would avoid assassination. The temple couldn't afford another mysterious disappearance.

Yet, she'd also serve as a scapegoat to restore the temple's authority

After all, the temple governs the people through faith and authority. divine power is supreme, and the sanctity of the gods' beautiful and holy presence must remain untainted.

Her interrogation might be poised to become one of the most vibrant and grand spectacles in history, likely attracting common folk from across the entire diocese. Should she choose to reveal the truth and voice her grievances at that moment, it would severely challenge the temple's authority.

This plan is a risky maneuver, a delicate game where each step relies on the precise action of every participant, including herself. Any deviation from the plan, and her life would be at stake.

For instance, if she fails to make a lasting impression or win the people's affection, or if the diocese's priest, in a moment of indifference, decides not to pursue the investigation and instead arbitrarily condemns her to be burned, she would need to find another way to escape. The most critical factor is whether the parents of the young girls, intimidated by the temple's authority, will have the courage to testify. If they remain silent, her entire plan could fall apart.

She is placing her bets entirely on the capability of Loire, who stands by her side.

During their brief confrontation, she challenged Loire to strip the priest of his reincarnation rights and send him to hell, as a way to test his abilities.

She is wagering not only on Loire's capabilities but also on her own judgment.

If her assessment is wrong, she risks losing everything.

Margo was convinced of Laurent's resolve. However, she couldn't help but wonder if she, in Laurent's shoes, would have the courage to take such a gamble. Her answer was a resounding no. She lacked confidence in how the parish priest would react, doubted her ability to win everyone's affection, and questioned Loire's capabilities. Margo didn't have the nerve to stake everything when the future was so uncertain.

The queen, Laurent, seemed truly daring, even to the point of madness.

Margo recalled a disturbing memory: the queen had once taken her to a grim execution chamber. While ordinary nobles would steer clear of such a dark and foreboding place, the queen sat nearby, watching intently. Her topaz-like eyes shone with an intense brightness, and her cheeks flushed with a vivid blush, resembling a child discovering the allure of dolls for the first time.

At that moment, Margo thought Laurent's interest was because she was like a "toy doll" to the queen. However, in hindsight, it became evident that Laurent's gaze was never truly on her. Instead, Laurent was captivated by the strange and varied instruments of torture, which were the real "toy dolls" she longed for.

This realization explained Laurent's impatience with the priest's matter—she craved the thrill of risk and the benefits it promised.

Yet, Margo worried: could Laurent's ally, Loire, truly withstand the temple's might?

There was no record of a creature like Loire—a being with human-like intelligence and speech—in the Roman Empire's monster compendium.

What was Loire's origin, and why did he ally with the queen, consuming her blood?

Margo's imagination wandered: was Laurent harboring a world-ending secret? Was Loire using her for a larger scheme? But if Loire had the power to disrupt the world's order, why rely on Laurent? Wouldn't it be more strategic to align with the Roman Empire's warriors?

The Roman Empire revered strength. Loire could easily ascend to power, win the king's favor, and dominate the world.

Yet, Loire's ambitions were simpler: he desired Laurent's company and blood.

His allegiance was driven by appetite, not conquest.

The following morning, Margo was taken aback by Laurent's annotated name book.

She couldn't discern any pattern in Laurent's markings.

With information tightly controlled by the Holy Light Empire, most people relied on local churches for news. Margo speculated that Laurent prioritized compensating families closest to the church, ensuring they'd be the first to testify during her trial.

However, Laurent's annotations seemed random, as if she casually selected names while enjoying breakfast.

Concerned for the queen's safety, Margo sought clarification. "Your Majesty," she began, "why compensate this family first?"

Laurent, engrossed in her breakfast, corrected her, "Call me Master, not Your Majesty. We must avoid slip-ups." She continued, "Why don't you understand?"

"Okay, Master," Margo said, puzzled. "I really don't understand. This family lives so far from the church. Any news announced by the church in the morning would only reach them by sunset at best. Why not choose a family closer to the church? They also lost a daughter, and they're still a wealthy family."

Laurent took a bite of her buttered bread, syrup glistening on her lips. She replied casually, "A wealthy family? Did you check their surnames in the register?"

Margo nodded. "Yes, there's a parish registry on the bookshelf. Their second daughter died. The eldest daughter is married to a baron, and the youngest brother is studying at a seminary, planning to become a priest after graduation. The family was devastated by the second daughter's disappearance, especially the mother, who nearly drowned herself. That's why the younger brother chose to become a priest—to save his sister's soul. He wants to use everything he's learned to bring peace to his sister soul. Isn't this the best choice?"

Laurent, savoring her bread, responded, "Wealthy families might seem ideal, but they're also the worst choice."

Margo, surprised, asked, "Why?"

Laurent pointed out, "Their title—Baron—is the issue."

Margo remained confused. In her view, nobles wielded more power than commoners. If nobles wouldn't testify, how could commoners?

Laurent saw through Margo's thoughts and carefully wiped her mouth with a napkin. "How was the Kingdom of Light established, and how did it stand firm amid so many threats?" she mused. "In the past, confined to my boudoir, I thought it was through military might and strategic alliances. But now I realize that what truly made the Kingdom of Light invincible was faith, ideology, and the deity that the temple invoked, whether it existed or not."

She continued, reflecting on something Margo had once described about the God of Light. "The Romans have been watching us for so long. In their lands, magic, witchcraft, and demons are free to develop. Logically, they should have overrun our kingdom long ago. Yet, they haven't figured out how to breach the heart of the Kingdom of Light. Is it because they lack strength?" Laurent shook her head, her voice sweet with a hint of mirth. "No, it's because they don't know how to dismantle the temple."

Margo had never considered this perspective. She assumed the Romans couldn't conquer the Kingdom of Light because they weren't strong enough.

Surprised, Margo asked, "So, the Romans tried to invade the Kingdom of Light with force and still couldn't rule the entire kingdom?"

Laurent nodded with approval. "You're right. The Supreme Temple's messengers only allow servants of the gods to inherit the throne. Without faith, the Romans would never agree to become servants of the gods."

She sipped her chocolate and continued, "Why do some oppose my succession to the throne? Besides their many prejudices against women, they fear violating the authority of 'God.' In their mythology, women are seen as servants to men and slaves to their husbands. But if God allows a female servant and slave to serve him, it disrupts their dogma. They're afraid my existence will lead to questions, so they sought to strip me of my inheritance rights."

"Even the royal family cannot challenge divine power. Do you think a mere baron would dare defy the gods?"

Margo realized that the baron would never allow his wife to accuse the priest. If rumors of the priest consuming maidens were true, it would create a crack in the temple's authority. While it might not immediately impact the temple, it could lead to more cracks in the future.

The temple desired an unblemished reputation. It didn't matter if the royal family crumbled; if the temple fell, the Kingdom of Light would cease to exist, and noble titles and wealth would vanish overnight. Even though barons weren't as wealthy as marquises or counts, they still had hereditary assets. Why would a baron sacrifice his wealth and support his wife in exposing the priest's wrongdoings?

"That's why I chose a poorer household," Laurent explained, gently setting down her cup.

Margo finally understood the queen's strategy.

When the priest's scandal becomes public, those with prominent backgrounds, even if they've lost loved ones, will stay silent to protect their titles and property. But the poor are different. Whether there's a temple or not, they suffer the same.

For the impoverished, divine or royal matters are irrelevant. They endure life, cold and numb, in tattered clothes, barely surviving. The temple's rise or fall means little; they seek only food and clothing.

If told their missing daughter was killed and consumed by a prominent figure, they might accept compensation. To gain more, they'd need to sign a joint indictment against the priest. Thanks to the temple, each indictment carries a slight divine power. A willing handprint enhances its efficacy, with sincerity amplifying the effect.

Before this, Laurent would have Margo explain the situation clearly: the lawsuit's target, their daughter's tragic death, and how she was commodified. Some might fear the priest's influence and refuse to testify; others might have moved on. But most, living day-to-day, would find a handprint worthwhile for a little more security.

Whether they signed or not, the temple's reputation would still be tarnished. Laurent planned to use those accusations like termites, gnawing away at the temple's foundation.

In Illuminati terms: "Thanks to the benevolent God, she encountered the infamous priest and the loyal, powerful Loire, saving her much time in her schemes."

This was just the first step in her act of blasphemy.

She hoped the temple's response wouldn't disappoint her.

ELEVEN

Loire, hidden on Laurent's wrist, observed her as she read, studied, and convinced people to take legal action against the priest.

She possessed a mysterious and sweet charm. With just a few gentle words, people believed everything she said.

He witnessed her persuade a timid woman to poison her neglectful husband.

This woman's husband was a gambler who used his charm to engage in numerous flings. He spent his time at dance halls and gambled away their money at taverns, often resorting to pawning her clothes when he ran out of funds. Due to his reckless behavior, she hadn't been able to buy new clothes for years. Her hands, worn and calloused from relentless labor, bore the marks of hardship, resembling those of an old blacksmith.

By day, she worked at a laundry, her hands red and swollen from the hot water. By night, she cleaned hotel floors and counters, returning home to care for her husband and two children.

Her only wish was not to be beaten. Her mother had once said that a husband who doesn't hit his wife is a good husband.

Her husband had promised not to hit her before marriage. Yet, after marrying, he beat her so severely that she coughed blood and was often covered in bruises.

He broke his promise, but she felt guilty for losing their first child—a robust, beautiful girl with blonde hair.

This guilt kept her from resisting him, and over time, she let him treat her like a docile pet.

Laurent changed her life.

Hearing of the woman's plight, Laurent approached her, removing her deerskin gloves to hold the woman's rough, red hands with her warm, delicate ones.

Under her hood, Laurent's pale face and petite figure made her appear like an innocent child. Yet, her golden eyes shone with a captivating light.

Leaning in like a legendary witch, Laurent whispered in a voice as sweet as a silver bell, "Your husband deceived you. He sold your daughter to a priest for twenty Golden Johns. But your life didn't improve because he gambled it all away."

Initially, the woman couldn't believe it, but she recalled key details: her husband had no job, relied on her support, and after their daughter vanished, he splurged extravagantly. He drank and dined lavishly, even inviting others to join him in lowly dance venues, flirting with dancers. When she timidly questioned his newfound wealth, he claimed he earned it at the casino and insulted her for doubting him. Fear silenced her.

But now, she realized it was her daughter's life that had funded his indulgences. Wracked with unprecedented pain, she covered her face, unable to stand.

Laurent gently wiped away her tears, asking, "Do you want to save your two remaining children? Or yourself?"

Confused, the woman asked, "What do you mean?"

"If you stay with him, you and your children face doom," Laurent replied, tucking a tear-soaked strand of hair behind her ear. "Has he beaten you before?"

"He beats me daily, sometimes in front of neighbors," the woman admitted. "I've stayed with him since I was fifteen. I have no one else. My children need a father, and I need a husband."

"You have options," Laurent insisted, her deep gaze penetrating the woman's timid eyes. "You're more hardworking than he is, earning more. You not only support two children but also a useless gambler. It's not you who needs a husband; it's he who needs you."

The woman's tears cleared. She realized she was the breadwinner. Why did she think she couldn't survive without him? He squandered her earnings, attracting attention with her money. If she stopped supporting him and spent on herself, she could enjoy life too.

"But how can I leave him?" the woman despaired. "He's stronger. If he catches me, he'll kill me."

Laurent smiled faintly, whispering sweetly, "Then kill him first."

The woman recoiled, eyes wide, shaking her head. "No, killing is illegal. I'll go to prison."

Laurent stepped closer, pressing a finger to the woman's trembling lips. "If you don't act, he might sell your remaining children and even you. Your home is already stripped bare. When there's nothing left, you'll be his next bet."

"But—"

"No buts," Laurent said, placing cantharidin powder in her hand. "Put this in his drink, and you'll be free. I'll give you money to start anew."

The woman hesitated, torn between refusal and acceptance, seeking strength in Laurent's eyes.

Laurent stood poised at the edge of the eaves, a striking figure caught between sunlight and shadow, embodying the balance between light and darkness. For the woman before her, accepting the bottle of bufotalin powder meant a pivotal choice: the chance to escape the pain and nightmares that had haunted her for over a decade. It was an opportunity to step away from the shadows of her past and toward a brighter, more hopeful future. This moment held the promise of liberation, a chance to reclaim her life and rewrite her story.

Her children wouldn't grow up amidst cries and anxiety.

With newfound resolve, she closed her eyes and clutched the powder. "I will avenge my daughter. I don't need money; use it to help others. I can earn it myself."

Laurent shook her head. "I'm giving you money because I need your help. I have a favor to ask."

"Anything," the woman replied earnestly.

"Sign this indictment," Laurent said, handing it over. "My sister was also sold and eaten by the priest. I want to sue him. Even if it's a slim chance, I must try."

Tears welled up in Laurent's eyes, her cheeks flushed with emotion. Her vulnerability stirred the woman's maternal instincts. She signed the indictment, embracing Laurent like a mother comforting a child.

A white light flashed, activating the indictment.

"Don't cry," the woman soothed. "You're the strongest girl I know. You can avenge your sister. What else can I do?"

Laurent leaned against her shoulder, glancing at the indictment with a subtle smile. "Just stay alive. That's the greatest help."

She stood, kissed the woman's cheek, and promised, "Tomorrow at six, wait outside the town. I'll take you to a new life."

Then she turned and left.

Clutching the powder, the woman watched Laurent's retreating figure and touched her face, warmth spreading through her.

She never imagined a child's words could transform her life. Her husband claimed women were petty and wouldn't sacrifice as men did for friends.

But meeting Laurent, she realized she had been deceived.

Never again would she be fooled.

Hatred for her husband and dreams of a new life fueled her resolve.

Laurent was right. Without action, she and her children would remain mere pawns in her husband's gamble. She should have realized this sooner.

Now, she would make him pay the price he deserved.

***

Margo stood to the side, captivated by the queen's mesmerizing influence over everyone around her.

The queen possessed an innate talent for charming newcomers, effortlessly enchanting both men and women with her captivating presence.

As Laurent leaned in to kiss another woman's cheek, Margo felt a pang of envy and almost quipped, "Your Majesty, you haven't kissed me yet." Thankfully, she held her tongue, avoiding any potentially awkward glances from the queen.

Unbeknownst to Margo, she wasn't the only one under Laurent's spell. A wisp of mist was similarly captivated by her allure.

Loire had dispatched this wisp of black mist to watch over and protect Laurent, not anticipating that it would absorb negative energies along the way and develop a mind of its own. No longer under Loire's control, the mist began to affectionately interact with Laurent, much like a playful puppy, even attempting to enter her parted lips as if seeking to devour her from within.

Loire was left speechless by this turn of events. He swiftly decided to eliminate the rebellious mist. Witnessing this, the other wisps of black mist became agitated, crackling with anger like flames, and screamed for Laurent's judgment, questioning why Loire could monopolize her while they could not.

Loire and the misty entities were born in the same manner, both originating from desire. Yet, while Loire could savor Laurent's essence and allure exclusively, the entities were denied this privilege.

As long as Loire remained with Laurent, these entities would persist. However, he had no intention of sharing Laurent and possessed the power to eliminate them entirely.

Listening to their desperate cries only solidified Loire's resolve, stirring a cold and merciless intent within him.

These creatures were merely low-level beings created by him casually, autonomously conscious due to his influence.

Just as he had granted them life, he could also bring about their extinction. The black mist was a realm within his mind, and with a fleeting thought, he extinguished half of the screaming entities.

The remaining wisps quivered in terror, huddling together and sobbing as they sought refuge with Laurent.

Sensing their turmoil, Laurent glanced down at the snake bracelet on her wrist.

At some point, the black snake awoke, its tongue flickering with menace, eyes cold and tail thrumming with agitation.

Mistaking its restlessness for hunger, Laurent tenderly kissed its head and whispered soothingly, promising to feed it later. The snake gradually calmed under her touch.

The little wisps of black mist managed to escape unharmed, mimicking human gestures as they nervously wiped away imaginary sweat. Despite their relief, a few of them couldn't help but gaze at Laurent with evident greed and longing.

"Laurent is truly amazing!" they thought, entertaining the idea of one day overcoming the formidable Great Black Mist to have her all to themselves.

However, as soon as this thought flickered through their transparent forms, they were abruptly crushed, like caterpillars underfoot.

The remaining mists, now thoroughly cowed, dared not entertain any further ambitions.

Loire's mind settled into a state of tranquility, his authority undisputed.

TWELVE

Laurent didn't spend all her time on persuasion alone.

After seeing off a woman and her child, she convinced several households to endorse the indictment with their fingerprints. She then entrusted Margo with the responsibility of this matter, as she had other pressing tasks.

She needed to memorize texts like "Ode to the Light Sutra," "Record of the Words and Actions of the divine messenger," and "Record of Creation" within two weeks.

Resting her chin on her hand, Laurent recited and pondered.

The temple's methods were more sophisticated than Laurent had anticipated, cleverly promoting its teachings by inspiring benevolence among people. For instance, a wealthy believer in the God of Light might, after hearing the priest's teachings, feel compelled to follow divine directives and assist the poor. Once aided, the poor would feel gratitude not just towards the wealthy benefactor, but also towards the divine. They would believe that it was the priest's guidance that prompted the rich to offer their assistance, reinforcing their faith in the gods and the temple's teachings.

Moreover, both the rich and the poor indulge in the fantasy that universal belief in the God of Light would create a utopian world free of troubles, fostering love and harmony. Even skeptics, seeing their neighbors engrossed in discussing divine texts, would join in to integrate into the community.

The temple's teachings advocate kindness and benevolence, seemingly for the people's and country's benefit. However, those who defy these teachings or express disbelief are taken to the temple court and face severe punishment.

The temple's doctrines are like honey-coated poison; compliance brings sweet rewards, while resistance results in deadly consequences.

The Roman people's loss of faith stemmed from the kingdom's past, where diverse beliefs led to constant wars and suffering. They eventually overthrew their gods, leading to a culture valuing strength.

Laurent mused that if the temple continued feeding its people honey-coated poison, it too would crumble like the temples of the Roman Empire.

She planned to expedite this downfall with her own schemes.

Laurent, with her quick wit inherited from John II, memorized the required texts in just a week.

When her father was young, he was a remarkable ruler with exceptional wisdom, fluent in reciting the "Ode to Light Sutra" in any language. He skillfully deceived the messenger from the Supreme Temple with a facade of devoutness, eventually securing the crown of the Holy Light Empire. However, as he aged, he grew fearful that his son's intellect might surpass his own and that his son might inherit his ruthless nature. Consequently, he deliberately hindered his son's intellectual growth with poison.

John II likely passed away never realizing that his sharp intellect, brilliant yet ruthless military acumen, unmatched linguistic abilities, and eccentric methods were not passed on to the son he feared, but rather to his overlooked daughter.

In his early conquests of neighboring territories, he was renowned for his calm and calculated approach, never underestimating his foes. Even when facing countries with only a fraction of his own strength, he attacked with unwavering resolve and fierce determination.

Ironically, his downfall came from underestimating his own daughter.

Laurent, demonstrating her inherited brilliance, memorized the necessary texts within just one week. Left with some free time, she began perusing other books from the priest's bookshelf.

A hardcover book without a title, slotted diagonally at the back of the bookshelf, drew Laurent's attention. She stretched up on her toes to retrieve it and began flipping through its pages casually.

The book detailed the origins of the Skull Society. It seemed the priest considered the Skull Society a last resort.

Founded in 1544, the Skull Society initially emerged to combat the Temple Court's brutalities. However, as its influence expanded, the knights who once fought against tyranny began to mirror the very institutions they opposed. They adopted the temple's strict rules and practices, even imprisoning dissenters in miasma-filled rooms, watching them suffer and die from grotesque sores.

Laurent twirled a soft strand of black hair around her finger, her eyes alight with a sly, mischievous interest. She found herself quite intrigued by the tale of this society and its transformation.

***

Her interest awakened Loire.

He transformed into a snake-like black mist, slithering along Laurent's arms, shoulders, and neck, entwining itself in her thick, abundant hair. It extended a part of its body forward, releasing dark, hissing whispers.

During this time, he had absorbed numerous evil thoughts, growing stronger, yet still far from his true self.

He discovered a new emotion—jealousy.

Through these malevolent thoughts, he began to understand the distinctions between men and women and the nature of desire, akin to the primal instincts of wild beasts.

Just as wild beasts mark their prey with distinct bite marks to assert ownership, he too had left his mark on Laurent.

The teeth marks on her palm were a symbolic claim, indicating that in his eyes, she belonged to him.

This primal instinct, akin to a predator's, underscored his possessive nature and the deep, unspoken connection he felt towards her. To him, Laurent was not just a person of interest; she was his, marked and claimed in a way that was both intimate and territorial.

Yet, she never seemed to focus on him.

Was that book truly more captivating than he was?

He felt an intense fear of the book in her hand, much like a male creature fearing another male.

When threatened, a snake's tail vibrates loudly. Loire, having adopted snake form, mirrored this behavior.

Laurent turned her head to find Loire staring intently at the book in her hand, his snake tail sizzling with irritation, and his purple-blue eyes radiating a fiercely cold light.

Laurent: "..."

She blinked twice, puzzled by the little snake's apparent resentment. After a moment's thought, she gently patted his head and, in a casual, soothing tone, asked, "What's wrong, my little snake?"

Her attention, though momentarily diverted, quickly returned to the book.

Loire managed to suppress the urge to destroy the hateful book, opting instead to scan its contents with a cold and swift glance.

The book was written in four languages: Holy Light, Latin, Romance, and a rare script of wavy lines and dots.

As Loire absorbed more evil thoughts, his knowledge expanded exponentially. Concepts that would take ordinary people a lifetime to comprehend took him mere seconds to grasp.

He quickly spotted the words "Skeleton Society" within the text.

Loire's mind lingered on the words: Skeleton Society, miasma, becoming a god.

The memories of the woman's remarks danced in his thoughts, and his purple-blue eyes gleamed with cunning.

He realized that if he were to disclose everything to Laurent now, it would only result in a pet-like reward from her, which was no longer sufficient for him.

He desired something more, though he couldn't yet define what that was.

He believed that once he captured the essence of the Skeleton Society and consumed more evil thoughts, he'd gain clarity on the reward he truly sought.

***

Meanwhile, Desmond Pierre, a minor leader in the Skeleton Society's border branch, stood in a shadowy fir forest, patiently awaiting the deepest part of the night.

As the darkness enveloped the surroundings, he surveyed the area before raising his hands, signaling the start of the sacrificial ceremony.

The tall members of the Skeleton Cult gathered around an open coffin, chanting complex mantras over the thick blood within.

These followers were all physically robust white men, as the Skull Society, much like the Temple, excluded women and people of color from their ranks.

Clad in long black cloaks, they each held bloody skulls in their hands, still warm as if freshly taken, with strands of pink flesh clinging to their eye sockets.

The coffin was filled with human skeleton, steeped in animal fat and blood. Following the sacrificial ritual, the devotees lined up to drink from the coffin as a demonstration of their loyalty to the God of Darkness.

This ritual was nothing out of the ordinary. Just as the Temple had waited in vain for a response from the God of Light, the Skeleton Society had gone over two hundred years without a sign from the God of Darkness. Yet, they held onto the belief that with sufficient offerings and unwavering devotion, a miracle from the God of Darkness would eventually manifest.

Desmond Pierre, despite being a leader within the Skull Society, did not partake out of genuine belief in the God of Darkness. Instead, he relished the freedom his position afforded him to act wickedly without consequence.

As he observed the fervent believers around him, he couldn't help but scoff at what he perceived as their foolishness.

"How can there be a god in this world?" he thought, dismissing their devoutness as naive and misguided.

The Temple Court had executed nearly 6,000 pagans in a year, employing brutal methods such as whips, wheels, and wooden horses as common punishments. Those deemed severe offenders endured even harsher fates, having their nails stripped, being roasted alive, and having molten lead poured into their mouths, ears, and noses.

Yet, the Skull Society's methods were even more merciless than those of the Temple.

Desmond Pierre pondered the irony of belief. If a god truly existed, why would they not intervene to protect the people from such evil believers?

His skepticism, however, wasn't rooted in sympathy for the misguided individuals but rather in his disdain for the devout, whom he viewed as pawns of the church.

"How foolish," he thought, "to be so blindly devoted to a god, while I, who show no such reverence, have ascended to my current rank."

Reflecting on this, Desmond felt a surge of pride.

He anticipated that the day's sacrifice would proceed as uneventfully as those before it. But as the chanting ceased, an ominous black mist began to rise from all directions, unlike any ordinary night mist.

Before it could fully envelop the area, Desmond felt a sharp, chilling sensation that made him shiver involuntarily. The atmosphere shifted dramatically, hinting at an otherworldly presence.

The black mist swept across the landscape like a relentless plague, transforming mountains, fields, and forests into impenetrable darkness. Even the bright moon above could not escape its consuming grasp.

The world plunged into an abyss of shadow.

Desmond's mind raced with disbelief as he tried to comprehend the unfolding scene.

Could it truly be that a god of darkness existed in this world?

His once rebellious thoughts seemed dangerously close to being acknowledged by a higher power, and he couldn't shake the feeling that his disbelief had been exposed.

A dense layer of cold sweat formed on his forehead as the gravity of the situation settled in.

As the coffin radiated a cold, sinister, and dazzling white light, the once lifeless skeleton within began to stir with an eerie vitality.

The human skeleton, drenched in blood, slowly rose to its feet, moving with an agility and lightness that mirrored that of the living.

Its head turned, and it scanned the members of the Skull Society with eyes resembling evil spirits—red, fleshy voids that seemed to pierce through their very souls.

Desmond trembled uncontrollably, breaking out in a fierce cold sweat.

Though the skeleton did not physically touch him, he felt his spirit and energy being rapidly drained. In an instant, he collapsed like a withered plant, his plans for post-ritual cruelty forgotten. The skeleton seemed to devour his evil thoughts completely, leaving him utterly exhausted and filled with nothing but fear.

"This world really does have gods!" he thought, his disbelief shattered. "Who else but a god could wield such power?"

His knees buckled, and he knelt on the ground, overwhelmed by the revelation.

One by one, the other believers followed suit, kneeling in submission.

Loire, observing the scene through the skeleton's eyes, looked down at his skeletal hand, newfound understanding dawning upon him. He had learned to distinguish between beauty and ugliness, realizing that his current terrifying appearance would surely repel Laurent.

He knew he needed a powerful and perfect body, one that matched Laurent's aesthetic preferences, before he could present himself as a human male to demand the reward he desired. Lowering his chin slightly, Loire spoke in a hoarse voice, "From today on, I am your master. You will fear me, believe in me, and offer sacrifices in my name, and I shall bless you. Betray me, reject me, and ignore my commands, and you will face my punishment."

Desmond was the first to pledge his allegiance, his face alight with fanaticism.

The other believers quickly followed, fervently kowtowing before their newfound master.

Loire gazed at his skeletal hand with a touch of surprise, reflecting on the transformation that had just taken place.

The realization that he could wield such influence and power—drawing not only from the malevolent thoughts he had consumed but also from the fervent faith of these followers—was both unexpected and intriguing. The skeletal form, though initially perceived as terrifying and grotesque, now represented a newfound potential he had yet to fully explore. This revelation was promising, hinting at the possibility of achieving his ultimate goal: becoming a figure worthy of Laurent's attention and the reward he sought.

With this understanding, Loire's path forward seemed clearer, albeit fraught with challenges yet to be encountered.

... very good, he thought.

The leverage for seeking the reward he desired had just increased significantly.

CHAPTER
THIRTEEN

Half a month later, Margo completed the task Laurent had assigned her.

They hired a sedan chair with two horses to make their way to the parish temple.

The coachman, smoking his pipe, couldn't help but steal glances at Laurent, captivated by her striking presence.

She wore a wide-brimmed straw hat adorned with white egret feathers, her thick black hair woven into a heavy braid resting on her shoulders. The hat's brim obscured much of her face, leaving only her straight nose and thin red lips visible, yet even this glimpse hinted at her exceptional beauty.

The coachman, known for his unscrupulous behavior, entertained wicked thoughts. His past misdeeds involved exploiting noble ladies who, bound by societal expectations of chastity, remained silent about his transgressions. Today, he intended to repeat his tactics.

However, when Laurent suddenly lifted her brim and shot him a malicious glance, he was taken aback. The pure malice in her eyes was unlike anything he had seen before, as if possessed by something evil. Caught off guard, he swallowed hard and wiped the sweat from his brow. By the time he looked back, Laurent's demeanor had changed completely. She appeared innocent, childlike even, twirling a silk headband around her neck.

Perhaps he had misunderstood. The coachman considered his past experiences with noble ladies, who would typically blush or shy away when caught under his gaze. No noblewoman had ever returned his look with such malice. Surely, he had misread the situation.

He took another heavy puff from his pipe, ready to continue admiring his beautiful passenger. But once more, Laurent's gaze met his, and this time he was certain—there was no mistake. Her sweet dimples belied the cold, predatory sharpness in her eyes, akin to a hawk's, one that had already ensnared its prey.

She held his gaze with a chilling malice, idly playing with a small, sharpened knife in her hand. Her demeanor was anything but innocent, and the presence of the knife only reinforced that fact. Clearly, if he continued to leer, something dire would surely happen.

Realizing the potential danger, the coachman quickly averted his eyes, pretending to busy himself with patting the horse's neck. Yet, a cold sweat began to seep down his back.

Laurent was unlike any girl he had encountered before— strangely intimidating.

He resolved that no matter what, even if Laurent initiated conversation, he would not dare to look at her again. His life, after all, was far more important than indulging his curiosity.

***

Laurent remained blissfully unaware of the coachman's internal turmoil. Her intention had simply been to warn him to keep his focus on driving the carriage and to curb any inappropriate thoughts. Who would have guessed that a mere glance would render him as obedient as a scolded dog?

She shook her head, amused by the unintended effect, and settled back into the carriage.

The journey to the parish temple would take about three hours, and as the scenery passed by, Laurent found herself absentmindedly caressing the snake bracelet wrapped around her wrist.

Loire, the entity within, had been unusually restless and agitated lately. Even minor conversations with Margo seemed to provoke him, causing his tail to tremble defensively.

Laurent, though fond of snakes for their appearance, was not well-versed in their behavior (aside from the infamous snake venom). She couldn't help but wonder if Loire's agitation signaled some sort of mating season impulse.

But then again, Loire was essentially a black mist—could such an entity even experience reproductive urges?

This line of thought left Laurent feeling slightly out of her depth, as if she had stumbled into an unexpected gap in her knowledge.

Puzzled but pragmatic, she decided to set aside her curiosity about Loire's behavior for the moment. There were more pressing matters at hand, namely her plans at the temple, which occupied her thoughts entirely.

She resolved to address Loire's mysterious impulses once her current tasks were complete.

Four hours later, the carriage emerged from the dark, secluded fir forest and into the domain of the parish temple. The sight before Laurent was breathtaking—a sprawling white building complex nestled in lush greenery.

The first thing that caught her eye was the expansive green lawn, leading to an open square and a castle-like palace of ivory-colored stone with towering peaks.

These temples, meticulously designed by architects, were positioned so that sunlight would naturally illuminate their interiors, casting a divine glow. This temple was no exception, bathed in a radiant golden light, as though it were a dwelling fit for gods.

As they approached, Margo leaned in and whispered, "Master, there are Demon Forbidden Stones everywhere here, you must be careful. I'll be waiting for your message at the parish hotel."

Laurent reassured her with a gentle pat on the hand. "Don't worry," she replied confidently. With Margo's concerned eyes watching her, Laurent alighted from the carriage and made her way toward the temple's side entrance.

Each day, the temple welcomed numerous goddesses recommended by bishops or priests—girls who often came from families that did not fully value them, sent here in hopes of gaining divine favor for their households.

Clad in white cloaks, these girls walked quietly and humbly through the side entrance.

Laurent presented her recommendation letter to the guard, who, after a brief review, permitted her entry.

As she stepped toward the entrance, she cast a glance at the temple's grand main doors. A quiet determination filled her heart; one day, she vowed, she would walk through those doors openly and with pride.

Submitting the recommendation letter was only the initial step in Laurent's path to becoming a goddess. The process required her to undergo a personal examination, which involved disrobing completely for the old goddess, who would meticulously record her body's dimensions.

The old goddess, accustomed to seeing young women anxious and self-conscious during this procedure, was taken aback by Laurent's composure.

Contrary to expectations, Laurent undressed without hesitation and sat down, exuding an air of nonchalance as she casually flipped through a book. Her demeanor was one of complete confidence and ease, unbothered by her nakedness.

This unexpected display of self-assurance challenged the old goddess's preconceived notions. Laurent's lack of embarrassment and her calm presence stood in stark contrast to the usual nervousness of others, marking her as someone who defied ordinary expectations and commanded a presence all her own.

When the old goddess entered the room, Laurent acknowledged her with a nod, then stood gracefully, extending her arms as if inviting appreciation of her form.

The old goddess, maintaining an expressionless demeanor, scrutinized Laurent's physique. Coldly, she remarked, "You have a waist circumference of 22 inches. Are you from the countryside?"

Laurent calmly began dressing and replied, "Why do you say that?"

The old goddess explained, "Most of the goddesses here are noble ladies who have attended noble schools. These schools require girls to reduce their waist circumference by an inch each month. Some diligent girls compress their waists to 13 inches. With a waist as thick as yours, a noble would have been expelled long ago."

Laurent responded with a half-smile, "Is that so?"

The old goddess continued, muttering, "Do you think I'm lying, little village woman? Women's organs are fragile, especially the uterus. Without a waistband, it will move within your body! Don't think that beauty exempts you from wearing one. The uterus is crucial; neglect it, and you might end up an unwanted old virgin like me."

Laurent's brow furrowed slightly at first, but upon hearing the latter part of the statement, she relaxed, smiling faintly. "Really? You might not know, but my biggest dream is to live freely, like you. A life without a husband's control sounds quite wonderful."

The old goddess, often shunned by the younger generation for her rigid demeanor, was taken aback. She had expected Laurent to be as sharp-tongued as others, yet Laurent's words were genuine, devoid of any mockery. This unexpected sincerity shifted the old goddess's attitude, softening her view of Laurent and fostering a newfound respect for the young woman who defied expectations with grace and poise.

The old goddess, though initially rigid, decided not to make things difficult for Laurent after witnessing her composed demeanor. With a cold snort, she arranged for Laurent to have a room with ample lighting, a subtle acknowledgment of Laurent's poise.

In the privacy of her new quarters, Laurent donned the goddess's vestment—a simple yet elegant white silk dress with gold borders, devoid of any patterns. As per temple rules, traditional adornments such as earrings, headwear, and bracelets were to be removed, except for one piece of jewelry that held special significance. For Laurent, that piece was the bracelet embodying Loire.

Interestingly, as soon as she crossed the temple's threshold, Loire seemed to quiet down, as if the temple's atmosphere placed him in a state of tranquility or perhaps some form of confinement. Laurent felt no concern over this; for her, Loire's presence was a mere bonus. She maintained confidence in her ability to navigate the temple's challenges with or without him.

***

Meanwhile, deep in the fir forest, Loire was engaged in his own pursuit. He consumed the coachman's spirit and evil thoughts, driven by an intense aversion to anyone who dared to covet Laurent. Even the slightest notion of desire towards her was intolerable to him, prompting him to act decisively.

This duality between Laurent's serene acceptance and Loire's fierce protectiveness illustrated the unique bond they shared, each navigating their respective paths with an understanding of their own strengths and purposes.

Loire turned his gaze toward the temple, visible just beyond the fir forest.

He sensed something intriguing—an energy emanating from the temple that seemed to feed him, a blend of faith and human desire. Lust, greed, and an insatiable appetite, manifestations of the seven deadly sins, pulsed through the temple's atmosphere, providing him with nourishment.

His power grew, the black mist surrounding him thickening to almost a tangible form.

This connection to the temple sparked a curiosity within him—it might hold clues to his origin. Driven by this possibility, Loire moved swiftly, infiltrating the temple with the speed and stealth of lightning.

He seized a young priest, merging with him and taking control of his body.

As he settled into this human form, Loire furrowed his brow, realizing the male body was more fragile and susceptible to desire than he had anticipated.

This vulnerability was a stark contrast to the detached composure of his snake form.

Simply thinking of Laurent in this new body stirred an unfamiliar anxiety, accompanied by a throbbing pain deep within his bones—sensations he had never experienced before.

This new form presented both challenges and insights, revealing the complexities of human desire and emotion. Loire's determination to understand his connection to the temple and his purpose in relation to Laurent only deepened as he navigated these new experiences.

At that moment, the door swung open, and another young priest entered, addressing Loire in the guise of Clyde. "Clyde, you're in great luck! The bishop has assigned you to lecture the new girls, and there's one named 'Laurent.' She's quite the beauty, though I question her ability to grasp all the material. But, you know, women are naturally—"

Before he could finish, Loire grasped the young priest's collar with a firm hand. The movement was not aggressive, but the cold, penetrating glance Loire gave him spoke volumes. "Pay attention to your words," Loire said, his voice low and commanding.

The young priest, though unsure of what exactly he had said wrong, recognized the change in "Clyde." This was no ordinary rebuke; the aura emanating from him was one of absolute authority and intimidation. Clyde's once gentle and noble features now bore an icy, oppressive beauty that demanded submission.

The young priest quickly backtracked, his voice trembling with fear. "I was wrong, I was wrong... I won't speak recklessly anymore. Please, let go, Clyde, I truly understand."

Satisfied, Loire released his grip, not sparing another glance at the chastened priest. He adjusted the white collar within his long robe with a calm, deliberate motion and strode out of the room, exuding an air of unapproachable power.

The young priest stood there, stunned and bewildered, as he watched Clyde walk away. The way Clyde had adjusted his collar and carried himself exuded an aura that was both majestic and commanding, imbued with an inviolable, noble charm. It was as if a powerful force had taken residence within him, compelling those around to hold their breath in his presence, not daring to disturb the air with even a whisper.

The young priest couldn't shake the feeling that Clyde had been possessed by something beyond the ordinary.

The thought was unsettling—how could such an entity exist within the sacred walls of the temple? Was it possible that an evil spirit had taken hold of Clyde, or was this simply an illusion, a trick of the mind brought on by stress and fatigue?

Dismissing the notion as fanciful, the young priest shook his head to clear away the lingering doubts. After all, the temple was a place of holiness and sanctuary, protected from such dark forces. Whatever transformation Clyde had undergone, it was best left unexplored, at least for now.

He returned to his duties, though the memory of Clyde's transformation lingered, a haunting curiosity that would not easily fade.

CHAPTER

FOURTEEN

As Laurent entered the classroom within the temple, a hush fell over the room, the lively chatter among the girls ceasing abruptly. They turned their attention to the newcomer, examining her with a mix of curiosity and intrigue.

These girls, all around sixteen or seventeen, bore the marks of the temple's strict aesthetic standards. Their waists were cinched tightly by corsets, and their faces, painted with white lead powder, held a ghostly paleness. This artificial pallor, meant to embody the temple's ideal of demure femininity, left them looking fragile and sickly.

In stark contrast, Laurent's appearance was vibrant and full of life. Her skin, though fair, radiated a healthy glow, with a delicate rose tint gracing her cheeks, neck, and earlobes. Her lips were a deep, natural red, accentuated by the gleaming white of her teeth—a vivid splash of color that seemed almost rebellious in its vitality.

Laurent's presence was a contradiction to the temple's ideals.

The institution preached meekness and submission, encouraging women to adopt a demeanor of quiet obedience, their faces free of any "sinful" embellishments.

Laurent, however, exuded a fierce vitality, her natural beauty a silent defiance against the imposed norms.

The girls exchanged unsure glances, hesitant to approach or greet her.

Laurent, unfazed by their indecision, acknowledged them with a slight nod, maintaining an air of calm composure. She gracefully chose an empty seat, picked up a book, and began to read, seemingly indifferent to whether their reactions were of admiration or apprehension.

This quiet confidence set her apart, establishing an unspoken authority that challenged the expectations placed upon them by the temple. Her mere presence suggested that there was another way to exist—a possibility that perhaps not all were ready to embrace, yet could not entirely dismiss.

The round-faced girl, with a friendly demeanor, quickly took a seat beside Laurent. She leaned in, whispering softly, "Don't mind them. It's not that they're ignoring you; it's just the rules of the temple..." After a moment of hesitation, she pulled out a small can of lead powder and discreetly handed it to Laurent, "the priest and Sister Catherine are coming soon. When Sister Catherine sees your mouth turn red like this, she will whip you with a vine! Hurry and apply it quickly!"

Laurent accepted the jar, twirling it between her fingers with casual curiosity. She turned toward the girl, mimicking her conspiratorial whisper, her voice laced with a kind smile, "Do you know this is poisonous?"

Her tone was gentle, like honey, soothing yet carrying a weight of truth that landed softly in the girl's ear. The girl's cheeks flushed immediately, a mix of embarrassment and concern. "I... I don't know... is this really poisonous?"

Laurent's response sidestepped the question, her tone still light. "How long have you been wearing this?"

"Not long," the girl replied, glancing down. "Only one or two months."

Laurent continued, her voice soft but probing. "After applying it, do you feel restless, lose your appetite, or experience gastrointestinal colic?"

The girl looked at Laurent with surprise, her eyes widening. "How do you know? Do you have these troubles too? Sister Catherine calls it the disease of wealth and status, saying it's punishment for our laziness and greed. She claims that if we eat less and tighten our waists, we won't have these problems."

"Silly girl, it's not laziness or greed, but the lead in the powder causing your discomfort," Laurent sighed gently, her voice carrying a note of genuine concern, "your body is reacting to the poison. My mother passed away when I was very young because of it. It's important to value your health over these imposed standards. "

Hearing this, the round-faced girl was immediately convinced. No one would ever joke about the loss of a parent.

Her eyes widened with empathy and understanding as she nodded, "I'm sorry, it reminded you of something sad. I promise I'll wear this less in the future. Thank you for telling me."

With a gentle touch, Laurent lifted the girl's chin and carefully wiped away the innermost layer of lead powder from her lips with a handkerchief. She offered a warm smile, "You're welcome."

Laurent's presence was naturally charming and approachable, a likable energy that drew people in. When she chose to connect with someone, this charisma became even more potent, creating a bond that was hard to resist.

For a moment, the round-faced girl felt her admiration for Laurent swell, her heart brimming with newfound fondness. Laurent's kindness and authenticity had not only imparted important knowledge but also forged a connection that left the girl feeling seen and valued.

The girl absorbed Laurent's words, the seeds of doubt about the temple's teachings beginning to take root. Laurent's quiet rebellion against the norms offered a glimpse of an alternative—a path where one's well-being was prioritized over rigid conformity. It was a perspective that, while new and perhaps daunting, carried the promise of empowerment and self-worth.

***

As the priest and Sister Catherine entered the room, a hush fell over the classroom, the silence so profound it was as if one could hear a pin drop.

The priest was strikingly young and handsome, clad in a simple long robe fastened with silver buttons from hem to collar. Beneath it, he wore a white robe, fitted horse pants, and polished leather boots that gleamed under the light.

His expression was one of detachment and indifference, an aloofness that seemed to lack any warmth or human touch. Compared to him, even the most remote divine messenger would appear more compassionate and approachable.

He nodded slightly in response to Sister Catherine's words, his cold, measured gaze sweeping across the faces of the girls seated before him.

Eventually, his eyes settled on Laurent, drawn perhaps by the contrast she presented. Unlike the other girls, Laurent's demeanor was relaxed and self-assured. Her attention, however, was not directed toward him. She rested her cheek on her fist, listening with genuine interest to Sister Catherine's discourse, seemingly unfazed by the priest's scrutiny.

Sister Catherine's voice resonated throughout the classroom, her words carrying the weight of divine expectation. "When you enter the temple, you become God's lifelong servants. This is your honor and blessing. You must love God with all your love, and only when you love him wholeheartedly can you become a true goddess. Remember, God is omniscient and omnipotent, and if you are even the slightest bit impious or unclean, he can see you."

Her gaze swept across the room, scrutinizing each girl with the intensity of a hawk. Her eyes landed on Laurent, piercing through the room's silence. "You, the new goddess," Sister Catherine's voice was cold and accusatory, "didn't you read the 'Ode to Light Sutra' before coming here? Why did you paint your mouth so red? Don't you know that God dislikes red the most?"

All eyes turned to Laurent, a mix of confusion, mockery, and indifference passing through the girls. Some were puzzled by Laurent's audacity, while others seemed eager to witness the impending reprimand. Many simply looked on out of habit, docile and detached.

The round-faced girl, still untouched by the temple's rigid conditioning, quickly spoke up, "Mammy, you know she's new here and it's normal for her not to be familiar with the 'Ode to Light Sutra.' Besides, she didn't intentionally paint her lips red! Her lips are naturally red like this."

Sister Catherine's reprimand was swift. "Shut up. Did I let you speak? Or do you want to be punished with her?"

The round-faced girl shrank back, silenced by the harsh rebuke.

"If you're born with a red mouth," Sister Catherine continued sternly, "apply lead powder. You're not the only one with a red mouth here. If you come from a poor family, come to me for a can of lead powder on credit, and I'll ensure you repay it with interest in the future."

Laurent realized the underlying motive—an exploitation of the girls' insecurities for profit.

She chuckled softly, unfazed by the confrontation, and gracefully stood up. With a composed demeanor, she performed a standard goddess priestess ritual, bowing her head slightly toward Sister Catherine.

Her action was a blend of compliance and subtle defiance, a quiet assertion of her own identity and values. Laurent's calm response left an impression, hinting at her resilience and the quiet strength she carried within herself, a strength that would not be easily subdued by the temple's stringent norms.

Catherine had fully intended to chastise Laurent, expecting to find fault in her manners and thus justify a punishment— perhaps making her roll out and stand as a lesson in humility and obedience. However, much to her surprise, Laurent's execution of the goddess ritual was impeccable. Each movement was precise, each gesture aligned with the highest standards of etiquette, leaving Catherine with no room to criticize. Even the most exacting etiquette teacher would have been hard-pressed to find a fault.

Frustrated but unable to show it, Catherine managed to say, "There's no need to bow in class." Her voice carried a hint of irritation. Yet, she knew that had Laurent not bowed, she would have wielded it as a reason to expel her from the class for disrespecting elders.

Laurent, observing the subtle nuances in Catherine's demeanor, understood the trap laid before her.

Laurent's smile was soft, but there was an unmistakable edge of confidence in her gaze as she addressed the silent priest. "Father, I have to say some honest but unpleasant words next. Please protect me from punishment."

Loire observed her with calm attentiveness, recognizing her intelligence and sharpness. Even without direct eye contact, she could sense his special attention, and she had no qualms about using it to her advantage.

He was very willing.

He nodded slightly, murmuring, "Okay."

Sister Catherine, skeptical and defensive, retorted with a sneer, "God tells us that honest words must be pleasant. I'm curious, how can you say something honest but not pleasant?"

Laurent's smirk was mischievous as she answered, satisfying Catherine's curiosity. "Mammy, have you been experiencing a dry throat, unexplained sweating, stomach cramps, and difficulty in urinating lately?"

Catherine's demeanor shifted immediately. Laurent's words hit home, accurately describing the symptoms that had plagued her for years. Though she had sought the doctor's help, the symptoms persisted, leading her to fear divine punishment and forsake further medical assistance. Her condition had worsened to the point where her face began to rot, forcing her to conceal the blemishes with makeup.

Feeling exposed and defensive, Catherine raised her voice. "So what? Don't you see how old I am? Which elderly person doesn't have health issues?"

Laurent shook her head gently, speaking with soft certainty. "You're not sick, Mammy."

Catherine's anxiety heightened. "If not sick, then what?"

"It's poisoning," Laurent stated plainly. "The lead powder you apply contains arsenic. Not only you, but many girls here suffer from various degrees of poisoning. If you stop using it and take the antidote, perhaps you can save yourselves."

As Laurent spoke, several girls began wiping the lead powder from their faces.

Sister Catherine, though aware of the truth about lead powder's toxicity, was unwilling to relinquish her profitable venture. The potential financial loss from her unsold hoard of lead powder was too significant to ignore. She clung to her vested interests, determined to maintain her authority and income.

"Stop it all, don't wipe it!" she commanded, her voice sharp and authoritative. "Have you all forgotten my teachings? God is the greatest, and as long as he disapproves of red, you must apply this lead powder! What's the point of it being poisonous? If God knew you were afraid of this toxin and gave up your reverence for him, would he still care about you when something really happened to you?"

As Sister Catherine's words echoed through the room, a cold sweat broke out on her forehead. Her internal conflict was palpable; she was torn between her desire to maintain her lucrative trade in lead powder and the personal fear of poisoning. The reality of her own vulnerability struck her, prompting a frantic mental note to cleanse herself thoroughly later. Yet, she remained uncertain about the future—should she continue using lead powder, or finally heed the warnings?

In her mind, she clung to a naive hope: perhaps arsenic poisoning wasn't as dire as Laurent claimed. Maybe regular visits to the doctor could manage the symptoms. This wishful thinking allowed her to avoid confronting the full implications of her actions. The potential poisoning of the girls was something she conveniently pushed aside, considering it outside her concern.

Laurent's words shattered her fantasy: "Mammy, arsenic is a highly toxic substance, and some types can even cause instant death. Moreover, God has never said that he does not love red." After speaking, she smiled and took out a copy of the "Ode to Light Sutra" before Catherine Mammy could respond. "If you don't believe me, I can recite all the words of God inside." Sister Catherine was speechless: "..." This little girl is too arrogant!

The girls who wanted to wipe their mouths but were scolded were also stunned: "..." Are they wiping their mouths, or not?

The round-faced girl was stunned too. She didn't expect Laurent to not only have beautiful, aggressive eyes but also be prickly like a rose thorn. Laurent left Sister Catherine, a notoriously mean nanny in the temple who often made the girls bleed for trivial matters, speechless. Catherine couldn't punish Laurent because she had said herself, "Honest words must be pleasant,"and indirectly admitted that 'lead powder is poisonous."

Now, Laurent had taken out the "Ode to the Light" again, and unless Catherine could prove that Laurent's recitation was wrong, she could only stand there in silence.

Sure enough, Sister Catherine was surprised and walked over to take the "Ode to the Light Sutra." She sneered, "Is that so? It seems like you're a genius. It's a pity to be a goddess. You should become a theology professor. Reach out your hand, spread it out, yes, that's right. Memorize it. If you get a word wrong, I'll lash you with the vine and let you know the consequences of speaking big."

Laurent calmly followed suit.

Loire set his gaze on Sister Catherine.

His gaze was no longer indifferent and observant but became extremely deep and terrifying. Only when the devil wanted someone to go to hell would he show such a cold and icy expression.

FIFTEEN

When Laurent finished reciting the "Ode to Light Sutra" word for word, the entire classroom fell silent. Not only had she memorized God's words, but she also remembered every detail that led up to them.

The girls had their copies of the "Ode to Light Sutra," making it easy to verify her accuracy. Despite only having memorized excerpts themselves, they understood the difficulty of mastering the entire text. The book was more of a detailed chronicle, recording dialogues between God and believers from different eras, each with unique backgrounds, identities, and circumstances. They had received many lashes for getting dates wrong, but Laurent didn't miss a single number. Sister Catherine was right—she was indeed a genius.

Watching the girls throw admiring glances at Laurent, Sister Catherine's hands trembled with anger. This was not the outcome she wanted. She had hoped to see the talkative girl punished for any mistake. However, she could only muster a forced smile and say, "You recite very well, even better than a theology student. But look, there's not a single sentence that says God likes red."

Laurent nodded playfully. "Yes, there's not a single sentence that says God likes red, nor is there one that says God doesn't like red. So, Mammy, how do you know God doesn't want to see our mouths red?" she asked innocently, tilting her head.

Catherine's forehead broke out in a cold sweat. Indeed, the "Ode to Light Sutra" didn't mention that God disliked the color red. It was the temple authorities who equated red with evil, tricking the girls into using the lead powder they sold.

Both the old and new religions believe fertility was a divine punishment for women, with menstruation being proof of their sins. The girls, enduring this bloody punishment, believed that blood was dirty and trusted the temple's rumor.

No, it couldn't be considered a rumor. Red had always symbolized demons. God had said his eyes did not see wickedness or falsehood. Red, as the color of demons, was heretical and illusory.

Thinking of this, Sister Catherine breathed a long sigh of relief.

She tried her best to express these views with a kind and benevolent expression.

The girls listened attentively, nodding along, thinking her words made sense. Despite being mistreated by her, they didn't hold any resentment and still believed every word she said.

Unexpectedly, as soon as Sister Catherine finished speaking, Laurent smiled with great interest, as if waiting for this exact moment.

Catherine's heart skipped a beat.

"Sister, red symbolizes demons—it's just a folk belief. How can folk belief represent divine will? Or do you think that gods tend to be biased and believe whatever others say?"

"Of course not..." Sister Catherine retorted, her voice still weak and unconvincing.

"Roses are red, does God forbid people from using roses as a symbol of love? Flames are also red, does God prohibit the judgment court from burning heathens? Sunshine is sometimes red, does God prohibit people from sunbathing?" Laurent's smile became sweeter and her voice gentler. "I advise Mammy to retract those words just now. If someone were to carry those words to the ears of the divine messenger... Mammy would lose more than just money."

As she spoke, Laurent gave her a meaningful glance.

Catherine, on the other hand, was struck by the realization.

This seemingly naive girl knew everything! She not only had an excellent memory but also remarkable eyesight. She immediately saw through her and knew that she forced those girls to apply lead powder for money.

For a moment, Catherine's face turned whiter than paper. If the divine messenger found out about this, she would lose more than just money—she might lose her life!

As she approached Laurent, her mind was swirling with thoughts. She was almost hunched over, trembling slightly. In a low, almost inaudible voice, she asked, "You're too smart... You're not here to be a goddess. A goddess lives alone in the temple for eternity. What are you doing here?"

Laurent smiled faintly and replied, "You're mistaken. I am here to become a goddess. I want to be the goddess of the Supreme Temple."

"There are no goddesses in the Supreme Temple," Sister Catherine challenged, looking directly into Laurent's eyes. "You can recite the 'Ode to the Light Sutra.' I can't believe you don't know this."

"I do know," Laurent admitted, "and that's precisely why I want to be one."

Sister Catherine regarded her thoughtfully for a moment before saying, "I will introduce you to the divine messenger of the parish."

Laurent nodded slightly. "Thank you, Sister. In exchange, I will pretend not to know what you've done. But you must stop letting these girls use lead powder," she said with a sudden intensity. "They are already suffering from illness."

Sister Catherine sensed the complexity in Laurent's tone but dismissed it, thinking she was just feeling sorry for the girls. What she didn't realize was that Laurent felt no compassion at all.

"I understand," Sister Catherine said, "I'll buy some wine to help detoxify them." She knew that wine was indeed an antidote to arsenic poisoning.

Laurent clapped her hands in agreement, and with that, the issue was put behind them.

Catherine exhaled deeply, deciding to introduce Laurent to the divine messenger, hoping never to see this troublesome girl again.

As the class neared its end, Sister Catherine spoke briefly on stage before announcing a break and leaving with the young priest.

Laurent curled her lips into a smile and picked up the "Ode to the Light Sutra" from the table. Just as she was about to return to her room, she was suddenly engulfed by the enthusiastic embrace of the other young girls.

This was exactly what she wanted: to enter the temple and make everyone notice her, adore her, and lay the groundwork for her audacious plan. Yet, when she was genuinely kissed and embraced by these girls, she couldn't help but feel bewildered.

She had never seen so many people her age. Pretending to be an innocent girl for years, at that moment, her face truly reflected innocence.

***

Sister Catherine hummed a tune as she walked.

Laurent had promised not to reveal anything to the divine messenger. Relieved of a significant burden, Catherine felt cheerful, never considering that without Laurent, she wouldn't have these troubles at all.

As she rounded a corner, she suddenly realized someone had been following her.

Initially, she thought nothing of it. It could be someone just taking the same path. After all, this was a temple, and no one would dare commit violence under the watchful eyes of the gods.

Unexpectedly, as she entered the shadow of the arcade, a strong hand grasped her neck firmly.

Sister Catherine gasped in surprise, turning to see a familiar, handsome face—it was the young priest who had been with her during the class!

She knew him well! His name was Clyde, a devout and respected priest. He was known for his simplicity, often praying for poor families and helping them with weddings and funerals. He never sought money or indulgence.

Yet, at that moment, his gaze was icy and detached, as if he were looking at an animal to be slaughtered. He had a murderous intent and wanted to kill her!

"Father Clyde..." Sister Catherine croaked, "Why are you doing this?"

Why?

Because I sensed your malicious thoughts towards Laurent. Even for a mere few seconds, I will destroy you.

Loire's expression remained unchanged as he tightened his grip.

"Father Clyde... Is it because I let the children use lead powder for money?" Sister Catherine guessed desperately. "I know I was wrong! I'll take them to the best doctor and pay for their treatment... Please, spare my life... I want to live."

Her face turned crimson as air escaped her lungs, her frail hands fluttering helplessly.

Loire remained unmoved, his grip unwavering, regarding her with a chilling indifference reminiscent of a deity looking down on mortals.

Why would a god show mercy to mortals?

Had the heavens, earth, mountains, rivers, or seas ever shown mercy to humans?

Sister Catherine closed her eyes in despair, her withered hands falling limp.

This was her retribution.

There was indeed retribution, and everything gained through greed would be returned. She knew her wrongs, felt her repentance, and vowed never to seek small gains again... If the merciful God was listening, she implored forgiveness for this moment. She would never dare repeat her misdeeds.

This was perhaps the most devout moment of Catherine's life. Her veins pulsed with sincere blood, her chest filled with fervent religious emotion.

People only become impassioned about repentance when absolutely necessary.

Her breathing weakened, but her silent prayer grew more devout. Never had she despised her former self more, and if given another chance, she would never commit the despicable act of selling lead powder.

Suddenly, a rush of fresh air filled her lungs.

Catherine collapsed to her knees, her hands on the floor, coughing violently.

Her prayers were answered.

Thanking the merciful God for sparing her life, she vowed never to do evil again.

But who had just attacked her? She had no memory of it at all.

***

Loire strode out of the arcade.

He walked to the fountain in the temple's center, supporting himself on the cold marble, closing his eyes tightly.

He had heard Sister Catherine's silent prayer, and it had compelled him to let go.

Her prayer ignited a trace of divinity within him, awakening him. He didn't understand why he possessed divinity or why he had to let go. He only knew he seemed to have made another mistake. Why "another"?

Had he ever harbored desires, impulses, jealousy, or even aspired to become a man before?

Yet, he should never have become a man.

Gender brought weakness.

He should transcend gender, remain detached from worldly matters.

Yet, he attempted to become a man, observing the world through a man's eyes and understanding desire through a man's mind.

He felt a crack in his spirit, unable to return to his former sacred state. But who had he been before? He couldn't find the answer.

There were many questions left unanswered. Why had he turned into a black mist? Why did he feed on evil thoughts?

Most importantly, why was he drawn to Laurent?

If he only devoured evil thoughts ordinarily, he would never desire to become a man, or feel jealousy.

He began exploring worldly affairs because of Laurent, and it was because of her that he experienced impure emotions like jealousy.

It was as if he was destined to be seduced by her.

Loire sat down on the marble, resting his forehead in one hand.

What exactly was he doing?

He vaguely realized Laurent was merely his creation.

When he created her, he had no emotions or preferences.

Her gender, her flesh and blood, her bones—were as ordinary as countless other creations.

He hadn't created her for himself; rather, he became a tangible man for her.

In this moment, being in a male body and contemplating this matter with a male mind was the ultimate proof.

The male body was savage and fragile, easily deceived by desires.

This trace of divinity hadn't completely awakened him but instead introduced a new emotion—regret—plunging him further into the abyss of desire.

What was more terrifying was that he would still return to Laurent's side, remain loyal to her, and let his soul be carried away for her sweet desires.

The difference was, with this trace of divinity, he would clearly and deeply realize that all of this should not have happened.

Then, with clarity, he would watch himself continue to sink into depravity.

SIXTEEN

Laurent's rise to fame was not unexpected.

Practically everyone knew of the new goddess named Laurent, who was not only beautiful but also possessed a remarkably quick mind. With just a few words, she had managed to silence the stern Sister Catherine.

The most remarkable thing about Laurent was her humility. Despite her intelligence, she never let it make her arrogant or condescending, even after outsmarting Sister Catherine. She treated everyone with kindness and gentleness, drawing people to her. The girls felt comfortable around her and sought her company.

But just like how Sister Catherine wasn't the only one who sold lead powder, not everyone likes Laurent either.

The other older women, whose income streams Laurent had disrupted, despised her. They harbored such hatred that they wished they could silence her forever.

Though Sister Catherine had sincerely urged them to find alternative ways to make money, asking them to discard their lead powder stocks was like asking them to cut off a limb.

They could have amassed a fortune, and it was all because of that meddling Laurent!

Gathering together, the older women plotted to punish Laurent.

Having contacts and means to supply and sell goods, they began to concoct a plan. Inspired by ancient texts, they devised a devious scheme—to have Laurent drink a "love potion," thereby ruining her reputation and getting her expelled from the temple.

The older women were thrilled with their plan, convinced it would work.

Imagine a respectable, intelligent girl, suddenly engaging in promiscuous behavior—perhaps even with a chaste priest. The scandal would be devastating. She would still be torn apart by rumors and insults, even if expelled from the temple. Her beauty and intelligence would mean nothing if branded a disgraceful woman.

Fueled by excitement, the women set their plan into motion.

They acquired ingredients for the "love potion" from a peddler—nettles, poppies, crocodile eggs, rhino horn powder, and lizard eyes. The recipes were found in ancient texts, some from Assyrian tablets, others from the mysterious East.

The temple forbade medicine-making, with severe penalties for those caught.

The women huddled in a cramped room, guarding the alchemy furnace day and night, determined to ruin Laurent's life.

The room was so tight that they sat amongst the herbs. Soon, their skin was irritated by nettles, and the furnace's heat left them drenched in sweat and on the brink of fainting.

After three grueling days, the "love potion" was finally ready.

Despite their exhaustion, dark circles under their eyes, and nettle-stung limbs, they were giddy with anticipation of Laurent's downfall.

***

Laurent awoke from an unsettling nap, her mood sour. She stretched lazily and donned her robe.

She had dreamed of her late mother.

She always thought her mother had little impact on her, but now realized she never forgot her mother's pale face.

Her mother was a beautiful yet simple woman from a noble family. Her superstitions led her to believe in omens from dreams—snakes foretold bad luck, mice a warning of harm, a kitten bite signaled infidelity.

In her pursuit of beauty, she used lead powder and arsenic-laced whitening pills and even endured leeches on her face to maintain pallor.

In the Holy Light Empire, girls came of age at fourteen, boys at sixteen. Laurent lived with her mother until she was fourteen.

Every morning, she heard her mother's cries as maids tightened her waist.

Obsessed with a slim figure, her mother imposed waistbands on Laurent too, lamenting any lack of slimness.

When she was thirteen, her mother died beneath a fiery maple tree.

Late autumn didn't deter her from wearing thin dresses and velvet slippers revealing her toes, her face adorned with starry stickers that no longer hid blemishes.

No one harmed her.

She died for beauty—a senseless death.

Laurent felt no sadness—she didn't know how. She just hoped her mother would be wiser in the next life, abandoning futile beautification.

She always thought her mother was like a few sparks bursting out of a bonfire—shining suddenly and disappearing into the darkness.

It wasn't until she saw these girls that she realized she had never forgotten that beautiful, superficial woman.

Over the years, she has hardly applied makeup or pursued a slender waist and pale skin, all because of her mother.

Outwardly, she sought ambition and power, seemingly indifferent, yet within, she battled unfair fate.

She refused to repeat her mother's fate or see other girls fall to it.

This was perhaps her only righteous belief.

Laurent frowned slightly, feeling her heart's beat.

It was surprising that she had a compassionate heart.

Her thoughts were interrupted by a knock.

She stood up to open the door.

An amiable old lady stood outside the door, holding a steaming bowl of liquid. Even from a distance, Laurent could detect the distinct aroma wafting from it, unmistakably the scent of an aphrodisiac.

Laurent: "......"

She blinked her long black lashes. "Mammy?"

"I heard you recited the 'Ode to the Light Sutra' in full," the lady praised. "Remarkable! No goddess has recited it before. You're the best among this group, and the divine messenger will notice your talent."

Laurent smiled. "I'm honored by your approval."

"This is a potion from the divine messenger," the lady offered. "Drink it, and you'll hear divine secrets... Only the most outstanding goddesses enjoy such a gift. Drink and thank His Excellency."

Laurent smiled gently.

The old lady felt a foreboding chill.

Laurent would never drink the potion.

Though she had some immunity to poisons, she wouldn't willingly consume anything suspicious.

"Mammy, do you know why I came here?" Laurent asked, fixing her gaze on the old nanny with the tone of an obedient little girl. "It's because I'm not a good girl. My heart is quite wicked, filled with malicious intentions."

She leaned closer, whispering softly into the old lady's ear, "I poisoned my father and brother. My mother believed I was beyond redemption, so she sent me to a respected priest, hoping I would repent and find the right path... And guess what happened?"

At that moment, the deep bell of the temple rang out.

Its sacred sound was like a magnificent epic, resonating through the clear afternoon sky.

Laurent, meanwhile, appeared like a pure elf conjured from the bell's chime—her eyes innocent and pure, framed by delicate, fan-like black eyelashes. Her cheeks were pink, and her small, bright red lips resembled rose petals, creating an impression of innocence and harmlessness.

Yet, this seemingly harmless elf spoke words laced with venom: "I killed the priest too." She mimed a handgun with two fingers and a slight thumbs up, "With a bang, he fell down."

Afterward, Laurent tilted her head and blew away imaginary smoke from her index and middle fingers.

The old lady was so terrified that it felt as if her heart might burst.

Having served the temple for many years, she had witnessed the Inquisition and seen truly vicious criminals. She could distinguish between real and fake menace in Laurent's eyes—this girl indeed had blood on her hands.

Her palms turned cold and damp, like those of a dead person. She opened her mouth in shock, stumbled back a couple of steps, and trembled like a leaf, desperate to flee.

Meanwhile, Laurent stepped forward.

Seeing Laurent's face up close, the old lady was so frightened that her spirit seemed to leave her, goosebumps rising all over. She completely forgot her own malicious intent. In a panic, she waved her hand helplessly, trying to ward Laurent off, but accidentally dropped the bowl of soup, shattering it.

"Sister, this bowl of soup wasn't sent by the bishop," Laurent said softly. "If I present these broken pieces to him and claim you attempted to frame me with an aphrodisiac, what do you think he'll do to you?"

The old lady, suddenly recalling the contents of the soup, quickly squatted down to gather the scattered porcelain pieces.

Laurent watched her amusedly for a moment. As it was getting late and her afternoon class was about to start, she stepped on the back of the old lady's hand that was tiding the shards and walked out.

The broken porcelain shard pierced into the old lady's palm, causing her to grit her teeth in pain as sweat poured down her face. Though she wanted to scream, she feared attracting attention and causing a scene. Instead, she could only moan softly in agony, using her bloodied hands to carefully gather the shattered pieces.

This arrogant, vicious girl!

She vowed to make Laurent pay for her arrogance.

"Kill the priest, did she?" the old lady thought, her mind racing. "That's a grave sin, one that could lead her straight to the gallows. I'll report this to the divine messenger and let the law bring her to justice!"

CHAPTER

SEVENTEEN

The afternoon class was led by Father Clyde, the young man who had been watching Laurent with such intensity that day.

He still wore his black velvet robe, complemented by a white ribbon at the neck, high-waisted trousers, and polished boots, exuding an aura of elegance and dignity. His cold blue eyes seemed to impart a sense of superiority and compassion wherever they landed.

Laurent found herself deeply intrigued by him.

During her confrontation with Sister Catherine, his gaze had been unwavering, hotter than a volcano. Yet today, as she sat close enough for their eyes to meet, he didn't spare her a single glance.

If he wasn't merely playing hard to get, it only made him more interesting.

She had no idea when the older women would report her to the parish priest. Until then, she could only find amusement to distract herself.

This didn't mean she had developed any romantic interest in Father Clyde. She was merely curious about his motives and found his expressions amusing.

His demeanor had a detached coldness, as if he observed everything yet was unmoved by anything. But beneath that façade lay a sense of regret, especially when he discussed the Sutra of Light, almost bordering on self-loathing.

It seemed he was trying to rid himself of something but was simultaneously tempted by it.

If he wanted to forget her, she'd be happy to help, ensuring he never thought of her again.

As class concluded, Father Clyde held up the Hymn of Light Sutra and led the girls in prayer. As a goddess, she prayed thrice daily—morning, evening, and before bed.

After the prayer, Laurent noted the remorse in his eyes had deepened, along with his self-loathing. What exactly was he regretting and hating?

As the bell rang to signal the end of class, Laurent's leisurely appreciation of Father Clyde came to an end.

With a smile, she stood up. Before she could leave the classroom, she was surrounded by a group of sweetly fragrant girls.

Since she had helped them break free from Catherine's oppressive grip, this scene played out nearly every day.

The girls embraced her warmly, kissed her cheeks, held her hands tightly, and softly showing her warmth and concern.

Initially, Laurent had been a bit taken aback by their affection, but after a few more experiences, she regained her composure, handling their enthusiasm with grace. Though her ears turned a shade of red as they kissed her cheeks one by one.

Occupied with the affectionate girls, Laurent was unaware that the "Father Clyde" she had been observing was also observing her.

In truth, he had been watching her all along. Outwardly, he appeared not to notice her, but in reality, as long as he desired, everything in the world served as his eyes and ears, allowing him to see her.

The gentle breeze rustled the oak leaves, their sound a soft whisper in the air. Each leaf served as his eyes, vibrant green hearts encircling her head, swaying softly by her ears with a rhythmic thump. The resin's fragrance was also a part of his sight, drifting close to her, permeating her very being, offering a perspective wider than the oak leaves themselves.

Beyond the fragrant oak trees, the omnipresent air, sunlight, and mist were additional extensions of his vision.

His senses encompassed the entire temple—or rather, the temple itself was an extension of his senses. Even with Father Clyde's eyes closed, he could see every detail of her with keen precision.

She was undeniably beautiful, but was her beauty truly unique? What about her captivated him so? Was it her black hair and fair skin, or those wolf-like eyes brimming with malice and determination?

It had been two days since he regained a hint of his divinity. In that time, he had delved into many books. This was a perilous endeavor, for the more he learned about creation, the more he understood emotions. He knew he should not further explore his creation, yet he was compelled to continue.

Strangely enough, as he learned more about creation, his obsession with her grew stronger, and his curiosity about her deepened.

From a societal standpoint, she was far from perfect. She was deceitful, greedy, despicable, and ruthless, with ambitions greater than most men. Her bold desire for power would shock many if revealed.

She was a rose and a gun simultaneously.

In the lives he created, no other being was as unique as her.

She was unparalleled, even her blood uniquely sweet.

Thinking of her blood, Loire closed his eyes, his Adam's apple moving involuntarily.

He once again felt the inconveniences of inhabiting a male body. Men, he realized, were often too easily influenced by their emotions, with rationality swiftly overshadowed by feelings. As he contemplated the allure of Laurent, a sudden and intense thirst began to rise from his throat to his abdomen, sparking a flame of desire that felt almost sinful.

He had to grip the book in his hand tightly, taking deep breaths to quell the flickering desire.

He lamented choosing a male form. Returning to a misty state would mean losing human emotions and this overwhelming feeling. Mist had only appetite, while humans experienced myriad desires, blending human and animalistic traits.

He recognized his hypocrisy. He was greedy, desiring both divine solemnity and human experience.

How could he call Laurent greedy? She had clarity in her purpose—to become a devil and fulfill her ambitions. He, on the other hand, wanted to be both an extraordinary god and a flawed devil.

At that moment, Laurent exited the classroom.

He set down the Sutra of Light and followed her without hesitation.

To his surprise, Laurent didn't go far. After passing the tree-lined path, she stopped in a jasmine field, leisurely appreciating the flowers and giving him a playful glance.

She awaited him.

No, she awaited Father Clyde.

Loire closed his eyes, jealousy stirring within him.

What did this man have to earn her favor, beyond his handsome looks and tall physique?

Laurent was unaware of his inner turmoil. She had lost interest in the person, but his pursuit piqued her desire to tease him.

Sometimes, her mood led to unsettling, mischievous whims, much like scaring the priest's maid or lying to the old lady. These whims were her sudden, wicked amusements.

Yet Loire misunderstood her intentions, believing she held special affection for Father Clyde, and his jealousy intensified.

Meanwhile, Laurent approached him.

"Father," she asked with a smile, "do you like me in the way I think you do?"

Loire frowned slightly, turning his head to avoid Laurent's probing gaze on Father Clyde's face.

Laurent coldly turned his face back toward her, "Answer me, Father Clyde."

Her palm lightly touched Father Clyde's chin, a gesture that sent a shiver through Loire, almost allowing cold fury to spill into something irreversible and terrifying.

He paused for a significant moment, wrestling with his emotions, before finally responding in a hoarse, low voice, "Yes." Then, unable to suppress his jealousy, he added, "Does Miss Laurent like me?"

He thought if she said "yes," regardless of truth, he would end Clyde tonight.

Unexpectedly, Laurent withdrew her hand, pulled out a handkerchief, and wiped her fingers with a nearly wicked smile. "I don't like you, not at all. What I despise most is the priest, especially a hypocritical one like you. Outwardly, you've renounced desire to serve the gods, yet inwardly, you crave human pleasures. Let me guess, Father—you desire me and want to mate with me, don't you?"

Loire, momentarily relieved that she didn't favor Clyde, was stunned by her final words.

He understood the implication but hadn't expected it. A dry heat spread across his cheeks.

He turned away, his Adam's apple sliding visibly.

Before Loire could respond, Laurent flicked the handkerchief at him with a malicious chuckle. "I suggest you abandon this unrealistic fantasy. I'm not here to find a husband but to desecrate the gods. If every woman needed a mate, I'd choose your gods over you."

After delivering her parting words, Laurent disdainfully tossed the handkerchief at Loire as if it were refuse, then turned on her heel and walked away.

It wasn't until her figure vanished amidst the flowers that Loire came back to his senses.

He crouched down, carefully picking up the jasmine flowers with two fingers. He was not Clyde; he didn't perceive her words and actions as derogatory. Instead, he grasped a singular meaning from it all—Laurent was more intrigued by gods than by men.

—Could he possibly be a god?

Whether he was or not, divinity resided within him.

If he regained all his divinity, he might have a chance to win her over.

CHAPTER

EIGHTEEN

On the other side, the old lady, injured by the broken porcelain shards, finally seized the opportunity to meet with the parish priest.

The divine messenger's assistant informed her she had only ten minutes.

This was a privilege bestowed by the messenger on the faculty—each member, regardless of rank, had the chance to meet him and confess.

Covering her injured hand, the old lady bowed to the assistant and hurried into the lavishly decorated room.

The messenger sat by the French window, hands clasped, his demeanor calm. Clad in a deep purple robe with a golden ribbon at the neck, his appearance was youthful and handsome, though his age lent him a deep, steady temperament. His eyes, sharp and lively, belied his years.

He regarded the old lady kindly and extended a hand.

The old lady approached and respectfully kissed his gemstone ring.

"Dear Sophia," the messenger addressed her by her religious name, "what brings you here? You seem distressed."

Aunt Sophia burst into tears, "Oh, Your Excellency... I almost couldn't see you! There's a devil in the temple! She confessed to killing her father, brother, and even the priest who tried to guide her back to righteousness. She's a devil, and you must bring her to justice!"

The messenger's expression remained unchanged. "Calm down, Sophia. Who is this devil you're speaking of?"

"A girl named Laurent," Aunt Sophia replied through gritted teeth. "This little girl is really scheming. She's made quite a name for herself in just a few days."

"Interesting," the messenger mused. "Your friend, Sister Catherine, also mentioned her, but with a completely different account. Who should I trust?"

"I swear I'm telling the truth. She confessed with her own mouth."

"Have you considered she might have been joking? Her name is the same as the notorious queen known for such crimes," the messenger sighed, with a hint of humor.

"You must understand, Sofia," the messenger continued, "your actions could be perceived as rash and uninformed. Bringing such a matter to me without sufficient evidence could make us both appear foolish in her eyes. If I were to summon her based solely on your claims, it might give her the opportunity to mock us."

Though his tone was not reproachful, Aunt Sophia's heart skipped a beat.

She knelt quickly, apologizing, "I'm sorry, Your Excellency. I acted foolishly. I apologize for disturbing you."

"Don't worry, my Sophia," the messenger reassured. "I won't get angry. Just don't make such mistakes again, alright?"

"I won't, Your Excellency!" Aunt Sophia promised, trembling. "I'll reflect on my actions."

"I'm glad to hear that," the messenger smiled.

After she left, the messenger's gentle demeanor vanished, replaced by disdain. His forgiveness was superficial, masking his contempt for her rashness.

As for Laurent, she seemed no better, trying to deceive him. But he was no fool, and saw through her game.

He held this position not by mere chance but through a calculated understanding of his responsibilities and influence. Unlike those priests who were swayed by the affection of women, he remained steadfast, never succumbing to temptation despite his striking looks and the attention he garnered. To him, the allure of the flesh held no sway; he found no interest in women beyond their biological roles.

In his view, women offered little of value beyond their capacity for reproduction.

When noblewomen came to confess, he listened with a polite smile, yet inwardly he found their voices grating and their confessions trivial. To him, women were confined to the roles of wives and mothers, existing primarily for the sake of family and progeny.

He saw women as impulsive, irritable, and lacking competence. The simplest tasks seemed to exhaust them, and he regarded their daily routines as frivolous. In his eyes, they barely qualified as true beings.

He took comfort in knowing that the Supreme divine messenger shared his views, ensuring women would never rule the Holy Light Empire. The thought of living under female rule seemed a fate worse than death to him, as he believed it would undermine the very fabric of society.

Fortunately, the Supreme divine messenger shared his views, preventing women from ruling the Holy Light Empire. Under a woman's rule, he thought, life would be unbearable.

The messenger dismissed his contemptuous thoughts and summoned his assistant. "Find out who recommended Laurent."

"Reverend Fletcher, sir."

"Find him. I need more information."

The assistant hesitated. "We haven't heard from Reverend Fletcher in weeks. Yesterday was the time for him to pay the town tax, but the priests knocked on his door without receiving a response. We suspect that he has already..."

The divine messenger recalled Aunt Sophia's words and raised his eyebrows in disbelief. Did priest Fletcher really get killed by that girl?

He immediately instructed his assistant to investigate the whereabouts of Reverend Fletcher and then ordered someone to summon Laurent.

Ten minutes later, Laurent entered the room.

She clasped her hands before her and lowered her lashes, allowing the divine messenger to take in her appearance with a serene and gentle demeanor.

Her beauty was indeed extraordinary, surpassing even the expectations he might have had. Yet, it wasn't her physical allure that truly captivated him—it was the look in her eyes and the strength of her character that piqued his interest.

He observed in her gaze a determination and resilience typically associated with men, an unusual combination of grace and a sharp, penetrating aura. This rare blend of attributes set her apart from others he had encountered.

The divine messenger found himself admiring Laurent, recognizing in her a confidence and strength that were seldom seen in women. Her composure and self-assuredness were qualities he respected, even though it challenged his preconceived notions about women's roles and capabilities.

Laurent presented a paradox that intrigued him, making him reconsider the rigid views he held about the nature and potential of women.

If she is willing to sincerely apologize like Sofia, he is prepared to give her an opportunity to explain and correct herself, even allowing her to become his personal goddess—a great honor that many goddesses have begged for but cannot obtain.

"Laurent, do you know why I summoned you?" he asked gently.

Laurent's response was unexpected. With a slight smile, she calmly stated, "Your Majesty, I want to repent."

The messenger frowned, perceiving her words as abrupt and perhaps lacking the decorum he expected. In his mind, this was typical of what he deemed the weaknesses of women—ignorant and incapable of strategic thought.

Had she responded with the insight and cunning he would expect from a man, he might have questioned whether there was a different spirit residing within her, one that defied the delicate exterior.

"Okay," he replied, his tone laced with condescension, "then let's hear what you want to confess."

Laurent, unfazed by the disdain in his voice, remained composed. She was aware of his low opinion, but it mattered little to her. She was there with a purpose, and his underestimation would not deter her from executing her plan.

If Margo were with her, she would have noticed that the queen's plan was already halfway to fruition.

Laurent had been at the parish temple for less than three days, yet she had already gained the admiration of the goddesses and had been summoned by the parish divine messenger—a rare and significant occurrence.

The parish messenger held a position of considerable authority within the diocese, akin to a small monarch who wielded control over its resources and operations. From his elevated vantage point, he oversaw the spiritual and administrative affairs of the diocese, listening to the confessions and concerns of its people with an air of detached authority.

In the hierarchy of power, his role was crucial, though it sat just below the exalted status of the Supreme divine messenger. The Supreme divine messenger's influence extended beyond that of a king, and the parish messenger's power, while not as expansive, still surpassed that of a typical courtier. His decisions shaped the lives of many, and his judgments carried significant weight within the ecclesiastical community.

This unique positioning allowed him to act with a degree of autonomy, managing the diocese's affairs with a blend of spiritual guidance and practical governance. Those who were summoned to his presence understood the gravity of such an audience, often approaching with reverence and humility, aware of the influence he wielded and the potential impact of his decisions.

While he outwardly presented himself as open-minded and willing to hear the confessions of clergy, few dared to approach him without significant cause.

His time was highly valued, and those summoned typically expressed profound gratitude and deference, marked by a respectful kiss to his gemstone ring.

Laurent, however, did not display the expected reverence. Instead, she met his gaze with a playful defiance, her black eyelashes fluttering as she curled her red lips into a mischievous, almost wicked smile. "I want to repent for the sin of murder," she declared, her tone carrying a mix of mockery and boldness.

Her words, laden with a provocative charm, challenged the very authority she stood before, hinting at the depth and audacity of her intentions.

"Do you realize what you're saying?" the messenger's smile vanished.

"Of course I know what I'm talking about, sir," Laurent smiled lightly. "I also know that you summoned me because someone reported that I recited Ode to the Light Sutra. Ah, perhaps not only the Ode to the Light Sutra, but also that I killed people, including family members and priests. You are curious about me, so you summoned me. Am I correct?"

Absolutely correct.

The messenger stiffened. She saw through him, as if he were transparent.

Being seen through was unsettling, especially by a woman he deemed incompetent.

"Did you bribe them to speak against you?" the messenger asked, his tone laced with accusation.

"Of course not," Laurent replied, lightly tapping her temple with a finger. "Why use money when wisdom suffices?"

Her response, while appearing innocent and straightforward, was imbued with an undeniable arrogance.

Except of arrogance, the divine messenger discerned irony, subtly mocking him for his assumption that influence could only be exerted through something as crude and tangible as bribery.

The divine messenger always believed that his wisdom and vision could only be compared to the Supreme divine messenger, so he rarely got angry. But now, he was gritted by the provocation of a sixteen or seventeen-year-old girl.

She saw through his temperament at a glance and accurately stepped on his weak points with every sentence.

The messenger took a deep breath and finally calmed down. This little girl was just good at grasping people's hearts. She was too confident and completely unaware that this was a dangerous conversation. Any minor carelessness would send her to the gallows by him

"So, are you here to repent for Reverend Fletcher's murder?" he asked, feigning compassion.

"No, sir," Laurent laughed. "My only sin was not killing him sooner."

"But you said you came to repent for murder," he pressed, hating her control of the conversation.

"Yes, if I'd killed him earlier, fewer would have died," she said. "Fletcher was a serial killer who murdered hundreds. I have proof, and I want a public trial."

The divine messenger fixed Laurent with a dark, brooding gaze.

The notion of publicly trying the case, thereby elevating her to a heroic status for exposing and punishing a serial killer. No way! He was poised to deny her request outright and condemn her to be burned at the stake for "plotting against a clergyman."

However, just as he was about to voice this decision, a sudden realization coursed through him. Laurent had already made a name for herself within the temple; nearly everyone knew of her. A rash decision to sentence her to death could provoke unwanted scrutiny and questions from others.

Despite his position as the de facto monarch of the diocese, the divine messenger knew his power had its limits. It wasn't enough to silence every voice or quell every whisper of dissent. His role wasn't hereditary; it was earned by capability. As such, many within the ecclesiastical hierarchy, those aspiring to succeed him, watched keenly for any misstep that might topple him from his perch. This made handling Laurent a delicate matter—one not to be approached hastily.

The thought of agreeing to a public trial sent a chill through his heart.

Laurent seemed to have maneuvered herself into a position where each move had to be meticulously calculated. She had refuted Sister Catherine publicly, gained the favor of the goddesses, and made a name for herself within the temple. It was as if she had orchestrated these events to ensure he would tread carefully when dealing with her.

He began to wonder if their meeting was part of a grander strategy. Had she anticipated his every reaction, even threatening Aunt Sophia with tales of murder to provoke his summons? The idea that her machinations extended so far was both unsettling and impressive.

The divine messenger found himself grappling with the notion that Laurent's mind was far more cunning and strategic than he had ever credited a woman with being. Her ability to navigate and manipulate the intricate web of temple politics was alarming. How could she possess such formidable wisdom and foresight?

The divine messenger shook his head, dismissing the unsettling thoughts that had momentarily clouded his judgment.

He decided that a public trial would be the perfect stage to undermine Laurent's credibility. By portraying Reverend Fletcher as a virtuous and respected figure, he intended to sway public opinion against her. He would invite the entire parish to witness the proceedings, confident that the weight of communal judgment would crush her.

He didn't believe that an isolated girl like Laurent could withstand the tide of scorn that would follow. Her hard-won reputation would crumble, and those who admired her would be appalled to see her painted as a vile murderer who had slain a beloved clergyman.

"Okay," the messenger said with a light chuckle, masking his intentions with a veneer of sincerity. "As you wish, a public trial will be held."

Laurent responded with a soft, enigmatic smile, her demeanor calm and assured.

She could see through the messenger's plan and felt a twinge of pity for his naivety. He underestimated her resolve and cunning.

She knew that the higher he elevated Fletcher, the more devastating the fall would be when the truth was revealed.

Laurent was eager to witness the unraveling of the messenger's carefully laid plans.

Inwardly, she mused about the irony of the situation. If there truly was a God of Light, why would HE not intervene and save HIS people from the deceit woven into their beliefs? Instead, the divine messenger's arrogance blinded him to the storm Laurent was about to unleash.

NINETEEN

Loire wandered through the temple, holding Laurent's handkerchief as he entered the sacred space where worshippers gathered.

As soon as he stepped inside, a sense of clarity enveloped him, and the tumultuous desires that usually clouded his mind seemed to vanish.

Although he could still detect the faint scent of desire, its sweetness no longer lingered on his senses. It was as if the temple's sanctity had cleansed him, rendering his lips and tongue incapable of tasting desire.

In that moment, he forgot everything, even Laurent.

With closed eyes, he moved forward guided only by intuition. The fragrance of desire gradually gave way to the scent of fragrant oil, and Laurent's expressions seemed to merge with those of the devotees around him. They passed by, worried, and he could feel their suffering, empathizing with their pain, though he couldn't offer help—not even once.

Divinity forbade his interference in mortal matters.

For mortals, having a god in their world was the ultimate solace.

At the heart of the hall stood a grand pipe organ, towering into the dome. With over ten thousand pipes and four rows of keys, it resembled a majestic silver-white edifice. When played, its music reverberated like a flood, audible from twenty kilometers away—a magnificent, awe-inspiring hymn.

In this atmosphere, Loire felt an unprecedented calm.

For a moment, he believed he could manage everything, even his desire to possess Laurent.

It was as if he returned to an original state, devoid of gender, and thus, free from desire.

Without desire, the world appeared as a unified whole to him. He no longer saw individuals as separate entities nor felt inclined to show favoritism. He was free from the entanglements of emotions and desires that individuals often provoked.

By preserving this sense of calm and sanctity, he believed he could regain his invincibility, rediscover his former self, and return to his supreme position.

But could he?

His mind and body had adapted to human ways, and he still clutched Laurent's handkerchief. Its warmth and softness were almost like her skin.

His mind had grown accustomed to human ways of thinking, and his body had adapted to living like one. Yet, he still clutched the handkerchief Laurent had given him. Its soft fabric felt as smooth and comforting as her skin. Holding it felt intimate, as if brushing against her lips.

He wondered if her lips would feel the same.

As this thought crossed his mind, a flood of memories he had tried to suppress surged back, overwhelming his reason like a wildfire.

Her smile, her gaze, her dimples, and her voice filled his senses again.

The longing to possess her reasserted itself, and he found himself imagining the sensation of kissing her. Could he even dare to kiss her? It was ironic—despite creating her life and the world she inhabited, controlling every facet of her existence, he couldn't know the taste of her lips. How paradoxical.

What was the point of holiness? Before he created the world, did holiness and impurity even exist as concepts?

Why is abstinence considered pure while indulgence is deemed dirty? If his desire to kiss her signifies depravity, does suppressing these impulses mean he is pure?

The answer was becoming increasingly clear. Despite his thoughts and attempts to escape, he yearned to become human and win her over. He admitted to feeling a romantic impulse toward her, wanting to possess her, kiss her, and understand her as a lover would.

He realized that he should have faced his desires with calm acceptance, acknowledging his wish to control everything. His desires were complex, encompassing both light and darkness, beauty and terror, reason and passion, holiness and impurity, divinity and humanity—he craved them all. It was no surprise that he was drawn to the alluring Laurent; in many ways, they were kindred souls, sharing similar desires and complexities.

Kindred souls.

He mused over the notion of being the same kind of person and chuckled at how quickly he identified himself as such. Just then, a voice interrupted his thoughts: "Father Clyde, are you here for the celebration too?"

Loire turned to see a round-faced girl who admired Laurent. He remembered her clinging to Laurent like a kitten and coldly replied, "No."

The round-faced girl was visibly anxious, seemingly oblivious to Loire's cold demeanor. She had been searching for Laurent for quite some time without success, and speaking to Loire was her way of calming her nerves. Although they had known each other for less than three days, Laurent had quickly become her favorite friend, and the girl's anxiety grew whenever Laurent was out of sight.

Pursing her lips, she looked at Loire hesitantly. Determined to try anything, she decided to ask for his help. "Father, please forgive my abruptness... Do you remember Laurent?" she asked. When Loire nodded, she continued, "She's gone! I've been searching everywhere for her, but I can't find her. She was here at the temple not too long ago, and I'm worried she might have gotten lost in its vastness."

As she spoke, her anxiety deepened. "And, as you saw that day, she's so straightforward and doesn't always know how to speak tactfully. She accidentally offended Catherine in front of everyone. I'm not trying to imply anything negative about Catherine, but I'm genuinely concerned for Laurent's safety. What if someone retaliates against her?"

Loire interrupted her gently, "I know. I'll find her."

"Thank you, thank you! You are such a good person," she replied, relieved.

But in truth, there was no need for a search. With a mere thought, Loire knew exactly where Laurent was.

She was in a cell at the parish court, awaiting a public trial in three days. Soon, the parish messenger would announce that she was suspected of murdering clergy members. Although she had pressured the messenger into agreeing to a public trial, this didn't mean the diocesan messenger had relinquished control over the situation.

The diocesan court was notorious for its hidden corruption, filled with dangerous criminals, many with blood on their hands.

Laurent shared a cell with a woman who claimed to be the reincarnation of Tofana—a clever and perilous figure who had murdered her husband and son for insurance benefits, leaving a trail of death wherever she went. This woman was rumored to have crafted a legendary ring capable of killing with mere thought.

The parish priests had likely placed Laurent with such a dangerous inmate in hopes they would destroy each other.

Laurent needed Loire, and he felt compelled to return to her side.

Once this thought emerged, he realized that all his previous reflections and struggles had been futile. He had never truly forgotten her or escaped her influence.

Whether or not he wished to become a man, Laurent's need for him was undeniable. From the moment he first encountered her desire, he belonged entirely to her.

Regardless of whether he wished to become a man or not, the fact remained that whenever she was in danger or needed him, he would find his way back to her side.

Perhaps from the moment he savored her desire for the first time, he became entirely hers.

From the beginning, he was filled with an insatiable appetite for her, eager to savor her essence. But now, beyond mere desire, he longed to hold her entire being within his embrace.

TWENTY

When Loire returned to Laurent's wrist, the first to notice wasn't Laurent, but the little black mist he'd left behind.

Little Black Mists: "......". How did this annoying thing come back?

Despite their grumblings, they made room and warmly welcomed him back. Some of the mist had grown plump on Laurent's desires in his absence, standing out awkwardly among the others.

Little Chubby Mist: "..."

Other Little Black Mist: "Why can't we just get rid of this stupid thing?"

Just as they were about to hide the chubby silly mist, Loire's cold glance made those who dared steal Laurent's desires explode on the spot.

The remaining small black mist quivered so intensely that the entire fog seemed ready to explode from fear. Was it just their imagination, or had the Big Black Mist truly become more formidable after his journey?

Previously, the Great Black Mist had been stern yet tolerant, allowing their presence as long as they held no ill intentions. But now, he wouldn't even permit their desire to siphon anything from Laurent, his possessiveness growing alarmingly intense. Could they continue to exist under such a shadow of his dominance?

With these thoughts swirling, the little black mists curled into a tight ball, trembling with both fear and frustration. Loire, however, paid no attention to their turbulent emotions, focused solely on his presence with Laurent.

Transforming into a sleek black snake, he coiled around Laurent's wrist, his bright red tongue lightly brushing her skin.

Laurent felt his touch and without looking down, gently stroked his head. "You're awake."

Having missed her touch, Loire's snake form shivered with anticipation. Laurent's slightest touch sent waves of excitement through him.

Laurent, however, didn't pay it much mind. She simply tapped the snake's head lightly twice to signal him to calm down.

Her mind was occupied with other thoughts.

She was acutely aware of her situation.

It seemed that the parish messenger had compromised and was willing to publicly address the priest's case. However, it was clear that he wouldn't easily let go of a woman who had outmaneuvered him.

The prison cell was the clearest evidence of that.

Her hands were stained with the blood of priests. Typically, a convicted criminal like her wouldn't be housed with other inmates. Yet, the court placed her in the same cell with a slender blonde woman.

This could only mean one thing: this woman was also a convicted criminal with blood on her hands.

The parish messenger likely wanted them to kill each other.

With this in mind, Laurent tilted her head slightly, observing the woman with interest.

The woman appeared to have been in prison for a long time. Her once golden hair was greasy and clumped together in strands, resembling the slender tail of a mouse. Beneath the disarrayed hair was a captivating face. No one could deny she was a classic blonde beauty.

With a wide-brimmed hat, jewelry, and a beautiful silk dress, she would be the kind of woman men dream of marrying. Regardless of love, seeing her reclined on a leather sofa, smiling and eating crystal-clear purple grapes would evoke a profound sense of satisfaction.

Laurent continued her scrutiny with great interest.

The woman's fingers were adorned with bright red nail polish, which was quite striking. However, prison life was far from glamorous. Inmates had to labor tirelessly, shackled with iron balls. Even when there was no work, the priests found tasks for them, such as loading and unloading heavy stones from carts repeatedly.

As a result, her nail polish was chipped, revealing dirty and darkened nails beneath.

Laurent chuckled softly.

"What are you laughing at?" the woman asked, frowning.

Just ten minutes earlier, a cloaked priest had told her that if she killed this girl within three days, she would be acquitted.

According to the legal code, even if convicted criminals are released, they must wear ankle shackles and have their charges and sentence clearly marked on their passports, stamped with a "very dangerous" red seal.

Over the years, she had been assisting the temple in "dealing" with prisoners who were inconvenient to bring to trial, but none had ever offered her the privilege of a "not guilty" release.

The priest promised that if she found a way to poison Laurent, she would not only live a free life but also receive substantial compensation.

Thinking of the carefree and joyful life outside the prison, the woman gazed at Laurent with blatant murderous intent.

The priest had returned her poisoned ring. With this ring, killing was as simple as could be. She only needed to feign concern and pat Laurent on the shoulder, and this innocent, beautiful girl would wilt like a flower deprived of water, reduced to a heap of withered petals and leaves.

To the woman, exchanging another's life for her freedom wasn't unethical. She had long grown accustomed to walking over bones and corpses, building her golden wealth on the lives of others.

The woman leaned against the stone wall, lowering her eyelashes to conceal the fierce glint in her eyes.

At that moment, Laurent curled her lips and spoke in a sweet tone, "I thought of something fun, so of course I want to laugh."

The woman sneered but stayed silent.

In her eyes, Laurent was just a young girl with a touch of beauty, who had somehow offended a clergyman and found herself locked up in the courtroom.

As for why she offended the clergy, it was obvious to the woman—it must have been because she rejected the advances of some influential figure. That person, scorned, accused her of murder and had her imprisoned.

The woman had guessed part of the truth.

The root of it all was indeed Laurent's refusal of Fletcher, a priest's, affections.

The woman pondered for a moment. This girl wouldn't survive the next three days anyway, so why not exchange a few more words? Building a rapport might make it easier to kill her when the time came.

"So, what's this fun thing you thought of?" the woman asked.

Laurent tilted her head, revealing two sweet dimples on her cheeks. "You're poisoned and about to die. I'll soon be living alone in this cell. Isn't that fun?" she said.

As soon as she spoke, a chill wind swept through, causing the candlelight outside the cell to flicker and dim.

In the dim light, Laurent's lips appeared to glow with an eerie red hue. The strange glow gave her pure and beautiful smile a beguiling and sinister quality, reminiscent of the mythical monster disguised as a beauty, who lured people to their doom.

The woman's skin prickled with goosebumps.

No wonder this girl could captivate the clergy. Her face did seem to possess an enchanting power.

But poisoned? What kind of poisoning?

The woman snapped to attention and asked warily, "Poisoned? What are you talking about? I don't understand."

Just then, the cell's iron door was tapped twice. A small hatch opened, and a guard delivered hot broth and cereal congee.

While prisoners were required to eat in designated areas, she was granted the "privilege" of dining in her cell, a reward for assisting the temple.

To ensure the temple didn't silence her permanently, she demanded that all her meals be served in silver bowls and plates, threatening to withdraw her assistance if they did not comply.

The judge agreed to her request and tried to accommodate her tastes as best as possible.

However, her appetite was worsening, especially today. Laurent's cryptic words had left her deeply unsettled, and the prison food seemed increasingly unappetizing, resembling livestock feed.

Outside, she could indulge in any delicacy she desired and even enjoy half a gallon of white wine daily. But here, she was stuck with this revolting pig feed.

In a fit of anger, she flipped the plate over.

She glared at Laurent with eyes blazing with fury. "If you have something to say, just say it. I hate riddles. Keep playing tricks, and I'll strangle you. Do you believe that?"

Laurent remained calm, but the snake on her wrist, Loire, suddenly straightened, its purple-blue eyes flashing with cold menace as it flicked its tongue.

The woman stood up abruptly, taking a step back in disbelief. "Did you... bring the snake in here?"

Laurent gently patted Loire's head and whispered, "Calm down, don't be angry. I can handle her."

The black snake, which had been hissing threateningly, settled down, coiling itself around Laurent's wrist. Its cold, watchful eyes stayed fixed on the woman, ready to strike if needed.

On Laurent's fair palm, this fierce and terrifying snake behaved as docilely as a puppy, a surprising contrast to its menacing appearance.

The woman felt a shiver run down her spine.

She was thankful she hadn't acted impulsively, or she might have ended up dead.

Laurent wasn't in a rush to answer the woman's question. She lowered her head gracefully, gently stroking Loire's head, clearly pleased with his loyalty.

She really adored this obedient and powerful little snake. When she finally spoke to the woman, her voice was noticeably softer: "Think about how you are now, compared to how you used to be. Were you always this irritable and quick to flip things over?"

The woman was taken aback and instinctively began to reflect on her past.

She used to be calm and composed. How had she become so quick to anger and capable of overturning her plate in a fit of rage?

What had happened to her?

At some point, her temper had soured, and she found herself frequently roaring and cursing hysterically. Once, she awoke from a nightmare, saw her cellmate sleeping peacefully nearby, and was inexplicably consumed by fury, punching the cellmate and knocking out two teeth.

That was just the beginning. Her anger grew more intense, as if a fierce evil fire was burning inside her. This fire didn't just consume her rationality; it also extinguished her appetite and her normal desires. She often felt hopeless and would burst into tears without any apparent reason.

She had confided in the priest at the court about her worsening condition.

The priest claimed it was divine punishment for her sins and that only by continually serving the temple could she seek God's forgiveness.

She believed him. Each time the temple asked her to "deal with" convicted criminals, she complied diligently, yet her health continued to decline.

Just a few days ago, she was severely beaten by her former cellmate. Years ago, she could have knocked out their teeth with a single punch, but now she was so weak that she couldn't even muster the strength to defend herself.

Could she really have been poisoned?

She had insisted that all her utensils be made of pure silver to prevent poisoning, refusing to use anything else. So why would she still be poisoned?

Laurent gently pointed out, "There is indeed an issue with your tableware."

"Impossible!" the woman retorted instinctively. "I'm not foolish; I can tell the material of my tableware!" She picked up the pure silver spoon from the ground and bent it forcefully to demonstrate. "See, it's pure silver. How could there be a problem?"

Laurent shook her head with a smile and posed an unrelated question: "Have you heard of the ancient Roman Empire?"

"What does that have to do with anything?" the woman replied, growing impatient.

"It was once one of the most illustrious civilizations, unmatched by even the Empire of Light," Laurent continued. "But it eventually led to its own downfall. Do you know why?"

"I'm not a history professor. How would I know this useless trivia?" the woman snapped.

Unfazed by her frustration, Laurent explained calmly, "The ancient Romans adored a metal called 'lead.' It was soft like silver, gray-white in color, and used to make various items. They crafted cups, plates, and dishes from lead, and even used it in pills, dental fillings, and hair dye.

They discovered that using lead pots for wine made it incredibly smooth and sweet, so they exclusively used lead pots for storage. Sometimes, to enhance their wine's flavor, they added lead powder. But lead is harmful."

At first, the woman listened with impatience, but her expression gradually changed. "You mean...?"

Laurent smiled and continued, "Due to lead's overuse, the entire ancient Roman society became irritable, lost their appetites, and suffered from insomnia. Even the elite rarely lived past thirty, often dying from seizures."

At this point, she suddenly frowned and shook her head. "Oh, how could the decline and destruction of an empire be related to the materials of cups, plates, and dishes? Don't take my words seriously."

As soon as she finished speaking, she closed her eyes and lazily lay down on the bed, pretending to take a nap.

The woman fully understood her meaning—after being imprisoned, her mental and behavioral abnormalities were definitely related to this "lead."

No wonder the temple agreed to her request so quickly when she asked to dine with pure silver tableware.

The temple never thought of letting her leave.

divine punishment or forgiveness is all nonsense. From the moment she worked for the temple, the temple arranged for her to die from poisoning.

The woman's face turned pale; she grabbed her hair and let out a suppressed scream.

She wanted to go crazy, scream, and smash all these poisonous utensils. However, she couldn't. She couldn't let the temple notice that she already knew the truth.

On the surface, she still needed to work for the temple; only then could she find an opportunity to seek revenge.

It took a while for the woman to calm down from her intense anger. When she finally did, she lifted her head and met Laurent's admiring gaze. "Your willpower deserves respect," Laurent said. "What's your name?"

In a hoarse voice, the woman replied, "Sisina." She closed her eyes and offered a weary smile. "So what does respect mean? To the temple, I'm still just a ridiculous failure."

Laurent chuckled softly and replied, "What if I told you I have a way to turn the tables and make the temple the failure you speak of?"

If Sisina had heard this ten minutes earlier, she might have dismissed it outright. But now, as she regained her composure, she began to realize the formidable nature of this young girl.

Laurent appeared innocent and harmless, but her vision, knowledge, observational skills, and reasoning were truly remarkable — perhaps even intimidating. It seemed that Laurent had deduced from the start that Sisina was an assassin sent by the temple, and she was working to uncover her vulnerabilities.

Just then, a guard from the court brought food, and Sisina, in anger, overturned the utensils. Within less than five minutes, Laurent had already deduced, from examining the tableware, that Sisina was suffering from lead poisoning.

Remarkably, instead of directly revealing her conclusion, Laurent skillfully led Sisina to discover the truth on her own. People tend to trust conclusions they reach themselves.

How old was this girl? She seemed not even half Sisina's age, yet she had mastered the art of manipulation to an extraordinary degree.

Initially, Sisina had dismissed Laurent as a naive little girl, but now she felt a wave of embarrassment at her own arrogance. Laurent's sharp intelligence must have easily perceived Sisina's earlier disdain.

Yet, this remarkably insightful girl had still praised Sisina's willpower as being worthy of respect. The thought filled Sisina with a renewed sense of happiness. Looking earnestly into Laurent's eyes, she declared, "If you can make the Temple a failure, I will wholeheartedly support you, no matter what it takes. Whatever you ask of me, I will do."

Laurent raised her eyebrows slightly, surprised by the depth of Sisina's newfound trust in her.

She bowed her head, contemplating how to express her gratitude to Sisina for her trust with eloquent words. Yet, all she managed to say was, "I will show you that you made the right decision."

Sisina burst into laughter.

Ever since being poisoned by the temple, her spirits had been dampened and dark, rarely finding joy. But now, she laughed heartily and loudly.

She admired this clever and arrogant girl.

After all, intelligent people ought to have a bit of arrogance!

An hour later, the divine messenger studied the note handed to him by the court guard and frowned. "Sisina claims she couldn't find an opportunity to poison?"

Reclining on a walnut lounge chair, he absentmindedly fiddled with the ring on his finger as he pondered. "With all her experience in eliminating threats, how could she not manage to deal with a mere girl who is twenty years younger?"

His assistant chimed in, "You've seen how crafty that girl is. She's as shrewd as a fox, even daring to plot against you. Didn't you say she has a mind akin to a man's? Sisina is just a woman; naturally, she can't compete with her."

The messenger nodded thoughtfully but added, "Your analysis is correct, but it is still biased. I admit that she has many advantages that only men have, but she will never have a mind similar to that of men. Have you read the scriptures of the Old Testament? Eve caused the fall of mankind, Delilah ruthlessly betrayed Samson, and Jezebel persecuted the respected prophets of the ancient Hebrews. Our ancestors have never stopped telling us how shallow women's vision is, how simple their minds are, and how weak their willpower is."

With a sigh, he concluded, "Women can never be on par with men. Keep that in mind."

The assistant nodded in agreement, albeit with internal misgivings. "You're right. What should we do now? Sisina can't find a chance to target Laurent. Are we just going to let her safely pass the three days?"

The messenger glared at him as if he were dense. "There are still three days left, aren't there? If she can't find a chance today, perhaps tomorrow or the day after. There are many female inmates in the prison. Where there are women, there are conflicts. Can't you incite and provoke them into brawls and quarrels? I refuse to believe that girl can emerge unscathed in the chaos."

He heaved a heavy sigh, adding, "You should be more adaptable in your thinking. Don't let yourself be outdone by a woman."

The assistant continued nodding but harbored doubts within. He lacked the divine messenger's confidence. No matter how he rationalized, he couldn't measure up to Laurent and Sisina.

At only sixteen, Laurent had outmaneuvered the diocese's priest; meanwhile, Sisina, in just a few years, had married over ten times, amassing hundreds of thousands of silver coins through insurance schemes. Rather than squandering it, she invested in opening a business. If not for her wealth attracting envy and betrayal by those close to her, she might not have been imprisoned!

If he possessed the intellect of these two, would he still be an assistant?

However, he dared not voice such thoughts, keeping them firmly to himself.

After scouring the court's records, he finally found ten female prisoners guilty of murder. It had been a challenge.

Women were not like men, who were arrested as true heretics. Arresting a woman was easy; merely expressing an opinion on God, right or wrong, in church could lead to accusations of witchcraft.

The assistant inspected these ten female prisoners and felt discontent. The grueling labor had left them dull and lifeless, like overworked beasts of burden. Using them against Laurent felt like pitting a weak horse against a strong one. Unfortunately, he couldn't find more female prisoners with blood on their hands.

In some aspects, women may indeed be seen as less capable than men, and the divine messenger's words reflect this belief.

The assistant pondered this notion but then had a revelation. Isn't this particular aspect about aggression and violence? Surely, there's nothing commendable about being proficient in killing. In the animal kingdom, it's only the wild beasts that resort to violence without restraint!

The assistant glanced down at the court's records and noticed the stark difference: the pages documenting male prisoners were significantly thicker than those for female prisoners.

He had always been influenced by the divine messengers' teachings, believing men to be superior to women. Men were the preachers, the givers, the ones inspired by God to become messengers. Men were seen as rational, determined, and visionary, while women were considered foolish, weak, and simple-minded.

But if men are truly superior in every way, why do the records show so many more male prisoners than female? Could it be that the differences between men and women aren't as significant as he was led to believe?

Suddenly alarmed by these thoughts, the assistant snapped the register book shut. Such ideas were too dangerous to entertain.

The next morning, before dawn, Laurent was rudely awakened by the guards at the courthouse. "Up, everyone! Get moving, you lot of worthless goods!" The guard banged the gongs and drums. "Open your eyes and get to work. You're here to pay for your sins, not to relax! Show God your sincerity through hard labor, or you'll never receive His forgiveness!"

Sisina, also jolted awake by the commotion, listened to the guards' threats with a smirk. How she once believed those words! She trusted the priests, thinking their promises would be fulfilled if she worked dutifully. But instead of forgiveness, she was cast into despair.

From now on, she vowed never to trust those hypocritical priests again.

As she dressed, Sisina approached Laurent and whispered, "Be careful. If I can't kill you, the priests will send others. I know their kind well. They may appear kind, but they're more ruthless than anyone."

Laurent yawned, lazily stretching, and murmured, "Don't worry. I'm more ruthless than they are."

Sisina was taken aback. She looked at Laurent's long, dark lashes, rosy cheeks, and doll-like lips, finding it hard to reconcile such innocence with ruthlessness.

She conceded that Laurent was indeed smart, but "smart" and "ruthless" were not the same.

The priests might lack Laurent's intelligence, means, and keen observation, but their intent to kill didn't require wisdom.

The human mind is powerful and versatile, yet the human body is fragile—just flesh and bone. A sharp object can easily pierce the skin, causing blood to flow freely.

In the face of brute force and weapons, intelligence has little room to maneuver.

Sisina didn't want to admit to the temple that she had no chance to act, knowing that would only prompt them to send more assassins after Laurent. Better to deal with one group than two.

But how should a delicate, powerless girl like Laurent deal with the temple's assassins?

Laurent sensed Sisina's doubts. As she braided her thick black hair, she glanced at Sisina and said, "You'll see soon enough."

The movement startled the black snake coiled around her wrist. The sleek, dangerous creature slithered along her shoulder and neck, disappearing into her dark hair. In the dim light, it became nearly invisible, save for the occasional glint of its scales.

Sisina shivered. She had extensive knowledge of poisons but never dared to handle them. She understood the lethal nature of venomous creatures — frogs, lizards, scorpions, snakes. Especially snakes. Many believed they could be tamed, treating them like pets, only to be fatally bitten.

Yet Laurent allowed the snake such proximity, even letting it nest in her hair. Her skill in taming such creatures was impressive, but her courage to dance on the edge of life and death was truly remarkable.

Perhaps this girl isn't as fragile as she seems?

Just then, the guard began banging the drums and gongs again, shouting, "Why are you still inside? Get out and start working now. If you don't come out, you'll never get out!"

Despite her clever mind, Laurent found it difficult to use her intelligence for the labor assigned to her.

The guard gave her the filthiest and most back-breaking tasks, assigning a burly old woman to supervise her and ensuring Sisina couldn't assist.

Laurent spent the entire morning scrubbing the bathroom, holding a bucket in one hand and a mop in the other. She not only had to hold her breath to resist gagging but also reach into the pipes to pull out clumps of hair, all while keeping a watchful eye on Loire to prevent him from biting the supervising nanny.

By the time she finished, an indescribable exhaustion was etched on her face—more psychological than physical.

Sisina watched her with a mixture of pity and concern. Laurent seemed too delicate for such conditions; hardened female prisoners could easily overpower her.

Sisina was both worried and intrigued about how Laurent would deal with them.

Noon proved to be the most perilous time, with all the female prisoners gathered under the scorching sun, waiting in line for their meals.

Under the strict watch of the guards, they dared not speak, the only sound being the clinking of their heavy ankle shackles. But silence didn't equate to submission; they harbored anger that simmered beneath the surface.

Once the guards left to eat, the prisoners were left to vent their frustrations on one another.

Sisina used to feel superior to the other prisoners, having received her meals directly from the guards and not needing to line up like a beggar. However, she now realized there was no real difference between her and these other women—they were all oppressed by the temple.

Half an hour later, the female prisoners received their lunch.

The guard, with a stick tucked under his arm, inspected them. Satisfied that no one had eaten prematurely, he allowed them to start eating and left with a warning: "No arguing, no fighting, and don't waste food."

As soon as he left, chaos erupted. Prisoners began shouting and cursing, yanking at each other's hair over the slightest disagreement. Some with larger appetites gobbled their meals and then stole food from others, leading to more disputes and an incessant din of banging and shouting.

Sisina whispered to Laurent, "Be careful. I suspect the temple's people will make their move now."

Laurent, seemingly unfazed, nodded absently, sipping her soup.

Exhausted from the morning's work and the noon sun, she was too tired to speak. If not for wanting to reassure Sisina that she could handle things, she might have laid her head on the table for a nap.

Sisina was incredulous. "It's chaos out there! Anyone could be the temple's assassin, and you're not worried at all?"

Suddenly, a terrified scream pierced the din: "She's got a knife! Why do you have a knife? Help, Elsa's got a knife—run!"

The already chaotic scene descended into madness. Prisoners pushed, fought, screamed, and cried, spilling soup and water everywhere. It was more chaotic than an asylum, though this was its own kind of asylum.

Some began using tin utensils as weapons. The floor was slick with greasy red soup, causing many to slip and fall, their screams echoing throughout the room.

Laurent calmly finished her soup, licking the corner of her lips like a child. "Tin utensils have such a peculiar taste," she mused, putting the bowl down with a sigh.

Sisina was exasperated. "Is that even the point? Didn't you see that Elsa is pushing her way over here? She's got a knife!"

Elsa, the butcher's daughter, had grown up in a bloodstained apron, assisting her father in slaughtering livestock. Her nature was cold and unfeeling; she could slit a beast's throat without flinching. Built like a fortress, she could easily haul two frail men. Despite her strength, like many women, she was undone by a man.

Her husband, a scrawny man, had run off with another equally frail woman, taking Elsa's hard-earned savings to start anew in the Roman Empire. When Elsa caught them in the act, she suffocated them with their own blankets.

Sentenced to burn at the stake, Elsa was offered a reprieve by a priest: kill for the divine messenger and walk free. She agreed without hesitation. Why would she care why this girl had to die? Her only thought was to kill.

With a chilling gleam in her eyes, Elsa gripped her knife tightly as she advanced toward Laurent. Alongside her, nine other prisoners moved forward, each wielding a blade.

Laurent seemed doomed.

Sisina felt numb. She had warned Laurent, done everything she could.

One prisoner noticed the armed group heading for Laurent and began to back away silently. In fear, others followed, leaving a clear path.

Seeing this, Elsa laughed. She had thought it would be difficult to kill the girl, that ten were needed. The priest was overly cautious; she could crush this girl with one finger.

Sisina tried one last time to persuade Laurent. "There's still time to escape. I'll throw soup at Elsa's face, and you can hit her with a bowl or chair and make a run for it while she's distracted."

Sisina spoke with earnest urgency. "I know how sharp you are, but Elsa isn't me. She won't understand your cleverness... She's a butcher's daughter; she only knows slaughter."

Laurent nonchalantly glanced at Elsa and nodded. "So she's a butcher's daughter. No wonder she's so strong."

Sisina was exasperated. "You're missing the point again! Fine, if you want to die, I'll save myself!"

As Sisina turned to flee, Laurent calmly opened her palm and called softly, "Loire."

From her thick black hair, a slender black snake slithered onto her palm. Its eyes were fierce and cold, radiating an aura more terrifying than any beast, sending shivers down spines.

Several prisoners halted, fear paralyzing them. Why did she have a snake? How had it entered the prison? Was it venomous?

"I'm terrified of snakes... I don't want to be bitten," one prisoner cried. "I'm out!"

Elsa rolled her eyes, sneering at their cowardice. "Useless women, afraid of a snake? It's probably not even venomous. I won't be scared. I've killed every kind of animal. When I was chewing on venomous snakes, you were probably crying in your mother's arms."

Sisina paused, watching Elsa and Laurent, her mind racing. Should she run or wait to see how this played out?

Ignoring Elsa's taunts, Laurent stood gracefully, placed Loire on the ground, and stepped back. "Don't kill anyone," she instructed with a smile.

Elsa laughed, slapping her thigh. This girl was naive, thinking a small snake could stop her. To Elsa, it was no more than an earthworm. She didn't need her knife; a stomp would suffice.

But then, something terrifying happened.

The scales of the black snake began to ripple, releasing a mysterious black mist. Suddenly, its body began to expand, growing into a massive, nightmarish python that filled the entire dining hall. Had Laurent not commanded it to halt, it might have burst through the prison walls. Its enormous eyes, each as large as Elsa herself, glowed like ominous purple-blue lanterns, reflecting Elsa's diminutive form below.

Elsa, who moments ago believed she could easily crush it, was struck speechless. Her face turned a purplish-red, a mix of fear and embarrassment, as her trembling hands dropped the knife to the floor.

Everyone was paralyzed with shock. They gawked at the gigantic serpent, mouths agape, too terrified to scream.

Sisina, equally astonished, glanced at Laurent with disbelief. How could she possess such a fearsome secret weapon? Why had she wasted so much time trying to persuade her the night before? It became clear to Sisina that Laurent genuinely intended to free her from the temple's grasp. If Laurent had revealed this trump card earlier, Sisina wouldn't have dared to plot against her with poison.

Laurent had saved her from the temple's deceit, yet in the face of danger, Sisina had thought only of herself. Her perspective had been far too narrow, her gratitude too shallow.

As the room fell silent, Laurent stepped forward, and the colossal python lowered its head.

The onlookers gasped, their hearts nearly stopping as Laurent gently stroked the python's snout. Her pure, beautiful eyes radiated affection for the creature. "I won't be here for long," she said softly. "If you don't provoke me, I won't harm you. But if you dare challenge me again, even if you can't harm me, I will have no mercy."

With a slight smile, she lifted her gaze, looking around at the crowd. "Do you believe me?"

Everyone was struck dumb. How could they not believe her? Faced with such an extraordinary display of power, they were left with no doubt. Laurent had the capability to destroy the prison, yet she stayed among them. In light of this spectacle, what else could they possibly disbelieve?

TWENTY-ONE

The divine messenger furrowed his brow, disbelief etched across his face. "You mean to tell me you recruited ten female prisoners, all with blood on their hands, to assassinate her, and yet they all failed? Now, not a single one dares to approach her... How is this possible?"

He sank into his chair, trembling slightly as he turned the gemstone ring on his finger—an emblem of power and authority. "How could this happen?" he murmured to himself.

He couldn't fathom that both assassination attempts had failed, especially against a supposed delicate and powerless girl.

The assistant, wiping cold sweat from his forehead, replied nervously, "...I can't explain it either. I even arranged to have the guards withdrawn to ensure Elsa and the others could proceed without interference. But somehow, we still failed."

His nervousness stemmed more from fear of the messenger's wrath than the failed assassination. Secretly, he wasn't surprised by the outcome.

He had warned them: Laurent was a rare, exceptional figure—like a prized horse—while Elsa and her group were merely beasts of burden. How could overworked livestock hope to outrun a spirited racehorse?

The assistant wanted to shake his head and sigh. The messenger's arrogance had led him to underestimate Laurent. Had he acknowledged her as a worthy adversary and carefully strategized, they might not have faced two consecutive failures.

Yet, he kept these thoughts to himself, wary of becoming the messenger's target. He wasn't a woman; the messenger would show no leniency to him.

Swallowing hard, the assistant asked cautiously, "Your Excellency, what should our next step be?"

The divine messenger rubbed his forehead vigorously, exhaling. "If the female prisoners fear her, then send the male prisoners."

The assistant stared incredulously at the messenger. Had Laurent driven him to madness? Male and female prisoners were housed separately, unable to even approach Laurent. How could they possibly assassinate her? Was he suggesting they move Laurent to the male prisoners' cell?

That wouldn't be an assassination—it would be outright murder!

The assistant nearly reached out to shake the messenger's shoulders, urging him to regain his senses.

"Sir, what do you mean by 'send the male prisoners'? I'm not sure I understand," the assistant said, trying desperately to convey urgency and reason through his eyes.

The divine messenger didn't notice his subordinate's frantic expression. He rubbed his brow, sinking deeper into his chair, engulfed by a rare and overwhelming frustration. A sinister voice whispered in his mind: You can't even kill a girl.

No, he had failed to kill a girl.

Something had gone terribly wrong.

Yes, she must be a witch. Only a witch could possess such uncanny abilities and evade his traps repeatedly.

But the clandestine nature of the assassination left no evidence to accuse her formally as a witch; otherwise, he'd have her executed immediately.

Damn it, what was his next move? Would he really let her appear in court unscathed?

The thought of Laurent ascending the judgment bench, perhaps casting a contemptuous smile his way, mocking his failures, tore at the messenger's heart.

He closed his eyes, gritting his teeth, struggling to contain his frustration and anger, resisting the urge to slam the table. He had to eliminate this girl. He controlled the entire diocese; how could he not manage to kill a measly girl?

His previous failures stemmed from underestimating the situation, relying solely on women to handle her.

If women couldn't deal with that cunning snake, then men would have to.

Hadn't those male prisoners been deprived of female company for years? He recalled vividly when he last inspected the male cells...

In the dim confines of the male prisoners' cell, they were like caged beasts—rough-skinned, thick-fleshed, with a raw, masculine energy that radiated from their bodies. Their desires were base and primal, and even an innocent ewe wouldn't be safe amongst them.

The divine messenger was convinced that Laurent couldn't possibly emerge unscathed from an encounter with such men.

With newfound calm, the messenger turned his attention back to his assistant, his glare sharp. "Do you really think I'd send her directly into the male prisoners' den? No, we need someone specific. Who's the most dangerous among them?"

The assistant quickly replied, "Anders, sir. He was once a leader in the Skull Society at the border—a dangerous man and the only one we've captured."

The messenger relaxed considerably at this information. "Then let Anders handle Laurent."

"But sir," the assistant hesitated, "Anders isn't one of us. He doesn't believe in God or respect the temple. No priest dares approach him. He's like a wild beast in a cage, and even standing near him is a risk."

The divine messenger stopped fiddling with his ring and fixed a piercing gaze on his assistant. "Your thinking is so limited, my assistant. You've called him a wild beast in a cage. If you can't open it, lure him to break it himself. A true beast will find Laurent by the scent of blood. Do you understand?"

The assistant nodded emphatically, outwardly praising the messenger's cunning, though inwardly, he recoiled. The divine messenger's plan was ruthless—releasing the most vicious male prisoner into the female cell was bound to cause chaos. What had those female prisoners done to deserve this punishment?

He found the whole idea distasteful and unethical. It was already questionable to pit female prisoners against Laurent, but now to involve male prisoners?

If he had the power, he would have advised the messenger to reconsider. But he didn't. He was merely an assistant, obliged to carry out the orders given to him, including releasing the beast that was Anders.

Meanwhile, within the female prison cell, an unexpected peace had settled. Laurent had kept her word, and after the prisoners pledged not to provoke her, Loire had shrunk back to a small, harmless-looking snake.

For the first time, the prisoners were more compliant than ever, the fear of Laurent's power keeping them in check. The atmosphere was tense but harmonious, as no one dared to disturb the fragile peace she had established.

Some female prisoners who previously thrived on causing trouble found themselves subdued, allowing the less dominant prisoners to finally breathe a sigh of relief. Their gazes toward Laurent were filled with deep gratitude, recognizing the unexpected peace she brought.

When the guards, bribed by the assistant to step away, returned, they were greeted by an astonishing sight: the female prisoners, as docile and obedient as domesticated cats, were voluntarily cleaning the mess in the dining hall. Among them, the most diligent worker was, surprisingly, Elsa.

The guard rubbed his eyes in disbelief, struggling to comprehend the change. Elsa, notorious for her defiance and strength, had always shirked heavy work unless coerced by a guard's stick. Yet here she was, bustling around like a busy bee, tackling the dirtiest, heaviest tasks. She even helped a frail prisoner carry a bucket with a smile.

"What happened while I was gone?" the guard wondered aloud. "Did a miracle occur?"

Laurent watched the scene unfold with satisfaction.

She appreciated order and harmony, and this was precisely the result she desired.

Smiling, she lowered her head to kiss the head of the snake peeking from her sleeve. "Thank you, my little monster," she cooed, her voice filled with affection. "You did a great job. Without you, I wouldn't have known what to do."

The black snake, caught off guard by the kiss, had its scales bristle in response. Though its gaze remained impassive, its excitement was evident as it flicked its tongue more rapidly. Its tail trembled slightly, and despite its detached demeanor, Laurent's praise clearly thrilled it.

Sisina, observing the snake's reaction, couldn't help but think how easily animals could be swayed by such simple lies.

Had she heard Laurent's words hours earlier, she might have believed them. But now, knowing Laurent's cunning, Sisina was certain that the snake was merely a convenient tool to expedite Laurent's goals without exertion—especially after a morning of exhausting work.

Loire, the snake, knew better than to believe the flattery. Yet, he found himself moved by Laurent's sweet words, just as he couldn't control his scales from standing on end.

Loire felt torn between two sides of himself. One part remained aloof and detached, viewing Laurent with a sort of unrequited admiration, appreciating her as a perfect yet ordinary creation. The other part was gripped by intense desire, akin to a wild beast in the throes of courtship, utterly captivated by her every move.

Everything about Laurent—her intellect, her methods, her very presence—was an intoxicating lure. Though he knew indulging in these feelings might lead to his downfall, he found himself helplessly drawn to them, savoring the dangerous thrill.

He was aware of his own descent into obsession, watching it unfold with a cold detachment.

Yet, disturbingly, both sides of him found a thrill in this descent.

His desire to possess Laurent grew, consuming him like a flame spreading across paper. It was an urge he found increasingly difficult to resist.

Loire's desire to possess Laurent gnawed at him relentlessly. It was a primal urge that disregarded reason, whispering that he must have her, by any means necessary.

Each time he assumed his python form, the temptation to envelop her was almost unbearable. He had to muster all his self-control to resist the vivid fantasy of holding her within his coils.

Her recent kiss had nearly shattered his restraint. The brief contact ignited a predatory instinct within him, threatening to consume his rationality. He found himself closing his eyes repeatedly, struggling to calm the fervor that surged through him like a violent storm.

The thought that one day his possessive desire might overpower him filled him with dread. Would Laurent, in her wisdom and independence, cast him aside if he ever acted on these feelings?

Laurent remained blissfully unaware of the turmoil within Loire. Her world seemed brighter, her spirit lighter, and her confidence unshaken. She felt an unprecedented sense of well-being, buoyed by the harmony she had achieved in the prison and the companionship of her unusual ally.

She anticipated the divine messenger's next move with eagerness. Each misstep they took only made them more vulnerable, and she relished the opportunity to outmaneuver them. It was this kind of opponent—one who underestimated her—that she found most satisfying.

Yet, of all her achievements, Loire brought her the greatest joy.

In him, she saw the realization of a long-held desire for a companion who was both formidable and loyal, meeting her every expectation with his unique blend of qualities. His presence was a source of genuine happiness, and her affection for him was sincere, even if she was unaware of the depth of his feelings.

Laurent's admiration for it is heartfelt and genuine.

Without it, playing with these people is incredibly dull for her.

Sisina's voice echoed in her ear, "By the way, will those priests still attack you again?"

"Of course," Laurent replied with a smirk, "and they'll come tonight."

Perplexed, Sisina observed the female prisoner at work and asked, "But everyone knows about your abilities. Who would dare to challenge you?"

Laurent raised an eyebrow and glanced at her, "Think about it carefully; does 'everyone' really know?"

Sisina frowned, pondered for a moment, and then hesitantly said, "All the female prisoners are here... Are they trying to bribe the guards to poison you? But as far as I know, the guards aren't affiliated with the temple and won't meddle in its affairs."

Laurent nodded, "You're right. The parish temple knights and the court guards fall under the jurisdiction of the capital's knight Group. They have the authority to oversee the temple, but whether they exercise this right depends on the temple's influence locally. If the temple's power is too strong, the supervision is merely symbolic."

Sisina suddenly realized, "No wonder those priests never contact me through the guards." She frowned, puzzled, "But... besides the female prisoners here, there are guards. Those priests wouldn't send the male prisoners next door to kill you, would they?"

Laurent smiled faintly, her cheeks glowing with interest. She unconsciously licked her lips like a predator sensing prey.

Her eyes were gentle, her smile enchanting, yet her gaze held the excitement of a wolf ready to play with its prey.

"Who knows," she said softly and sweetly, as she caressed the black snake on her wrist with slender fingers, "I'm really looking forward to tonight."

Sisina thought, "....." What's happening? It's making her look forward to it as well.

TWENTY-TWO

As night fell, Anders dragged his weary body back into his prison cell.

He removed his sweat-drenched uniform and collapsed onto the bed, ready to succumb to sleep. But before he could drift off, something struck his forehead. Instinctively, he opened his eyes and caught the object—a small piece of paper.

"The prison door has been opened. Seize the opportunity to leave."

Instantly alert, Anders sat up and stared in disbelief at the cell door. The large lock was indeed gone.

What was happening? Had someone from the Skull Society come to rescue him? But how could they, given that Desmond had already seized control at the border and sent Anders to the temple's court?

Who had thrown this note?

Despite the confusion swirling in his mind, Anders' longing for freedom overpowered his doubts. He approached the open cell door. Just then, another piece of paper landed at his feet:

"Go to the women's prison. Laurent will take care of you. If she is already subverted by the temple, kill her."

Anders was bewildered. Who was Laurent, and why was he supposed to go to the women's prison? If the cell door was open, why couldn't he just escape through the men's section?

The answer became clear when he noticed the increased patrols everywhere except the women's prison. The male cell area was heavily guarded, making it impossible to escape unnoticed.

Reluctantly, Anders realized he had no choice but to head toward the women's prison.

As he moved, a strange heat spread through his body, filling him with a troubling impulse. His limbs felt weak, as if intoxicated. Supporting himself against the wall, he understood what was happening: a conspiracy.

Someone had drugged him, opened his cell, and lured him to the women's prison, hoping to frame him for prison escape—a capital offense. The mastermind was likely Desmond, the leader of the Skull Society's Border Branch.

Wow, Desmond has really extended his influence all the way into the court.

Anders slammed his fist against the wall in frustration.

Turning back was no longer an option. In the men's cell, he was accustomed to acting with boldness, but if other male prisoners saw him outside and reported him, he'd be in serious trouble.

For now, the women's cells seemed like a safer bet.

Anders pressed on, suspecting that Laurent was also connected to Desmond.

He found it puzzling since the Skeleton Society never accepted female members. How had Laurent managed to deceive Desmond into trusting her so deeply?

When he thought about it, he cynically assumed that women could only reach high positions by leveraging their charm.

Biting his tongue to stay focused, he decided that since Laurent was part of the plot against him, he would take her down with him. He hadn't acted on his baser instincts for a long time, but tonight he felt compelled to vent his anger.

With a surge of fury, Anders stormed into the women's prison. His face was flushed, his neck thick with rage.

A female prisoner, terrified by his presence, was about to scream when he grabbed her throat through the cell bars.

"Where is Laurent?" Anders demanded, his eyes blazing.

The prisoner, trembling, pointed him to the innermost cell. Anders tossed her aside, and she hit her head against the wall, losing consciousness.

Driven by anger, Anders continued his search. His steps were heavy, and he felt like a beast on the verge of losing control. Inside, a furnace seemed to be burning, fueled by his boiling blood and eroding sanity.

A timid female prisoner clung to the wall, sobbing uncontrollably. She wondered what they had done to deserve this. Earlier in the day, they had been terrified by a giant python, but at least it hadn't harmed them. Now, in the middle of the night, a menacing man had broken into their prison. Life inside was proving to be more chaotic than life outside, and they certainly didn't want this kind of excitement!

In contrast, the bolder prisoners, like Elsa, were unfazed. Grinning, Elsa held onto the railing of her cell door, watching Anders with a mix of amusement and curiosity.

"Looking for Laurent?" Elsa shouted with a smile. "She's in the innermost cell. Just go straight ahead. Hurry, or you'll wake the guard up!"

A fellow prisoner, sharing Elsa's boldness, slapped the railing and chuckled, "Elsa, why are you so wicked?"

"Wicked? How am I wicked?" Elsa replied with a smirk. "This man is stronger than me, and I'm sure Laurent will like him. We've only met twice, but I can already tell we're kindred spirits. I can see right through her preferences."

"Oh, stop exaggerating," another prisoner scoffed. "You're just trying to use him to settle a score."

At this, laughter erupted among the female prisoners. Some laughed so hard they struggled to catch their breath, clutching the railings of their cell doors to keep from doubling over. The corridor filled with their mirth, a stark contrast to the tension that had been building moments before. It was as if they found a strange sense of camaraderie and relief in the absurdity of the situation, temporarily forgetting their own predicaments.

As Anders observed the scene, a chill crept into his heart.

It was no wonder people often said that where there are women, there is war.

It seemed the prisoner named Laurent had somehow offended Elsa, prompting Elsa to eagerly direct Anders her way.

The other female prisoners seemed to find amusement in the situation, showing no concern for the betrayal happening before them.

Didn't they realize that one day they might also be betrayed in a similar manner?

Anders couldn't help but shake his head repeatedly.

He found women's thinking so narrow, focused only on immediate, petty gains. It was no surprise that the leader of the Skeleton Society refused to accept female members. Imagine if this place were the Skeleton Society, with Laurent as a core member and him as an infiltrator from the temple. Driven by jealousy and spite, these women might easily undermine her position.

The leader's decision was indeed insightful. Allowing women into the Skull Society might result in the organization's downfall at the hands of the temple within a few years.

Sighing, Anders continued toward Laurent's cell.

He felt a pang of pity for her.

He understood the sting of betrayal all too well. If she could reveal who had set him up, he would do his best to suppress the effects of the drug and ensure she faced her end with dignity.

That was the greatest mercy he could offer.

However, as he drew nearer to Laurent's cell, a growing sense of unease settled over him. Something felt off, and he couldn't quite put his finger on it.

The temperature around Anders had dropped to an unnaturally low level, and the candlelight on the walls grew dimmer with each step he took. What unsettled him most was the sensation of being watched by unseen eyes, trailing him like a shadow.

The gaze felt cold and unnerving, devoid of any emotion, as if he were nothing more than prey on a chopping board, scrutinized by a predator unseen.

Anders had never known true fear until this moment. A man of strength and vigor, he had always held the naive belief that any obstacle could be overcome with sheer force. But now, he was gripped by an inexplicable dread.

He kept glancing back, but saw nothing in the darkness. Yet, the feeling persisted—an ominous presence, like a python ready to strike, waiting for the perfect moment to ensnare him in a silent, cruel grip.

Trying to steady himself, Anders took a deep breath, attributing the unsettling sensation to the drug coursing through his veins, causing hallucinations.

He shook his head vigorously and pushed onward.

He blamed Laurent for his predicament.

If not for Laurent, Anders wouldn't have found himself in such a strange situation or felt such fear—a fear he equated with weakness. Blaming Laurent for his troubles, he quickly dismissed any thoughts of mercy he had entertained earlier. His focus shifted to punishing her as a way to restore his wounded pride.

Even as he tried to convince himself that the oppressive feeling of being watched was merely a hallucination caused by the drug, the sensation persisted, like a chilling shadow lingering over him, until he reached the innermost cell.

There, a girl stood leaning against the cell door, waiting for him.

She was petite, dressed in plain clothing, with thick, black hair flowing down like a waterfall.

Her features were strikingly pure and angelic, with eyes and eyebrows that seemed almost ethereal, lips that were small and doll-like, and cheeks as pale as apricot blossoms touched with a hint of red.

Yet, when she looked up, Anders detected a fierce intensity in her gaze that sent shivers down his spine. It was a stark contrast to her delicate appearance, and it made his skin prickle with unease.

Unable to control himself, Anders felt his body tremble as if caught in a cold war, his breath becoming labored and his throat dry, exposing his raw, beastly side.

"Are you... Laurent?" he asked, his voice rough. "You look like this... damn, no wonder those women outside are jealous of you."

Laurent tilted her head slightly, twining a strand of her black hair around her finger, and asked with a curious tone, "Are they jealous of me?"

Without thinking, Anders recounted everything that had transpired outside. Meanwhile, Sisina, sitting in the corner, couldn't help but roll her eyes at the unfolding scene - it wasn't that they were jealous of Laurent; they simply couldn't stand you. They wanted Laurent to toy with you, to punish you, to scare you senseless.

Anders continued, "I know you're with Desmond, and I know you helped him frame me... I despise being set up. I wanted to kill you to vent my anger, but seeing how... endearing you look, I hesitate."

He paused, his voice growing even more hoarse. "I'm giving you two choices. One, come with me, be my woman. I'll get us out of the court, and you'll live the life every woman dreams of. Two, I kill you, and you can continue working for Desmond in hell."

Laurent's lips curled into a slight smile as she clapped her hands. "Those are great options. But unfortunately, I have two things to tell you."

Anders felt his heart skip a beat.

At the same time, the sensation of being watched returned.

This time, the gaze was colder, more terrifying, and filled with hostility, almost suffocating him.

Anders knew it was just a hallucination, yet cold sweat began to bead on his forehead.

"First," Laurent said, "you've been misled. I'm not with Desmond."

Anders was stunned.

"Second," she continued, her smile turning wicked, "I'm not interested in escaping. If I wanted to leave, my little snake could take me out anytime."

As soon as Laurent finished speaking, a giant python appeared without warning.

In that moment, when Anders locked eyes with those eerie purple-blue snake eyes, he realized that this was the creature that had been watching him all along. The python loomed over him from above, its scales releasing a nightmarish black mist.

Its massive body made no sound nor caused any damage as it appeared. The narrow prison cell couldn't contain its full length, so it lowered its head and wrapped its thick coils protectively around Laurent, encircling her multiple times.

The python was unnervingly calm, not displaying the restlessness typical of apex predators, but its vertical eyes held a chilling, suppressed bloodlust.

Anders was left speechless. "Is this what she calls a snake?" he thought incredulously.

Finally, Anders understood why the female prisoners had been so eager to direct him to Laurent. They weren't jealous of her; they had complete confidence in her ability to deal with him. Otherwise, they wouldn't have kept the python a secret.

He recalled the saying, "Where there are women, there is war." If he survived this ordeal, he vowed to confront whoever first told him that.

Laurent regarded him with an amused smile. "Now, do you still want to take me out of the courtroom?"

Anders was at a loss. Could he now plead with her to help him escape instead?

His pride shattered, Anders slowly shook his head, then fell to his knees with a thud, answering her question with his actions.

In the early hours of the morning, as the sky remained dark, the divine messenger awoke. Before donning his deep purple robe, he was greeted with dire news from the court.

Although this was theoretically his third failure, and he should have been more composed than before, he found himself unable to remain calm.

He clenched his fists, took deep breaths, and repeatedly asked in his heart, 'Why, why, why?

Why is that?

Isn't Anders the most vicious prisoner in the male cell? Isn't he capable of making someone paralyzed with just one punch? Isn't he so strong that he can handle ten male prisoners?

Isn't he like a wild beast in a cage, so fearsome that people don't even dare to stand near it and speak to him?

If that's the case, why can't he even kill a girl?

Why, why?

The divine messenger closed his eyes and asked the air with extreme pain in his heart.

He despised women so much that he had never looked at them directly, but Laurent was not even a woman. Her appearance still carried a hint of innocence and childishness like a little girl. She was still a delicate girl!

He fell three times to this girl, which was a great shame!

For a moment, the divine messenger was so angry that he almost gasped for breath.

He had to dismiss the servant who had helped dress him and stumbled to the desk. Trembling, he opened the drawer, took out a bottle of heart-protecting pills, and poured dozens of them into his mouth in one go.

After several moments, the pills began to work, and the frustration, suffocation, and restlessness that had been overwhelming him finally eased, allowing him to breathe normally once again.

Though he had experienced failure before, never had it been so humiliating as this.

In his eyes, women were nothing more than livestock—dirty, sinful creatures whose contributions to society were no greater than those of beasts of burden.

Yet here he was, having stumbled three times at the hands of what he saw as lesser beings. What did this signify?

It suggested that his intellect, strategies, and sophistication were inferior to those of a single woman.

The thought pierced his heart like a knife.

Without the heart-protecting pills, he might have collapsed right then and there.

He sank into a chair, his face pale, awkwardly supporting his forehead with his hand. He was not only drowning in the despair of being outdone by a woman but also ensnared by an indescribable fear and panic.

He no longer dared to confront Laurent.

He was terrified of trying again and still failing. If he were to lose to Laurent once more, could he continue to believe that his intellect surpassed hers? Could he maintain his confidence in looking down on women?

He didn't have the courage to seek the answers to these questions, fearing that his confidence and self-esteem would be utterly destroyed by Laurent.

Can he really do nothing but watch her step confidently onto the trial bench?

Isn't this just another form of torture? Another failure would surely shatter his self-esteem, but wouldn't simply watching Laurent stand unharmed on the bench do the same?

The more the divine messenger pondered, the more the agony intensified, nearly causing him to faint. He gritted his teeth and rubbed his temples vigorously, as if trying to push his fingers into his head to alleviate the torment.

Time seemed to blur until he unconsciously bit through his soft palate, a trace of blood trickling from the corner of his mouth, slowly bringing him back to his senses.

He hadn't completely failed.

The divine messenger took a deep breath, repeating to himself like a mantra.

There was still a chance to strike back, and the ideal moment would be during the public trial of the priest's case.

This time, he resolved to set aside his prejudices and regard Laurent as a worthy adversary.

He would muster the same determination and patience he had shown when vying for the position of divine messenger, meticulously observing and analyzing her every move. If necessary, he would even seek counsel from his trusted advisors.

He refused to believe that even with such preparation, he could still fail.

Coincidentally, Laurent's three consecutive victories might have lulled her into underestimating him, thinking him an easy opponent. In this scenario, if he struck with all his might, he could catch her off guard and reclaim his honor.

The divine messenger slowly exhaled, released his grip on his temple, and fully regained his calm and composed demeanor.

TWENTY-THREE

The divine messenger's plan was promising, but he was unsure how to execute it.

He didn't know Laurent's weaknesses.

Typically, when he wanted to dismantle an opponent, he could quickly pinpoint their vulnerabilities, such as their family ties. Yet, despite his efforts, he couldn't uncover any information about Laurent's family.

It was inconceivable that someone could be without family. This only proved that Laurent was exceptionally skilled at concealing her identity.

He realized he shouldn't underestimate her as just another girl.

Even if she had no familial weaknesses, surely she had personal ones.

After contemplating, the divine messenger decided to spend a substantial amount of money to bribe a female prisoner to shadow Laurent, recording her every word and action. He hoped this would help him identify Laurent's weaknesses.

To his surprise, no female prisoner was willing to take on this task, even for a large sum.

When he learned of this, the divine messenger nearly twisted the gemstone ring off his finger in frustration.

Laurent had been in prison for only a few days, yet she had already cultivated such a formidable reputation among the female prisoners that none dared to accept the seemingly simple task of tracking her movements?

The divine messenger couldn't help but wonder if he could achieve such a fearsome reputation in the men's cell in just two days.

The answer was glaringly obvious.

He would likely be beaten, torn apart, drenched with cold water by the rough male prisoners, and the cycle would continue.

Given this, how had Laurent managed to command such respect and fear?

No matter how hard he tried, the divine messenger couldn't comprehend it.

He was stronger, older, and more experienced than Laurent. In every conceivable way, he was superior, yet he couldn't match her influence.

The most soul-crushing part was that Laurent was just a young, seemingly weak, and unknown girl!

The thought that he couldn't compare to a girl became an internal torment, seeping into his veins, causing him dizziness and intense pain.

He had always been efficient with his work, yet today he accomplished nothing beyond pondering Laurent and wallowing in self-pity. This had never happened before. He was losing his composure.

Finally, his assistant managed to persuade a female prisoner to monitor Laurent.

The cost was reducing her sentence by five years and rewarding her parents with two hundred Golden Johns.

Even with such incentives, the female prisoner hesitated, repeatedly confirming, "I'm just monitoring Laurent, right? Not planning to harm her, correct?"

The assistant sighed and reassured her, "Yes, yes, just monitor her and record everything she does. Note every detail—what she eats, who she talks to, her reaction to tasks from the guards, and whether she does her work diligently. Understand?"

The female prisoner hesitated about the amount of work but perked up at the mention of extra pay, eagerly agreeing to the task.

Although the divine messenger achieved his goal, he wasn't elated. However, the prospect of analyzing Laurent's weaknesses from the detailed report sparked his anticipation.

He believed that no one could maintain a flawless façade indefinitely.

The next day at noon, the divine messenger received Laurent's activity log.

To brace himself against potential anger, he preemptively took several heart-protecting pills.

Despite his precautions, his eyelids twitched as he read the record:

At four in the morning, Laurent awoke and yawned five or six times. The guard assigned her to clean the toilets. As she braided her hair, she murmured, "Why am I still cleaning the toilet today?" The guard replied, "You don't have the right to ask that question." Laurent nodded, asked no further, and proceeded with her mop into the toilet, staying there until noon.

The divine messenger reread the passage repeatedly, bewildered as to why Laurent accepted cleaning the toilets without question.

Did she not have the cunning, intellect, and means to avoid such a menial task? Why didn't she try to evade it?

The divine messenger found himself endlessly puzzled, unable to comprehend Laurent's actions no matter how hard he tried. It seemed that every encounter with her left him more bewildered. Was it that he was inherently incompatible with this girl, or were her actions simply beyond his understanding?

If it weren't for his three prior failures, he might not have thought this way. But having been outmaneuvered by Laurent three times, without even formulating a clear counter-strategy, he couldn't help but become fixated on the idea.

Was he overanalyzing the situation? Or was it possible that Laurent's actions truly defied his comprehension?

He spent the entire afternoon pondering why Laurent complied with the guard's order to clean the toilet, yet he couldn't arrive at an answer.

He knew this task was unlikely to be a point of contention, but the "what if" lingered in his mind—what if it was all part of Laurent's plan?

✳✳✳

Meanwhile, Laurent rubbed her eyes, yawned, and shuffled to the back of the line to receive her meal, feeling exhausted and drained.

It was all Anders' fault; she had only slept for an hour. While cleaning the bathroom, she had dozed off on Loire's smooth snake scales, finding a surprisingly peaceful sleep.

Her little snake, Loire, was incredibly accommodating.

Without needing words, he understood her desire for restful sleep. Transforming into a giant python, he wrapped his cold, thick body around her and slid his flat head beneath her neck, creating a haven of comfort.

Remarkably, he even managed to shield her from unpleasant odors, allowing her to sleep more soundly than on the wooden prison bed.

Upon waking, her complexion was noticeably more refreshed, all thanks to Loire. She couldn't help but treat him affectionately, rubbing her nose against his snout and cooing,

"You're wonderful... I love you so much, my little snake. There's no other snake as lovable as you."

Loire's scales bristled at her touch. Despite not being a real snake, he reacted with an animalistic response to her affection.

His reactions were undeniably snake-like: scales standing on end, body swelling, and tail twitching — all signs of excitement or readiness to strike.

Under her influence, he had learned human emotions and simultaneously awakened his animalistic instincts.

At times, he struggled to discern whether he preferred being an animal or human around her. Perhaps he desired to be both—a blend of the two.

After all, when driven by intense desire, the line between human and animal blurs.

Loire fixed his gaze on Laurent, gently flicking his tongue to brush her cheek. His longing continued to grow, spreading like wildfire.

Where once a brief touch or a whiff of her fragrance satisfied him, it was no longer enough. He craved more.

He wanted to coil his heavy body around her, as he had done earlier. A mere kiss or caress no longer sufficed.

He longed to continuously inhale her scent and feel her hand on his raised scales, to have her eyes and voice linger on him indefinitely.

Unconsciously, the possessiveness in his gaze towards her became palpable, almost tangible.

TWENTY-FOUR

Laurent was unaware that her small gestures had only deepened Loire's desire.

To her, Loire was just a lovable pet, obedient and endearing, without any other thoughts.

The messenger could never have imagined that Laurent obediently followed the guard's orders and cleaned the toilet, simply because she was too sleepy to bother persuading the guard to change jobs.

Meanwhile, the divine messenger was baffled by Laurent's compliance with the guard's orders to clean the toilets. He spent the entire afternoon trying to decipher her motives, only to end up with tired eyes and no answers.

His confusion grew as he reviewed Laurent's behavior, noting her strict adherence to rules and her kind demeanor toward other prisoners. How had she gained such a fearsome reputation while being so gentle?

Instead of uncovering weaknesses, the divine messenger found himself mired in more mysteries about Laurent, each one burning like a flame inside him.

He initially considered analyzing Laurent's behavior with his think tank, but hesitated.

The records portrayed her as ordinary, and he feared being seen as incapable of handling a simple girl. Yet to explain his predicament would mean reliving his failures in front of those who saw him as a leader.

The divine messenger found himself in a dilemma, torn between the potential ridicule from his subordinates if he revealed his struggles with Laurent, and the humiliation of being outsmarted by her once more.

Ultimately, both paths led to mockery. He decided it was better to face the laughter of his own people first, with the hope of reclaiming his dignity when confronting Laurent again.

Resolute in his decision, he reminded himself that enduring a short-term embarrassment was preferable to prolonged suffering. He needed the courage to face the situation head-on and find a solution.

After much internal deliberation, he finally mustered the courage to convene his think tank.

In order not to look too embarrassing, the divine messenger orchestrated a solemn and grand banquet. The long dining table was laden with a variety of exquisite appetizers, while slender-necked glass bottles brimmed with freshly squeezed orange juice.

The main dishes had not been served yet. The divine messenger's plan was to pretend to be nonchalant and ring the cowbell, asking the servants to present the rich ham, tender foie gras, and delicious, juicy salmon when he was about to tell his story of shame.

In such a grand atmosphere, even if his experience was funny and shameful, it would only get a friendly laugh.

Thinking of this, the divine messenger poured a glass of wine to toast his own intelligence.

But he remained ignorant of the absurdity of the event itself—in this opulent hall, the esteemed priests—all graduates of the empire's top universities—were about to deliberate on how to handle a young girl who was merely a third of his age.

Fortunately, the assistant had wisely cautioned the think tank members to maintain their composure and refrain from laughing outright; otherwise, they might not have contained themselves

These advisers, much like the divine messenger himself, harbored an inherent disdain for women. They believed women to be simplistic and impulsive, often dismissing their capabilities. Their encounters with women who attempted clumsy seductions only reinforced their biases.

Despite having female relatives—mothers, wives, and others—they clung to their prejudices. After all, when does a playboy hesitate to pursue beauty in shadowy alleys because he thinks of his mother?

With faint smiles, they took the report from the divine messenger and casually glanced through it before setting it aside. They assumed the divine messenger was jesting, unable to take the matter seriously.

The divine messenger's expression remained stern, wanting them to understand the gravity of the situation, but he found himself at a loss for words

Their dismissive reaction mirrored his own initial response to Laurent.

In that moment, the divine messenger experienced a profound internal conflict, as if he were two separate individuals. One part of him was consumed with anxiety over the upcoming public trial, feeling a strong urge to dump hot soup over the heads of his advisers to wipe away their smug expressions and compel them to take Laurent seriously; simultaneously, another part of him felt a peculiar sense of relief. It dawned on him that underestimating women was a common error among men, himself included. It was a universal oversight, and perhaps he need not feel quite so ashamed or angry for having fallen into the same trap.

Unable to stand aloof any longer, the assistant finally intervened, reminding the think tank in a quiet but firm voice, "Everyone, Your Excellency the divine messenger is serious. Please take a closer look at the records. This girl is not as simple as she seems. We've stumbled three times because of her."

The divine messenger cast a deep, appreciative glance at his assistant. The deliberate use of "we" struck a chord with him, making him realize the cleverness and loyalty of his assistant.

One of the younger advisers reopened the records, scrutinizing them with renewed attention. "But these records... do you see anything special about them?" he asked, genuinely puzzled.

The assistant nodded, emphasizing, 'That's precisely what makes her so frightening. You might not know this, but this girl didn't need to get imprisoned originally. She used very peculiar and frightening means to plot against the divine messenger, and, with his help, sent herself to the prison cell."

The assistant recounted Laurent's remarkable feats in one uninterrupted breath.

For instance, how she rose to fame among the new goddesses in just two days; how two seasoned Sisters mentioned her name to the divine messenger, piquing his interest in her; and how she cleverly maneuvered to have the divine messenger promise to address the priest's case publicly. She used the divine messenger to get herself into a prison cell, where she deftly evaded three assassination attempts orchestrated against her

As the story concluded, a hush fell over the room.

Everyone set down their knives and forks, staring at the records in disbelief. Could a girl with such a formidable mind still be considered just a girl?

The divine messenger observed the skeptical expressions of his advisors and grew even more impressed with his assistant's storytelling prowess.

He held his assistant in high regard. Such a potentially humiliating tale, when told by the assistant, seemed so matter-of-fact and natural. It was as if being outsmarted by Laurent and feeling embarrassed was entirely ordinary, with no cause for alarm or shame.

The messenger mused on why he hadn't recognized his assistant's knack for spinning narratives before.

The divine messenger was overthinking, and the assistant was just telling the truth.

From an ordinary person's perspective, Laurent outshines the divine messenger in intelligence, poise, and strategy. It's no wonder the messenger might struggle against such a formidable opponent, and there's no shame in it.

The divine messenger, perhaps unknowingly, had come to terms with the fact that he couldn't match Laurent. He indulged heartily in his meal, seemingly unbothered.

A mustached man, scrutinizing the records in hand, spoke cautiously. "Your Excellency, this girl is peculiar indeed. Fortunately, the locals hold Reverend Fletcher in high regard, and many have witnessed miracles under his guidance. Whether or not he killed those girls, how bad can someone favored by the divine truly be? In court, you just need to emphasize the priest's virtues. The onlookers will do the rest."

Another man added calmly, "I remember Lady Davis from the capital. She prophesied John II's death and was sent to a mental hospital for treason. This girl is smart, but if people don't fully believe her, her intelligence won't change anything."

"The divine messenger is really too kind, treating a young, inexperienced girl as an equal opponent." Many agreed with this sentiment.

Amidst the praise, the divine messenger found himself questioning whether he was overestimating Laurent. Despite her intelligence and skills, societal biases against her gender would hinder her credibility.

On one side stood revered priests; on the other, a cunning young girl. Naturally, people leaned towards believing the priests, who were seen as both reliable men and godly messengers.

But Laurent? She is merely a sharp mind with a silver tongue.

No matter how formidable her intelligence, how intricate her plans, or how ingenious her tactics, if people don't trust her words, can she really use witchcraft to sway them in public?

If she ever dared to practice witchcraft openly, there'd be no need for a trial—they could simply take her to the stake.

These advisors were indeed resourceful. Their words lifted a weight off his shoulders, and he realized he hadn't cultivated them in vain.

With renewed confidence, the divine messenger poured himself a glass of white wine. As the alcohol soothed him, his racing heart calmed, and he felt ready for tomorrow's public hearing.

Now that the divine messenger was eating, the assistant no longer needed to hover nearby.

Yet, the assistant couldn't shake the feeling that they were underestimating Laurent.

Although her gender would bring challenges during the trial, it also posed restrictions in prison. But was she truly restricted? She seemed to be thriving.

Watching the divine messenger's confident expression, the assistant hesitated but chose not to dampen his mood. After all, he'd already failed thrice—what was one more failure?

Meanwhile, Laurent wrapped up her exhausting day and finally lay down to rest.

She undid her thick braid and combed through her hair, settling comfortably in bed.

Beneath her lay a massive python, unnoticed by casual observers.

The snake, unfazed by her movements, coiled around her legs. Its tongue flicked near her arched foot, as if pondering a bite. Most would find this terrifying, but Laurent was used to this intimacy with her "little snake."

Without opening her eyes, she lightly kicked the snake's head, her toes grazing its mouth. "Be good," she chided casually.

Sisina, unaware that Loire wasn't a real python, was nearly frightened out of her wits. Snakes are known for reacting to movement—wasn't Laurent afraid it might suddenly bite her toes?

Not everyone could handle this "little snake" like Laurent, who trusted it implicitly. Even those who trust pythons usually keep a safe distance. Yet, Laurent seemed unconcerned, even eager to be close, much like those who adore pets to the point of smothering them with affection.

After Laurent's scolding, the python ceased its probing, instead curling up with its eyes closed at her feet.

Sisina, marveling at their bond, approached Laurent's bed but dared not get too close, wary of the snake's potential venomous response.

"Are you confident about tomorrow's public hearing?" Sisina asked. "Do you need my help?"

"Of course, I am," Laurent replied softly, eyes still closed. "As for help, if I need it, you'll know what to do without my saying."

"Won't you tell me in advance?" Sisina asked, surprised.

Laurent slowly opened her eyes and flashed a playful smile. "Well, whether you can help or not depends on how foolish my opponent is. As someone who considers herself smart, I still hope my opponent is even smarter."

Sisina: "..." She was still unsure about what Laurent needed help with, but she couldn't shake the feeling that Laurent's words were quite cutting, perhaps even a bit hurtful.

Deep down, she genuinely hoped that Laurent's opponent would indeed be smarter!

TWENTY-FIVE

The following day, nearly everyone in the parish was buzzing with the news of a public trial scheduled for noon, where justice would confront evil.

Naturally, the side of justice was represented by the parish divine messenger, who was set to prosecute the murderer of Reverend Fletcher before the townspeople.

To everyone's shock, the accused was a seemingly innocent young girl, alleged to have killed Reverend Fletcher.

The story went that she had been a destitute, homeless girl wandering the streets, almost run over by a carriage. Reverend Fletcher had taken her in, offering her a promising future by recommending her to the parish temple to serve as a goddess.

But, like Aesop's fable of the farmer bitten by a viper, she had turned on her benefactor, cruelly murdering the revered priest.

If such acts went unpunished, who would dare to perform selfless deeds like those of Reverend Fletcher again?

This girl not only killed Reverend Fletcher but also metaphorically killed the spirit of countless good people who might have followed in his footsteps.

Punishing a venomous character like her by mere burning wouldn't suffice; she deserved to be tortured in the Iron Maiden, pierced by sharp steel needles through her malevolent heart until she confessed her sins on the verge of death.

The divine messenger, fair and merciful, was gracious enough to allow this venomous girl the chance to speak in court.

In the midst of this overwhelmingly biased atmosphere, the divine messenger found his calm and confidence restored.

Dressed in a deep purple silk robe with a golden holy belt, and wearing the gemstone ring that symbolized his glory and authority, he regained his former elegance and dignity.

Adjusting his collar, he quipped to his assistant, "The people's eyes are sharper than mine. Had I listened to them earlier, I wouldn't have felt so helpless. Age must be catching up with me; in my youth, a mere girl would never have frightened me like this."

The assistant frowned and ventured cautiously, "Sir, pardon my impudence, but something feels off about the public opinion—it's as if someone is orchestrating it. We didn't know Laurent's backstory of being a homeless girl saved by the priest. If we didn't know, how did this news spread to the public? Is it possible that—"

The divine messenger cut him off with a cold stare, "Dane, are you suggesting you've been swayed by that girl? Your appearance makes it hard not to suspect."

Dane was taken aback but protested, "Swayed? I've done no such thing... Your Excellency, please trust my loyalty. I only seek to serve you."

The messenger sneered, "Oh really? Then why do I not feel your loyalty? If I hadn't consulted with our think tank, I might still be anxious now. On reflection, it seems you've been the source of much of my unease. I asked you to eliminate Laurent, but you failed thrice, and now you're shifting the blame onto me."

"As I prepare to approach the trial bench, you suggest that Laurent might be manipulating public opinion and trying to spread doubt within me once more."

The messenger turned sharply, grabbing Dane by the neck with force. "Do you really think I'm that naive, dear assistant? Laurent is locked away in a cell. How could she possibly influence public opinion from there? She allegedly told people that Fletcher saved her life, but what advantage does that provide her? I am baffled as to why you would betray me, someone whom I have promoted. Only yesterday, I was contemplating elevating you to the position of bishop. You've shattered my trust, Dane."

Dane was momentarily stunned by the divine messenger's accusations but soon regained his composure. Holding the messenger's wrist, he pleaded softly, "Your Excellency, I assure you, I haven't betrayed you. I merely wanted to highlight how peculiar this girl is. Please trust me! My loyalty to you has been unwavering."

"That's enough," the messenger replied with a weary shake of his hand. "I won't listen to another word from a traitor. Once I've dealt with your so-called master, I'll address you."

Completely at a loss as to why the situation had escalated in this manner, Dane knelt on the ground, his hands clasped tightly, and pressed his forehead against them in prayer, hoping for divine guidance and answers.

Although Dane disagreed with the divine messenger's views and methods, the thought of betrayal never crossed his mind. He was a grateful individual who always remembered those who had helped him rise.

Yet, the divine messenger had arrogantly and unjustly accused him of treachery.

For a devoted subordinate like Dane, nothing was more devastating than being accused of betrayal.

Oh my god!

Dane thought with exhaustion that he should have seen this coming. Over the years, the divine messenger had grown increasingly incompetent and obstinate, enveloped by the opulence and comfort of the temple. He should have realized sooner that his loyalty to such a person might lead to this outcome.

Dane understood the harsh reality of speaking truthfully and knew that it was unwise to dampen the spirits of a self-assured divine messenger.

But the wind of public opinion was strange. Fletcher was a border town priest, yet his reputation had spread to the parish court.

Dane knew the messenger hadn't orchestrated this, planning only to recount Fletcher's good deeds at the trial. Something was definitely amiss—why couldn't the divine messenger see it? Was it simply because Laurent was a girl?

Dane straightened up, rubbed his forehead, and let out a hoarse laugh.

If the messenger was disappointed in him, why didn't he feel an endless sense of disappointment towards the messenger?

He had turned a blind eye for too long to the messenger's arrogance, stubbornness, and folly.

In the presence of the divine messenger, Dane had always maintained absolute loyalty, humility, and obedience, carrying out orders without question.

His fervent loyalty was met with a hand around his throat.

Dane shook his head, stood up, smoothed out his wrinkled black robe, and made his way to the public trial.

The divine messenger, preoccupied with the court proceedings, hadn't stripped Dane of his title, allowing him to still function as an assistant. He moved smoothly to the audience's seating in the court.

Before seeing Laurent, Dane clung to a humble and naive hope: perhaps the messenger was correct, and he had been overthinking. If Laurent truly was a negligible opponent, then his repeated cautions to the messenger could indeed seem like a traitor's actions, undermining morale.

But the instant he saw Laurent, Dane realized all his suspicions were justified.

The whispers among the people had surely been orchestrated by this girl.

She stood at the defendant's seat, smiling with an air of elegance and composure.

After spending three days in prison, Laurent's thick, raven-like hair was slightly tousled, and her complexion was somewhat dull, lacking the porcelain-like pallor it once had. Yet, her features remained meticulously arranged on her oval face.

From behind, her swan-like neck supported her head gracefully, giving the impression of a pure and harmless girl. But as she turned, her beauty resembled that of diamonds encased in glass; the rough prison garb failed to dim its sharp brilliance.

She casually surveyed the people around her, her golden irises and deep black pupils framed by long eyelashes. A closer look into those profound eyes revealed depths akin to the well of Demetrius. Her small lips, beneath a high-bridged nose, curled into a sinister and playful smile.

It was clear she was confident about winning the public trial and even seemed to welcome the proceedings.

In that moment, all of Dane's naive hopes were dashed.

He realized that the divine messenger was destined to lose.

The three assassination attempts on Laurent were less about a struggle between the messenger and her, and more a testament to the clash between him and her.

Dane knew all too well how formidable this girl was.

Any other isolated and helpless girl in her position would have succumbed countless times under those three attempts on her life.

Despite the challenges, she always emerged unscathed, showing no signs of injury.

Why is the divine messenger reluctant to acknowledge that this girl's wisdom surpasses his own?

According to the scriptures of the old religion, Eve was blamed for humanity's fall, leaving women to bear the burden of original sin and the pain of childbirth. However, if men are truly superior in intellect, why didn't Adam prevent Eve from eating the forbidden fruit?

Eve was described as "bone of bones, flesh of flesh" from Adam, meaning everything about her originated from him. If she were truly foolish, ignorant, and lacking in willpower, wouldn't that imply the same shortcomings in Adam?

Even if we assume Eve was foolish, what relevance does that have to Laurent?

Dane couldn't fathom why the divine messenger insisted on using characters from ancient religious texts to argue that Laurent was foolish and incapable of defeating him.

Laurent, however, did not fall for the serpent's temptation nor did she steal the forbidden fruit from the Tree of Good and Evil.

The more Dane pondered, the more he realized it was the divine messenger who was truly foolish.

He rubbed his forehead, eager for the trial to commence, so he could speak on Laurent's behalf and affirm his role as a traitor.

Finally, under the watchful eyes of the public, the trial began.

The divine messenger sat at the center of the judgment bench, flanked by the parish court judge on the right and the Royal Knights' jury on the left.

Above them, an artistic depiction of the God of Light adorned the high dome, holding the light of order and gazing down at the court with a calm, indifferent, and pure expression. It seemed as though under those just purple-blue eyes, all sin and impurity would be revealed.

The messenger rose, joining the judge and the jury in devout prayer for a moment.

Then, he lifted his eyes and looked directly at Laurent, seated in the defendant's chair.

"Laurent," he began in a deep voice, "you stand accused of murder by a respected clergyman. Do you understand the immense manpower and resources required for a temple to nurture a morally upright priest?"

"What you have taken is not just a life but also the faith of countless people, the path to salvation, and the servant of God who spreads divine revelation to the world. More importantly, your actions have caused countless virtuous women to endure the world's suspicious gaze. Do you confess your guilt? Do you feel remorse?"

Laurent smiled faintly, lifting her gaze to the image of the Father God in the dome. She made a poised and serene gesture of prayer, as though ready to address the God of Light directly.

Yet, the words she spoke were sharp and defiant: "I do not confess my guilt, nor do I feel remorse. For even if God were here, He would endorse my act of killing."

Her words caused an uproar.

The divine messenger slammed the table and sternly rebuked her, "You are too arrogant! You have no right to speculate on divine intentions."

TWENTY-SIX

Not only the messenger but also the jury members looked at Laurent with disapproving expressions.

In human history, there are seven original sins: lust, gluttony, greed, laziness, anger, jealousy, and arrogance.

Among these, arrogance might seem the least severe, but it is, in fact, the most primitive and serious, serving as the root of all evil.

If humans had not been arrogant and had remained obedient, they would not have fallen. If dynasties had not been arrogant and enslaved their people, their flags would not have been hung upside down on enemy weapons. If Satan had not been arrogant and attempted to usurp God's throne, he would not have faced heaven's wrath and fallen into hell.

Despite her young age, this girl has already embraced Satan's ways, recklessly speculating on divine intentions. Can she truly understand God's thoughts, actions, and judgments of good and evil?

The crime of arrogance alone could warrant a ten or eight-year sentence, not to mention the grave offense of murdering a clergyman!

The divine messenger appeared outwardly furious, yet inwardly he was at ease. As he removed his glasses and wiped them with a flannel cloth, he thought disdainfully that his assistant was indeed a traitor. Laurent's arrogance was a fatal flaw, rendering her harmless.

Even he could not presume to understand God's will, yet Laurent dared to do so publicly, even making a prayer gesture as if to flaunt her defiance.

Her actions were so foolish that, if stupidity were an original sin, it would have added to her charges and led her to the gallows

Just when everyone expected Laurent to panic and confess, she tilted her head, expressing confusion, "I don't quite understand what you're talking about. Haven't you read the 'Ode to Light Sutra'?"

Calmly, she recited, "In the second sentence of the ninth chapter of the Ode to Light Sutra: 'He will not mistreat every good person, nor will he treat every evil person generously. One day, the evil will be punished.' And I..."

She smiled faintly, concluding, "It's the retribution of Reverend Fletcher."

As Laurent spoke, the jury members began to search through their hymnal book at hand. A tall, handsome knight gave her a surprised look and asked, "Can you recite specific chapters and sentences from the Ode to Light Sutra?"

Laurent nodded slightly, her words confident, "To be precise, I can recite every word of the Ode to Light Sutra, including chapters and sentences."

Intrigued, the knight closed his hymnal, flipped through a few pages, and asked, "What is written in Chapter Seven, Sentence Six?"

Laurent replied, "Under his palm, the throne crumbles, cities become desolate, land is occupied by enemies, houses are seized by enemies, and wives and children are killed by enemies. This is because they have committed the crime of arrogance, and God is punishing sinners with His angry palm."

Correct.

The knight nodded and turned back to the beginning, continuing to ask, "What is the nineteenth sentence of the first chapter?"

Laurent replied, "He creates light and darkness, judges the good and the evil, and whoever is wicked will be severely punished by his angry palm."

"Correct," he affirmed. "Chapter 20, first sentence?"

"He can have mercy on his people and also bring punishment."

"Absolutely right," the knight confirmed.

The knight proceeded to ask over a dozen questions in rapid succession, each drawn from the Ode to the Light Sutra. At times, Laurent answered even before he had fully opened the book or asked the question.

There had never been conflict between the Knights and the Temple. With a half-smile, the knight looked at the divine messenger and joked, "This girl seems to be more knowledgeable than your priests. I recall when my family passed away, you sent a priest to help. I asked him a few questions, and he fumbled through the Sutra of the Light, hesitating without a response. You shouldn't call her arrogant. Perhaps the priest who can't recite the Sutra is the one who's truly arrogant! You should appoint her as your first female priest to restore the temple's faltering reputation."

"Knight Edwin," the messenger spoke coldly, "please respect the court's decorum. Women can never be priests in the temple."

Knight Edwin spread his hands and smiled, "Don't be upset, Your Excellency; I was just joking. But this girl is so devout, knowing the chapters and verses of the Light Sutra so well. Could it be that God truly spoke to her?"

The messenger slammed the table and retorted impatiently, "Impossible! Women cannot receive divine revelation."

Knight Edwin, unfazed, replied, "I don't quite understand your point. Are you saying your priest isn't even as competent as a woman who supposedly can't receive divine revelation? Remember, your priest can't even recite the Sutra of Light."

At this remark, the knights on the jury bench burst into laughter. Meanwhile, the priests turned pale, clutching their prayer beads tightly.

As tensions rose between the two sides, the judge intervened, "Silence! Let's focus on matters related to this case."

Turning to Laurent, the judge asked calmly, "As you mentioned, only the wicked are punished. Do you have evidence to prove that Reverend Fletcher is a villain?"

Eager to regain control and convict Laurent, the divine messenger interjected, "If Lord Fletcher were evil, there would be no good people left in this world. Before this trial, I heard people lamenting the loss of a good man, fearing that no one would dare perform good deeds like Reverend Fletcher anymore. How could someone who took in a stranger girl, tirelessly preaching and giving, be a villain? She's simply trying to exonerate herself by slandering the priest."

The judge nodded slightly, "Yes, many have written to the court, expressing how they were helped by Reverend Fletcher."

"The people's eyes are sharp," added the messenger. "They can discern good from evil. You can't deceive or fool the masses."

Laurent maintained her smile and, once they finished speaking, stated calmly, "If I told you Reverend Fletcher took me in to rape and kill me, would you still consider him a good person?"

Her statement sent shockwaves through the courtroom, leaving everyone in an uproar. The onlookers exchanged incredulous glances, seeing disbelief mirrored in each other's eyes.

This girl is incredibly bold to make such a statement! And her tone—so calm and composed. It seems that, in her eyes, this matter is truly the fault of Reverend Fletcher, and she feels no shame at all for being suspected of being tainted.

Dane, standing among the audience, couldn't help but applaud slowly. Laurent was remarkable! She could easily have exposed Fletcher as the serial killer, revealing that this "good man" had killed nearly seven hundred girls over ten years, but she chose not to. Instead, she was savoring the process of dismantling Fletcher's reputation with a slow, deliberate approach.

Wonderful, amazing!

Looking at the divine messenger, who used to be his boss, Dane noticed the messenger sneering at Laurent, seemingly mocking her supposed self-destructive behavior. If Dane were still his subordinate, he might have rushed to his side, shouting, "This is a trap she set for you, don't fall into it!"

But seeing the messenger's disdainful smile, Dane realized he had already fallen into the trap. How had he not noticed before that this man could never see beyond appearances to the underlying truth?

Sure enough, his former boss spoke contemptuously, "I don't quite understand what you mean. Are you accusing a respected priest of attempting to rape you, or are you admitting to being a shameless woman trying to seduce a priest?"

Dane couldn't help but cast a contemptuous glance at the divine messenger.

Why didn't he claim that Laurent tried to rape the priest?

The messenger surely wanted to, but even he knew that was too far-fetched.

Yet, many people shared the messenger's mindset. Upon hearing his provocative words, they cast suspicious looks at Laurent. Some idle drunkards in the crowd even ogled her, seeing her as little more than a streetwalker.

Laurent maintained her faint smile, unfazed by the murmurs around her. She possessed a strong heart, unconcerned with others' opinions.

Only the weak care about such things.

She was a fearless, powerful individual—cold, calculating, and undeterred.

The whispers and pointing fingers aimed at Laurent would eventually become sharp arrows directed at the temple itself.

As the murmurs subsided, Laurent tilted her head slightly, her black eyelashes fluttering, and a playful yet piercing gleam in her eyes. She continued, "If I told you that Reverend Fletcher treated nearly seven hundred girls this way—raping them and then killing them, turning them into pills for profit—would you still see me as a shameless woman and him as a good person?"

The courtroom fell into utter silence.

Her words stirred up an even greater tumult than before.

If her previous statement had caused ripples, this one unleashed a tidal wave—a towering, hundred-meter-high wall of shock.

Everyone was left speechless.

The contemptuous smile vanished from the messenger's face, replaced by a bead of sweat that silently trickled down his forehead.

How had he forgotten this?

Earlier, he thought he'd caught Laurent in a lie, eager to brand her as a deceitful woman. But he overlooked the nearly seven hundred girls who had been killed.

The number was too large to dismiss. Even if it had been seventy or a hundred, he might have claimed they seduced him, but seven hundred? No one would believe it.

The divine messenger wiped his brow, nervously twisting the gemstone ring on his finger. Dane recognized this as a sign that the messenger was beginning to think.

Only now was he starting to think?

Dane shook his head in disbelief. What had he been doing all along? He'd often whispered warnings in the messenger's ear, "Don't underestimate Laurent." Yet, he still stumbled into her trap and, once caught, floundered until it was too late.

He accused Laurent of arrogance, yet wasn't he guilty of the same? The difference was that Laurent was both smart and arrogant, while the messenger was foolish and arrogant.

Reflecting on how he once served such a fool made Dane's ears burn with shame. Fortunately, the messenger had pushed him away; otherwise, he'd have likely followed him blindly to his own detriment.

After a long moment of wiping away sweat, the messenger finally composed himself and spoke with authority, "Do you have any evidence that Reverend Fletcher murdered nearly seven hundred girls?"

Confident that he'd ordered Fletcher's house burned, the messenger felt even more assured, his tone growing stern, "Without evidence, you cannot make such accusations. Otherwise, even if you didn't murder Reverend Fletcher, you could be sentenced for defaming a clergyman."

Unexpectedly, Laurent chuckled, "Of course I have evidence, and there's plenty of it."

The messenger's heart skipped a beat.

Once Laurent began her counterattack, she wouldn't leave her opponent any chance to recover.

Laurent turned to Knight Edwin on the jury bench and asked calmly, "I understand that the Order of Knights has the authority to oversee the temple. Could you confirm whether clergy members have the privilege to commit murder and defile virtuous women without consequence?"

"Of course not," Knight Edwin answered with interest. "Even His Excellency the divine messenger would be sent to the gallows if he committed murder."

A wave of fear washed over the divine messenger as he felt the situation slipping from his control. In desperation, he sternly rebuked, "Do not attempt to sway the jury! I demand the defendant be warned—she is clearly trying to seduce Knight Edwin."

Before the judge could respond, the knight captain, previously silent, glanced at the divine messenger and said, "Your Excellency, the men of the knight order are not as easily seduced as the priests of the temple. It's normal to have questions and answers during a trial."

His words implied that suggesting the temple's priests could be so easily influenced was laughable, particularly after Laurent's revelation about Priest Fletcher murdering nearly seven hundred girls. Accusing her of seducing the clergy seemed even more absurd. Could seven hundred young girls have all intended to seduce an elderly, frail priest?

Everything descended into chaos.

The divine messenger's cold sweat flowed even more freely as he struggled to maintain control. He pressed on, demanding, "You claimed to have evidence. Where is it?"

Laurent replied calmly, "The evidence is with my maid. I intended to request Knight Edwin's help in summoning her, but the divine messenger accused me of trying to seduce him. So now, I must ask the divine messenger to do it."

He'd been outmaneuvered again!

The divine messenger realized Laurent's intent; she had deliberately engaged Knight Edwin to provoke a reaction, ensuring the messenger himself would summon her maid. By having him request the witness, her evidence would appear more legitimate and credible, avoiding suspicions of tampering.

If the messenger hadn't intervened and accused her of attempting to seduce Knight Edwin, she wouldn't have gotten his help. But he had taken the bait.

She had anticipated his every move.

The divine messenger recalled his loyal assistant's warnings to be cautious of Laurent. But it was too late now.

He had stumbled fully into Laurent's trap and could only proceed along the path she had orchestrated.

Taking a deep breath, he attempted to wipe the sweat from his forehead but found his hand felt leaden. With a heavy voice, he asked, "What is your maid's name?"

"Margo," Laurent replied.

"Summon Margo," the divine messenger ordered, his tone heavy with reluctance.

He still harbored a ridiculous hope that the evidence Laurent claimed to have was merely a bluff and that she was only stalling her sentencing.

But as soon as Margo entered the courtroom, the divine messenger realized how naive and ignorant his hopes were.

Laurent had meticulously prepared all the necessary evidence for this public trial. She had been waiting for this moment to unmask Reverend Fletcher's crimes to the world.

Looking at the judge, Laurent asked, "Sir, may I step out of the defendant's seat to present and explain the evidence to everyone here?"

Just as the messenger was about to object, the judge nodded, "You may, but you must wear ankle shackles."

Knight Edwin, eager to stir things up, raised his hand with a grin, "Please allow me to personally place the ankle shackles on this just and intelligent young lady."

His request was promptly denied by the knight captain, who gave him a stern glare.

An elderly lady approached to place the shackles on Laurent. As Laurent lowered her head, she realized it was an old acquaintance—the same lady who had helped her measure her waist that day.

The old lady didn't make eye contact or speak to her. When she put on the ankle shackles, she chose ones lined with fine velvet, typically reserved for clergy guilty of minor offenses. Laurent's case could be seen as both significant and minor; after all, she had only served as a goddess for two days.

By doing this, the old lady was silently expressing her support.

Touched by this gesture, Laurent understood its meaning. After the shackles were secured, she quietly thanked the old lady before stepping forward to present the evidence Margo had brought.

In addition to the register, they had found numerous incriminating items at the priest's residence — expensive exotic treasures, a complete set of alchemical equipment, rare poisonous herbs in the garden, and unsold alchemical pills.

With each piece of evidence Laurent presented, the divine messenger grew paler. By the time she finished, his face was ashen.

He was unaware of how much evidence Laurent had gathered, and it left him panicked, sweat pouring from his forehead.

Desperately, he clung to the hope that if people didn't believe Laurent, no matter how clever she was, she would be powerless.

He accused her, "Are these items not something you fabricated? How can you prove they belong to Reverend Fletcher? I warn you, do not slander or defame the clergy."

But his words were met with puzzled glances rather than support.

A voice rang out: "Sir, do you think our Knights are incompetent? We too are God's people and have the ability to communicate with Him. We can use divine power to trace the past of this evidence.Whether these dirty things belong to Reverend Fletcher or not, just ask the Almighty God and you will know."The speaker was Knight Edwin.

The divine messenger had completely forgotten that knights could also wield divine power.

Recently, the Supreme Temple and the Royal Knights had grown increasingly at odds, with the temple limiting the knights' activities and authority. Few knights were still willing to borrow divine power to enhance case efficiency.

But in this situation, using divine power was an option.

Knight Edwin was eager to see the messenger humbled.

With the knight captain's approval, Knight Edwin left the jury bench and began reciting the spell to borrow divine power for the evidence.

The divine messenger panicked initially but soon regained his composure.

He reassured himself that not everyone could borrow divine power; it required unwavering and devout faith.

Currently, only a few temple priests could wield such power, and even he couldn't.

This carefree knight, often joking in court, seemed too frivolous to have such faith. Surely, he couldn't even recite the prayer, let alone borrow divine power.

Feeling more at ease, the messenger awaited Knight Edwin's failure.

Half a minute later, Edwin's attempt to borrow divine power indeed failed.

Unsurprised, he stopped and was about to offer a sheepish smile to Laurent before returning to his seat. But when he saw her eyes—filled with pure expectation—he hesitated. She seemed unaware of his failure, believing he could deliver justice.

Knight Edwin paused, glancing at the knight captain, "Sir, may I try again? I have a strong feeling I'll succeed this time."

The knight captain agreed.

The divine messenger sneered silently. Borrowing divine power wasn't like magic; it wasn't a matter of trying multiple times until it worked. If it failed once, it would fail ten thousand times.

After all, could God's will be so easily swayed?

He is as steadfast as towering mountains, with eyes so pure that cannot tolerate wickedness or bias. He seemingly never shows mercy to individuals, yet his mercy is boundless. Just as he never displays anger, but his presence alone can make mountains tremble and rivers quake.

In his perspective, there is only the order of the world to maintain, and he is unwavering in his duty to uphold it. How could a few words from a mere mortal sway such an unyielding force?

Order is the delicate balance of light and darkness, the cycle of life and death, the rhythm of tides, and the dance of stars across the night sky.

To him, a single person is as insignificant as a grain of sand, a leaf, or a ripple on a lake's surface.

The divine messenger was convinced that Knight Edwin would fail again.

Yet, to his utter astonishment, Edwin managed to borrow divine power!

The evidence floated up, bathed in a radiant white light, replaying past scenes for all to witness. Laurent clenched her fist, suppressing the smile that threatened to escape her lips.

Her little snake, Loire, was indeed remarkable.

Hidden in Laurent's thick hair, Loire's cold purple-blue eyes glanced toward the image of the God of Light on the dome. Loire knew he hadn't intervened—he hadn't needed to. It was the god on the dome, with his serene and pure demeanor, who had shifted his stance.

Loire flicked his invisible tongue, a sense of unease stirring within him.

There seemed to be an inexplicable connection between him and this deity, and he sensed that the god's intent was not benevolent — at least, not for him. The God of Light's presence felt ominous.

Instinctively, Loire coiled his body defensively, like a beast protecting its domain. He hissed a warning, his snake venom poised, as he met the God of Light's gaze with an icy, fierce hostility.

CHAPTER
TWENTY-SEVEN

The first piece of evidence, rare and expensive antiques, was brought to life in the white light, vividly revealing how Priest Fletcher "acquired" them. The scene showed the supposedly revered priest charming a beautiful girl, removing the jade statue from her neck, and then assaulting her with a sickening eagerness.

Initially, the men in the courtroom felt detached from the gravity of the scene, unable to fully grasp the humiliation and violation experienced by the young women. A few shameless individuals even looked envious of the priest's vile actions.

However, the divine messenger could not afford such indifference. The revelation that a respected priest was secretly a vile predator undermined the temple's reputation immensely.

The messenger realized, with growing dread, that the knights who often clashed with the temple could now leverage this scandal to assert their oversight authority. His face turned ashen, and sweat drenched his back, seeping through his robes.

Dane had been right all along. Underestimating Laurent had been a grave mistake.

By allowing a public trial, the messenger had essentially handed Laurent the weapon she needed to dismantle the temple's reputation. Regret twisted his insides; he should have heeded Dane's warnings and recognized Laurent's intelligence sooner. But now, it was too late.

The retrospective scenes in the white light were just beginning. Fletcher's subsequent actions were even more horrific and unethical. Even Knight Edwin, who usually wore a perpetual smile, frowned at the priest's despicable deeds.

How could such a person ever have been called a priest? The parish priest had even defended Fletcher, claiming his death would discourage others from doing good. Such assertions were now exposed as the ultimate irony and an affront to true goodness.

The scenes showed Fletcher methodically cutting open a girl's belly, smoothing her skin, and collecting her internal organs, fat, and blood in jars. His actions were deliberate, not impulsive, as evidenced by the numerous containers at his feet.

Fletcher's inhumane treatment of young girls challenged the moral boundaries of everyone present. They realized that as humans, with flesh and blood, they could not condone such a person's existence, let alone honor him as a good man.

A voice from the crowd cried out, "She's right, this is Fletcher's retribution! What fitting retribution!" The crowd erupted in agreement, their faces flushed with anger, chanting, "Retribution, retribution!"

The priest was branded a devil, and the temple's decision to allow such a monster to serve as a priest for decades was questioned.

A noblewoman, having previously purchased Fletcher's pills, covered her mouth in horror upon realizing what they contained.

The graphic scenes forced her to confront her complicity in the girls' fates.

Another wealthy lady, unable to bear the truth, fainted in her maid's arms.

The messenger's lips quivered as he sought words to salvage the temple's reputation, but none came.

In the face of undeniable truth, words felt inadequate.

The white light continued to unveil more evidence, each linked to a young girl's tragic demise. The girls varied in appearance and background, but all met the same horrific fate. Some were adorned with daisies, which quickly wilted like their lives, crushed and reduced to nothing.

Among the spectators, a couple recognized their daughter in the scenes and wept bitterly. They had believed she had simply run away with a young man, never imagining she had been violated, murdered, and reduced to a mere commodity for profit. The reality was far worse than any imagined elopement.

Even Baron Margo's family discovered a relative among the retrospective images, further deepening the tragedy and the scandalous revelation of Fletcher's monstrous deeds.

Laurent hadn't fully grasped the depth of emotion her evidence would unleash within the Baron family. Their missing daughter was not just any family member; she was the second daughter, adored by her older sister — the Baron's wife—like a cherished porcelain doll. After her disappearance, the elder sister often dreamt of her golden-haired sibling, so much so that she nearly drowned herself in despair, stopped only by the thought of her own children.

The younger brother, who once shared his deepest thoughts and theological discussions with his beautiful and kind second sister, found an irreplaceable confidante in her. With the elder sister married, the bond with his second sister grew even stronger, making her loss all the more devastating for him.

Their entire family cherished this devout blonde girl beyond measure, showering her with love and affection. The irony of her tragic death at the hands of a priest they had trusted so completely was a bitter pill to swallow.

Despite the Baron and the seminary professor's attempts to maintain decorum, their family's grief overcame them. Ignoring propriety, they rushed forward, calling out the name of their beloved second daughter with anguished cries. The depth of their sorrow was palpable, a testament to the profound love they held for her and the immeasurable loss they now faced.

The younger brother, eyes red and voice hoarse, shouted at the judge, "Our family donates tens of thousands of silver coins to the temple every year... After my sister died, we even donated a pasture for her peace. I never imagined the priest who killed her was the one she trusted the most..." He broke down, sobbing, "I wanted to become a priest to comfort her soul... What was I thinking?"

As more individuals lost their composure, the divine messenger found himself engulfed in chaos. The cacophony of grief and anger was deafening, leaving him unable to process the turmoil around him.

The room's energy shifted dramatically, and he could no longer discern individual cries or shouts, only the overwhelming tide of emotion that surged through the space.

His eyes, wide with disbelief and fear, conjured the image of a galloping carriage barreling through the darkness—a metaphor for the unstoppable force of justice and truth now unleashed. The carriage's thunderous roar symbolized the public's growing outrage, while its massive wheels mercilessly ground down the parish temple's long-standing reputation, much like the unforgiving way Reverend Fletcher had destroyed the lives of countless young girls.

As pale sunlight pierced through the heavy clouds, it illuminated the courtroom, dispelling the shadows of deceit and secrecy that had long shrouded the temple's actions. Everywhere he looked, the divine messenger saw the incomplete corpses of reputations and lives destroyed by the scandal, cradled by people demanding accountability.

The divine messenger trembled uncontrollably, his cold sweat giving way to a feverish heat that fogged his glasses, blurring the scene before him as if he were looking through tears.

The weight of public condemnation bore down on him, surpassing any anxiety Laurent had previously induced.

In that moment, the messenger realized that the tide had irrevocably turned against him and the temple. The people's righteous indignation was a force he could neither ignore nor quell, leaving him to face the consequences of his own inaction and the temple's complicity.

His fear was palpable, reaching new heights as he realized Laurent had more evidence to show.

Like a blow to the head, the realization that Laurent's arsenal wasn't yet depleted caused the messenger to tremble. He clung to his gemstone ring, once a symbol of the temple's authority, now a reminder of its impending downfall. He fantasized about discarding it, escaping the wrath that loomed over him.

In his heart, he feared the Supreme God's judgment, knowing he'd be punished severely for protecting Reverend Fletcher and ignoring Dane's warnings about Laurent. His regret was profound, but it was too late to turn back the clock.

The messenger, desperate to apologize and salvage the situation, found himself unable to stand. His mind raced—what should he do?

The divine messenger, overwhelmed by the situation spiraling out of control, felt the weight of his actions bearing down on him. He longed to apologize, to find some way to make amends, but his legs betrayed him, leaving him to collapse back into his seat before he could stand.

"What should I do... what should I do?" he muttered to himself, clutching his hair in desperation. "Stay calm, stay calm, don't panic, find a way... find a way to fight back. Call her a witch, claim she's a witch. Even in death, I'll drag her to hell."

His whispered plotting went unnoticed by the judge, but not by the keen ears of the knight nearby.

The knight shot him a cold glance, shaking his head in disapproval.

At such a critical moment, rather than reflecting on his actions or attempting to salvage the temple's reputation, the messenger's instinct was to slander Laurent and drag her down with him.

It was a testament to how the parish temple's reputation had crumbled under the leadership of such a divine messenger.

Dane, who knew the messenger better than anyone else in the diocese, didn't need to hear the muttering to understand the messenger's thoughts.

The messenger's inability to see beyond his malice and seek redemption was evident.

Perhaps it wasn't foolishness but a deep-seated malice that blinded the messenger, making him incapable of seeing any path but one of destruction.

His initial dismissal of Fletcher's crimes, driven by a vendetta against Laurent, had now led to his downfall. Was it possible that Laurent had deliberately provoked him, leading him into a trap that clouded his judgment regarding Fletcher?

But what could Laurent gain from such a maneuver?

Did she harbor a personal vendetta against the divine messenger?

Dane considered these questions but found no clear answers. He chose not to dwell on them, instead focusing on the messenger's impending self-destruction.

As the drama unfolded, the final piece of evidence—the register—completed its retrospective display.

As the register floated in the air, bathed in dazzling white light, it revealed a chilling truth: the priest's sinister satisfaction as he meticulously recorded the names of the girls, smiling as he caressed the pages. Each entry was a testament to his heinous acts, and the sight of it ignited a fierce anger in the crowd that transcended words.

In moments of profound grief, people may only be able to express themselves through primal cries, while those witnessing such pain can only respond with loud, anger-fueled shouts.

The divine messenger is correct in stating that the people's perception is sharp, whether regarding good or evil. They can discern the truth at a glance, and no one can deceive or mislead the public.

The final piece of evidence was quite enough to convict the priest of his crimes. Even if the messenger from the Supreme Temple arrived, it would be impossible to twist the truth and declare the priest innocent.

The divine messenger understands that the situation is beyond redemption and realizes his impending fall from grace. He is no longer concerned with anything else, except his desire to bring Laurent down with him, ensuring she doesn't leave the courtroom alive.

Gathering his remaining strength, he stood up and slammed the table, exclaiming, "Everyone, listen to me... I admit I erred in my judgment regarding Reverend Fletcher."

Someone in the crowd shook their fist and shouted, "Why call him a priest? That old man isn't fit to be a priest at all!"

"My daughter was killed by him... by the people of the temple. How can the temple compensate us? Does it honor our trust?"

The Baron's wife, overcome with emotion, covered her mouth and began to sob, saying, "If I could, I'd swap my life for my sister's. She was just 16 when she died, with so much still ahead of her. I wish I could give her my life to bring her back."

The Baron sighed as he approached his wife, no longer restraining her from expressing her anger and condemnation towards the temple. He gently embraced her, softly patting her back to provide comfort.

Many others shared similar criticisms of the temple, and the divine messenger couldn't bear to face them. In fact, he couldn't be bothered to even acknowledge them.

His gaze was firmly fixed on Laurent, filled with resentment, consumed by one thought: I'm finished, and you won't survive either.

"Listen to me, everyone," the messenger proclaimed loudly, attempting to regain the authority he once had during his sermons. "I made a mistake in judgment because this girl deceived me. She is a witch—an evil, terrifying, and beguiling witch. She deliberately led me to conceal the priest's crimes, intending to tarnish the temple's reputation. Please, believe me, and don't be deceived by her. I will provide a thorough explanation regarding Reverend Fletcher's case, but first, this detestable witch must be executed."

As soon as he finished speaking, Knight Edwin was the first to respond with a smile. He turned to Laurent, his blue eyes twinkling with amusement, and spread his hands, remarking, "This man is crazy."

Laurent simply curled her lips into a half-smile, dismissing the messenger's accusations without concern.

The messenger was aware that his accusation was baseless, but accusing Laurent of witchcraft was his only chance to convict her. To him, Laurent was undoubtedly a witch, and only by labeling her as such could he rationalize her intelligence and the fact that she had outwitted him from the start.

How could an ordinary woman's intelligence surpass that of a man? Surely, only a witch could achieve such a feat!

Laurent must be a witch!

And because she is a witch, she must be sentenced to the gallows!

He could lose his glory, power, and everything else, but Laurent must face the gallows.

The messenger glared at Laurent with a gaze more venomous than even that of the murderous Priest Fletcher.

The judge, however, was no fool and could easily differentiate right from wrong. Despite feeling strong impatience with the divine messenger's behavior, he maintained his composure, given their long-standing relationship, and said, "You cannot accuse her of being a witch without evidence. You need to provide proof. Simply saying she's a witch doesn't make it true."

With that, the judge picked up the gavel and struck the table forcefully, commanding, "Silence! The trial is not over. Everyone must quiet down. Those who are idle should return to their places, or they will be punished for disrupting the court."

The divine messenger mistakenly assumed that the judge's call for order was in his favor and quickly declared, "I have evidence! After she was imprisoned, I sent three groups to assassinate her... yet each time, she miraculously survived.

Summon those who attempted to assassinate her and ask if Laurent is a witch; the truth will be revealed!" He then looked at his old colleague with hopeful, almost childlike eyes.

The judge was taken aback: "......". In front of all these people, you've admitted to attempting to assassinate Laurent three times. Are you out of your mind?

The angry crowd wondered, "......". Does the divine messenger think he can act with impunity, or does he believe we are powerless against him?"

The public's protests grew even more intense.

From the moment he witnessed the carriage crashing and tarnishing the temple's reputation, he lost his mind and all sense of reason.

The only thing keeping him upright was his determination to personally witness Laurent being condemned to burn for allegedly being a witch.

Driven by this intense and singular desire, he persistently urged the judge to call upon Sisina, Alsha, Anders, and others to testify.

The judge quietly offered him some advice, but realizing there was no stopping his reckless intent to make a spectacle of himself in court, he simply shook his head and summoned the individuals he requested.

As Sisina entered the courtroom, she finally comprehended what Laurent had hinted at the night before.

"Because whether you can help depends on how foolish my adversary is."

She was called upon purely because the divine messenger had no other option but to tarnish Laurent's name by inflicting significant harm on himself in the process.

Realizing this, Sisina was secretly amazed. Could Laurent have become so astute? Even before entering the courtroom, Laurent had foreseen the divine messenger's irrational behavior following his defeat.

The divine messenger's strategy was straightforward—these individuals, like him, had been bested by Laurent and were likely harboring resentment, eager for a chance to retaliate. He was more than willing to provide them with an opportunity to strike back at her.

Anticipating Laurent's imminent conviction as a "witch," the messenger eagerly pressed the judge, saying in a hurried and excited tone, "Ask them if Laurent is a witch."

With a sigh of resignation, the judge complied, "The messenger asks if Laurent is a witch."

The divine messenger looked at Sisina and the others with hopeful eyes, yearning for the response he desperately wanted to hear.

However, the answers given by Sisina and the others were far from what he anticipated.

"Witch? What witch? She's just an ordinary girl," Sisina replied, looking genuinely puzzled.

"Nonsense, how could she be ordinary? Just look at how beautiful she is!" Elsa countered.

"Who's Laurent? I don't even know her!" Anders exclaimed. "Are you mad? I live in a men's cell. How could I possibly know a female prisoner?"

The divine messenger was on the brink of fainting from rage at their responses. "Were you bribed by Laurent? You clearly attempted to assassinate her!"

"Injustice, Your Highness, injustice!" cried Elsa. "We don't understand what the divine messenger is talking about. We are all upstanding citizens and would never commit such acts."

Reflecting on this "upstanding citizen" who had once been involved in a gruesome crime, the judge simply said, "......"

Unlike Elsa, Sisina wasn't bold enough to loudly claim to be a virtuous citizen. She frowned and said, "While I don't understand why Your Excellency the divine messenger claims Laurent is a witch, I believe there must be a reason for such an accusation. However, I truly have not done anything like assassinating her. In another six months, I will be released after serving my sentence. I can't risk breaking the law with my release so near."

Sisina's words, though gentler than Elsa's, were met with skepticism by those aware of the truth: Why had her sentence been reduced from death to release in six months? Wasn't it because she had aided in many assassinations?

Despite the messenger's plight, these individuals had no intention of defending him.

While the female prisoners feigned ignorance, Anders was adamant in denying any knowledge of Laurent. No matter how persistently the divine messenger questioned him, he insisted he didn't know her.

The divine messenger slumped in his chair, drenched in sweat.

He saw the carriage barreling toward him, destroying the parish temple's reputation and heading straight in his direction. His limbs felt as heavy as lead, rendering him incapable of evading the oncoming carriage, and he could only envision his demise beneath its wheels, with regret etched in his eyes.

Dejected, he held his forehead, struggling to accept that he stood on the brink of death, but unable to take Laurent down with him.

Then, a spark of inspiration struck him: his loyal assistant, Dane, who would surely help him. After all, he had promoted Dane and knew his character well. Dane possessed a foolish loyalty and would go to great lengths, even risking his life, for his superior.

If Dane could testify that he had recruited those people to assassinate Laurent, their lies would be exposed!

The divine messenger immediately shared this idea with the judge, requesting Dane's presence.

The judge sighed, "Stop this nonsense, Christopher," he said, calling the divine messenger by name in hopes of restoring his sanity.

Grasping the judge's wrist, the messenger pleaded softly, "Please summon Dane. He will help me. You don't want to see me humiliated by a girl, do you? Please, my old friend, have pity on me."

With another sigh, the judge reluctantly agreed, summoning Dane out of pity for his old friend.

Dane soon arrived at the courtroom.

The judge asked, "Dane, as Christopher the divine messenger's assistant, did you ever instruct Sisina, Elsa, Anders, or others to assassinate Laurent? This is what the divine messenger wishes to ask."

Dane glanced at the divine messenger.

His former boss was looking at him expectantly, seemingly forgetting that he had threatened him before entering the court.

This is clearly a foolish, contemptible, self-centered, and excessively inflated waste.

For years, the divine messenger's wisdom, composure, and elegance had been mere façades. His true self was so pitiful that a more astute Laurent had driven him to ruin like a collapsing building.

This was the person to whom Dane had once pledged allegiance—a selfish and despicable fool.

Now clear-headed, Dane would not risk his life for someone like that.

"Your Honor," Dane began softly, "I can swear that I have never seen these people or instructed them to assassinate Laurent. I don't know why His Excellency the divine messenger said that, perhaps because he resents me for our argument this morning. But nothing is nothing. I cannot falsely accuse these innocent people just to gain the divine messenger's forgiveness for my rudeness."

Dane's statement was the final blow to the divine messenger.

In an instant, the messenger crumbled to the ground like a wealthy man who had just lost a fortune.

He couldn't comprehend how he had fallen so far so quickly.

Why had everyone betrayed him for Laurent?

Three lowly prisoners and even loyal Dane had turned against him. Who would betray him next? Could it be the judge?

His heart felt as though it was being torn apart, and tears streamed from his eyes as he cried, his sobs reminiscent of a distraught old hen.

Before encountering Laurent, he had been filled with pride and arrogance, dismissive of women. When women approached him, eager to offer themselves, he would push them away irritably, fearing they might sully his perceived purity.

But now, he couldn't bring himself to meet the gaze of any woman around him.

For the first time, he experienced a profound sense of inferiority in the presence of a woman.

He realized how humiliating his defeat had been and how unbecoming it was to weep so openly.

Once, he had been remarkably handsome, with a tall and robust physique and a gentle, elegant demeanor. Women couldn't help but fall for him, yearning desperately for his affection and embrace.

But now?

No woman would love him—not even the most frivolous. Though he looked down on them, he needed their admiration to sustain his fragile male ego.

Realizing this, the divine messenger felt enveloped in darkness.

He had lost everything: reputation, power, status. Even the cheapest, easiest-to-gain admiration from women was slipping away.

All of this was Laurent's doing.

The law couldn't punish this shameless woman, so he would.

Touching the gem-encrusted ring on his finger, the divine messenger recalled having it modified after confiscating Sisina's poisoned ring. With a simple press, it could deploy an arsenic-tipped needle.

"This wretched woman is doomed!" he thought.

The divine messenger activated the ring's mechanism and charged toward Laurent with all the potential he could muster, moving with such astonishing speed that even Edwin Knight, who stood closest to Laurent, couldn't react in time.

But just as he was about to reach Laurent and drive the poisoned needle into her, a majestic and intimidating white light descended, abruptly separating them.

The divine messenger was hurled nearly fifty meters away by the white light, slamming into the wall before falling heavily to the ground.

He coughed up blood, filled with an overwhelming sense of frustration.

As a divine messenger, he immediately recognized the nature of the white light—an immensely powerful divine force.

The supreme god was protecting her.

When God chooses to protect someone, not even an army of thousands can harm a single hair on their head.

Since God had chosen to favor her and shield her with His omnipotent hand, who could possibly make Him retract that protection?

Christopher, the divine messenger, widened his eyes in disbelief and finally let out an anguished scream before collapsing.

His vacant gaze lingered on the spot where the white light had appeared. No one knew what thoughts occupied his mind in those final moments. Was he repenting for his sins? Seeking God's forgiveness? Did he finally understand where he had gone wrong?

No one would ever know.

All that was known was that the divine messenger was struck down by the omniscient and omnipotent God for sheltering priests guilty of heinous crimes and for attempting to assassinate the hero who had brought them to justice.

Now, Laurent was renowned throughout the diocese, her story becoming a legend.

To be continued.

www.ingramcontent.com/pod-product-compliance
Lightning Source LLC
Chambersburg PA
CBHW021037310726
48969CB00006B/1700